HANG ON

ANNIKI SOMMERVILLE

One More Chapter
a division of HarperCollins*Publishers* Ltd
1 London Bridge Street
London SE1 9GF
www.harpercollins.co.uk
HarperCollins*Publishers*
1st Floor, Watermarque Building, Ringsend Road
Dublin 4, Ireland

This paperback edition 2021
First published in Great Britain in ebook format
by HarperCollins*Publishers* 2021
Copyright © Anniki Sommerville 2021
Anniki Sommerville asserts the moral right to be identified
as the author of this work
A catalogue record of this book is available from the British Library

ISBN: 978-0-00-835172-4

Printed and bound in Great Britain by
CPI Group (UK) Ltd, Croydon CR0 4YY

My dear friend Faye, who has always helped me hang on when times have got tough.

Happiness = a renewed sense of purpose, a more intense experience of life, the reason we were put on this planet, a distraction from all that is bad, a feeling of success, love, family, filling a void.

A baby.

Chapter One

I awoke with a start. Someone was lying on top of me. Someone who smelt like Davidoff Cool Water and stale fags. Was I back in the 00s? Had I travelled back through time? As I ran my hands across his back (yes, it was a man) I felt hair bristle beneath my fingers. The weight of him was quite comforting but I needed to pee. In a few weeks I'd know whether I'd been successful or not. Already I was hoping not.

My head hurt and I'd a bitter taste of stale booze in my mouth. This was my first attempt, the first step in my plan, but I was worried I hadn't set the standards high enough. He was hairy, emitting an eggy smell, and had a terrible taste in home furnishings (who chose black furniture these days?). OK, I'm not perfect; I have a black hair that grows out of my left nipple (this is quite common, apparently, but repellent nonetheless). Each time I pluck it out, it comes back stronger. I have an index finger that is slightly shorter as the top came off in a door when I was eleven and I have thick legs, which make shorts out of the question.

In the bathroom, I breathed in the fresh, toilet-block smell that emanated from the loo. At least I wasn't going to be sick – I was not *that* hungover. I needed a pee, but if I was going to get pregnant, if it had actually worked, I needed to be careful that I didn't dislodge his sperm. Hairy had been drunk enough not to notice that there was a sizeable hole in the end of the condom. This hole I'd engineered with a safety pin before we'd got into things. I'd been surprised that he'd requested a condom as he'd been so drunk but luckily I'd been prepared for this eventuality anyway. I was ovulating but was no spring chicken. I would google to see what the stats might be this time. And perhaps it hadn't worked. I wasn't sure about passing on these super-hairy genes to my offspring anyway. Body hair was very unfashionable now, and I'd be cursing this future child to a lifetime of waxing and epilation fees. Although, if the climate was rapidly warming up, was more body hair a good thing to help regulate body temperature?

Last night had been the first step in the baby plan I'd formulated. I'd yearned for a baby for some time now. I got a pang whenever I was confronted with yet another photo on social media – the first scan, the gender-reveal party, cake with either blue or pink sponge inside, the bump accompanied by a playful sign denoting how many weeks along it was now, then the wrinkled baby and birth story (usually quite harrowing), and so it continued: the first day of eating solids, the nursery, school, holidays… If you didn't have kids then *what did you actually post about*?

At first I'd kidded myself that all was OK, that time was still on my side: *'Oh well, at least Lydia Sotherby isn't pregnant – I mean, at school she was popular but it looks like she's still stuck in a job she hates and has no partner.'* Then a couple of months later I'd see a grainy, black and white scan photo with the declaration: 'TWO BECOMES THREE!' and I'd be, *When had one become two let alone Three?* Scrolling through Lydia's photos, I'd realise there was a photo two years back of a wedding ring which I hadn't even noticed (why hadn't I been invited?) and I'd have to find someone else from my past that hadn't yet done what we were all supposed to do. *'Oh, at least Angela Rodgers hasn't had a baby,'* I'd chant to myself. But it wasn't just peer pressure. It was a biological thing. It was an *ache*. It was also the fact that my life was a pile of donkey manure and, without a child, it would continue on the same trajectory (one that was ultimately very dull) until it was game over.

Was Angela Rodgers pregnant? I made a mental note to

double-check on that. She'd been massively unpopular at school, had terrible acne and was tall – but not the kind of tall that men deal with easily.

Aged thirty-eight and time was running out. One older friend (forty-two) that I'd been to uni with was already a grandma! This wasn't ideal, but at least she'd benefit from all those comments on how amazing she looked, how lucky she was to have got all the parenting wrapped up already – though nowadays being a grandparent was tough and you were expected to pretty much do 50 percent of the childcare if you were capable. My twenties had been a blur of listening to Radiohead and staring out of various windows smoking – waiting for something important to happen. My thirties were when I started to realise that nothing important was happening and the onus was on me to make things happen. I'd never, in fact, felt a sense of agency over my life (this was changing now with my plan in place) but around thirty-five I realised the following:

1. I was never going to be discovered.
2. There was no such thing as a perfect man.
3. I would never wear denim shorts and get away with it no matter how many carbs I cut out from my diet.

Now my social media was awash with tiny, scrunched-up faces and love-heart emojis.

Eddie arrived at 5.08am this morning and we're over the moon #blessed

Tabitha came unexpectedly (how so?) *this evening and we can't believe how lucky we are # newparentslovedupbigtime*

We are excited to announce the arrival of our new baby. We can't stop pinching ourselves! # howluckyarewe?

Was it luck though? All these babies were planned, babies that arrived in long-term relationships. There was no photo of a woman staring into the camera with a blank expression on her face.

Kate is happy to announce that nothing has happened of note # nolife # norelationship # nobaby # nada

 # stillwaitingforsomethingtohappenbutnothing

Mum would have been disappointed. She'd always given me pep talks. 'You need to be the *director* of your own narrative. Enjoy life but make sure you have a great career and don't rely on anyone. Don't leave it too late. You have to plan and then plan some more.'

Her words echoed in my ears. She'd been worried about my lack of baby. In the later years, just before she'd died, she'd kept bringing children into our conversations.

'So … are you thinking about babies, Kate?' she'd say if we were watching a nappy advert on the TV.

I'd look at the mum on the TV's adoring, blissful expression and feel a hiccup of sadness.

'I've still got time, right?' I'd reply. 'There's no big rush.'

At that stage I'd been thirty-five. Thirty-five didn't feel too bad as it wasn't approaching forty. I was also in a relationship then. There was *hope*.

'I don't want you to put it on the back burner, darling. So many women seem to be doing that. I had my kids in my twenties. Now there must be an awful lot of women who are missing out.'

'And don't settle,' Mum would say. 'That was the mistake with your dad. He was good-looking but only interested in himself. I only realised when it was too late.' Dad had been a sound engineer and travelled around different studios, recording classical music. I didn't have any desire to contact him – what kind of person abandoned their children just like that? What kind of person never tried to stay in touch? No birthday cards, no Christmas presents…

'I hope I'll get married one day,' I'd said to Mum – I

wanted to have a different life, a more stable one. 'I want the whole caboodle – 2.4 kids, the lot.'

And she was right about lots of women missing out on having kids. There were plenty of news reports and statistics that showed that fact. Yes, of course it was fine if you didn't want to have kids – I read interviews with these women to see if I could make myself feel the same sentiments, but I didn't and couldn't share their conviction. The baby plan had been concocted one evening after I'd returned from drinks with an old school friend. She'd had her second baby, was six months in, and had invited all her old mates out to celebrate.

'I'm so tired! I sometimes wish I could be pushed around in that damn buggy all day,' she'd said to me at some point in the night, 'but Kate, I'm so happy. I mean, it's awful, but it's a happy kind of awful, and it's stopped me from obsessing about myself.'

'In what way?' I'd asked, curious. I was always obsessing about myself. I was like one of those telescopes where you peered down one end but instead of seeing lots of bright, sparkling colours you just saw an anxious, wide-eyed face staring back at you.

'I just don't have time. It's only when you have a kid that you stop thinking about yourself. It's liberating.'

'But awful, too?'

'Yes, sort of. And tiring. Did I tell you how tired I am?'

'Yes, you did.'

Something about this conversation made it all click into place. I'd always been too focused on *me*. This was the source of my anxiety, the reason why I woke every morning with a bad tummy and butterflies (on the good days) and heart palpitations and sweats (on the bad ones). One benefit of becoming a mum would be to shift the focus and perhaps shut off some of the mental chitter-chatter that drove me bananas.

The baby plan was simple.

1. Choose fertile times in the calendar with the aid of ovulation tests which were ninety-nine percent accurate; quite expensive but could be bought in bulk on Amazon.
2. Locate a man in a bar/gym/supermarket/wherever.
3. Have sex.
4. Repeat above until pregnant.

Another reason I wanted a baby was that when I thought back to happier times in my life (and there had been some) they involved taking care of someone else. I'd had a cat called Kipper when I was seven years old. He was a giant, orange, loved-up thing, very overweight and affectionate. I'd put a baby bonnet on his head, wrap a blanket around his body and push him around our tiny square of garden in a doll's buggy. Mum would watch and say, 'Be careful, I'm not sure he's enjoying that, Kate – he might scratch you.'

I felt perfectly calm when I was looking after Kipper. I knew that looking after a baby was different, but even looking after Mum in her last few months had given me a sense of meaning. Besides, what did women do if they didn't have a proper career? You could be one of those women who strode about the place getting shit done or you had kids. And yes, all the living in my own head was exhausting: the ruminating about small stuff, the endless hypothesising, the worrying. If I was going to be anxious all my life then it made sense to do it over something important rather than the fact I'd seen a small brown mark on my left thigh that might be cancer but might be a speck of Magnum that I'd dropped in my lap last night. I'd always been too earnest. The kid at the party watching. I was the classic 'old head on young shoulders,' Mum used to say.

Like many women, I'd assumed that having a family would *just happen*. For a while it had looked like I was on course.

Dear Carl,

What can I say? How come it hurts to think about you three years later? And do you know that every time I smell Le Labo

Santal 33 perfume I think of you (and it seems like everyone is wearing it these days – you always said it was the perfect unisex scent and I guess you were right on that one).

Kate

The truth was, we weren't compatible. He was an extrovert; I was quieter, more guarded. I realised that he was frustrated by my lack of communication skills. He thought girls should naturally be more open and chatty and didn't understand that we weren't all cut from the same cloth.

'You're more like a boy, really,' he'd say sometimes and then launch into a long and boring chat about his latest work gripe – how some young intern had been promoted and then given a lot of responsibility but had then failed spectacularly and Carl had taken the blame. He worked in PR, which seemed to be incredibly tough. At thirty-nine he was considered ancient, a dinosaur who struggled to keep up with the latest apps and buzzwords. I was secretly envious back then as he earnt a lot of money for sitting at a desk and drawing complex diagrams on Powerpoint that made no sense at all but gave the impression of being remarkably clever. His agency went on fabulous away-day trips to far-flung places like Bali to team-build. Carl was adventurous and wanted to go on holidays where you did bungee jumping or ate strange Mexican weeds so you could 'find yourself'. I wanted to relax on the beach and read a good book – maybe have a cocktail and then go to bed. I was scared of heights and fast fairground rides. He liked food that was tiny and had 'sea foam' on top which looked as though someone had spat on your plate. I liked fish and chips. It was easy to see how it wouldn't work out long term.

The last few months we'd lived in silence. He came home and grunted. We'd eat dinner in front of the TV. Our texts were purely about what we would eat later and how we would get hold of those ingredients. At night I'd brush my teeth and pull an old T-shirt on (usually with a large pair of grey but very comfortable pants) and he'd turn his back as he got undressed and I'd stare at his body in a way that felt functional rather than loving. He never got an erection and I worried about initiating sex in case he rejected me after this happened on at least two occasions. I recognised that this was a body I'd felt thrilled by once but now no longer felt anything about. I was sure he felt the same and didn't care. If I got my hair cut, he didn't notice. If I wore a new pair of shoes, he didn't see them. If I dabbed a different perfume behind my ears, he didn't smell it. It was as if all the feelings we'd had for one another had gone, *poof!* in one go. At night I'd listen to him breathing and think, *who is this person?*

It hadn't been like that at first, of course. We'd met at a karaoke bar. It had been my friend Meg's birthday and there'd been a group of us who'd staggered into the dingy underground bar in Soho. Meg and I were singing 'Islands in the Stream' when Carl came into our booth by mistake. He'd got lost on his way back to a client night out. He was wearing a T-shirt with a photo of Debbie Harry on the front and black skinny jeans. I could tell he was self-conscious about his hair as he kept running his fingers through it and looking off to one side.

'Do you want to join us?' Meg had shouted through the microphone as he'd made no attempt to leave. It was a bit like a romcom, the key difference being I had to excuse myself to throw up in the toilet and then vomited again in my mouth while I launched into 'Kid' by The Pretenders. I'd been drinking vodka which wasn't my usual tipple and had trouble even focusing on the bright neon words that jumped up on the TV screen.

'I haven't seen you so moody about someone in ages,' Meg had said, laughing, in the taxi on the way home.

Carl had given me his number. 'I need to tell you that I have psoriasis,' (it turned out he had a patch of it on his elbows and back) he'd said before we'd parted.

'Why are you telling me now?' I'd asked – it seemed such a strange and intimate thing to say.

'Just in case we get our clothes off one day. I mean, I'm guessing we will at some stage.'

'That's presumptive,' I replied.

'And did I tell you that you remind me of a Botticelli painting?' he said.

He was slurring as he staggered off in the direction of the night-bus stop. Later, I'd googled Botticelli and seen lots of angelic-looking women with hair down to their knees. It was obvious I bore little resemblance to these women and he'd been very pissed.

I also googled psoriasis, so I'd be prepared if we did meet again or things went any further.

We'd sat watching films together (anything 80s and a bit naff). We'd gone to gigs (we were both fans of bluegrass and Gillian Welch, which was odd as I'd never met anyone else that liked it). We'd eaten at the pop-up restaurants in East London where you had to queue for two hours to get a table and then were given a plate of food someone had spat on. Carl was always chatty and gregarious. He'd talk to the waitress: 'This place is super-popular, right?'. The people at the next table: 'Ooh, this looks nice but we've been queuing for days!'. The taxi driver: 'What kind of shift have you had, mate?' I frequently felt embarrassed by his chat; it was like being on a date with my late nan who had insisted on speaking Esperanto to everyone because she believed everyone was fluent in it, whatever their nationality.

For a while, Carl was perfect. For four years. After Carl left I'd dipped into online dating. There was a new app that twinned you up with nerdy men – these were my type, usually, men that looked like they read lots of books and liked arty films; and if they wore glasses, even better. The app was called Top-Nerd, but after going on a couple of dates I realised these men were just pretending. They went to the gym and exercised like loons. They liked House music. They weren't like Carl. Carl was an *authentic* nerd and collected Avenger comics and liked to make giant constructions out of Lego. There was definitely a part of him that refused to grow up. These mock nerds lied about their age and turned up looking twenty years older than their profile photo. One kept asking if he could kiss me, before launching himself at my neck, leaving a slobbery residue behind. It was like the wild west out there and I wasn't sure I had the stamina to work my way through all these men until I found the right one.

Where did this leave me if I wanted a child? Still, I'd given it a good eighteen months before I went on dates again – I couldn't be accused of not trying to find another relationship. My brother George had said it was best to 'get straight back on that dating bike'.

If I was honest (and people weren't) my dating profile would have read thus:

Appearance: Goldie Hawn if she'd grown up in London and never seen the sunshine.

Age: old but not so old as to be wearing sensible shoes or slacks from the back of Sunday supplements.

Living arrangement: with brother George aged 35 years. No parents – mother passed away three years ago and father walked out aged five.

Occupation: Deputy Manager at Franklin's bookshop.

Hobbies: reading crime books, watching TV, planning impending motherhood.

I wouldn't have mentioned the baby plan as that scared people. Nobody wanted a woman who was silently counting how many eggs she had left or was looking down at your crotch to size up whether you had healthy sperm.

I'd never considered *not* having children.

Having a baby was the thing that kicked it all off – the grown-up life. I also didn't mention on first dates that I was the kind of woman who preferred to watch from the sidelines. In a film, I would have been the one who hovers in the background and never jumps in the swimming pool to do the skinny dipping and perhaps gets killed off early on.

On my gravestone it would have read:

Nothing of note happened here.

Whenever I went to a comedy film with Meg she'd have to nudge me in the side to remind me to laugh. I found it hard to laugh because it required switching off all my anxiety and the anxiety was always present somewhere. It might have been something like: *'Why is that man with a rucksack sitting next to us on this carriage? Is he a terrorist?'* Or in a movie theatre it would have been: *'Is my popcorn making too much noise? Is the woman in front of me sighing each time I put my hand in the box? Shall I stop chewing it? Can she hear me chewing it? I need to swallow but when do I do that? Do I wait till the music gets loud again?'*

And I'd never been popular. I'd not been picked for the netball team and had spent many parties in my teens and twenties sitting on my own (cue Radiohead and an over-identification with Thom Yorke), being sarcastic (for protection) or waiting for a boy to ask me to snog him (most thought I was stuck up).

Mum had claimed Dad was a moody git, but I didn't have many memories of him. He'd left us just at the point when you start to develop strong memories. I'd seen photographs, though. He was good-looking and always wore a long leather jacket. In one photograph – which I'd stuck to my bedroom wall somewhere where Mum couldn't spot it, next to the skirting board – he was playing the guitar and looking lovingly at Mum. I'd never felt that kind of love from a man.

However, it was also clear that that kind of love didn't stick around for long.

Fast forward to the Hairy One, who clearly wouldn't stick around – not that I'd want him to. When I got back into his bedroom, the air smelt terrible, of eggs and booze. I tried to remember what had happened the previous night.

'How do you undo this?' he'd asked, battling to get my bra off – it was front fastening.

Then: 'Do you like this?' as he climbed on top with zero foreplay.

He'd licked his palm and slid it over my vagina and I'd tried not to notice or say anything, but was this *actually* considered foreplay?

'Was that good?' he'd said afterwards, when it clearly hadn't been, but that wasn't a priority right now.

He'd also tried to get his willy in my bum. I knew pregnancy wasn't likely with this method so had tactfully moved it.

'Oh, OK,' he'd said sounding disappointed.

Men watched a lot of porn these days and thought all women were up for anal sex and gang-bangs. They would try bum sex if they thought they'd never see you again.

I picked up my clothes, trying not to rouse Hairy, and

went back into the bathroom and took a shower. I'd spent much of the night lying awake, waiting for morning, too tired to get up and go home, a thudding hangover developing with an underlying sense of fear. I also had an old John Denver song stuck in my head which Mum had sung to me as a child. There was a poster of Bob Marley on the wall, the one students had flirted with back in the day (it was either that or a poster of a Tarantino film, usually), and an overflowing ashtray next to the bed. A pair of boxer shorts was draped over the chair with a picture of Homer Simpson across the bum and a bottle of Southern Comfort had a half-burnt candle wedged in the neck. This was *not* Steve Jobs and this chap would live the life of a student until he died. He was possibly early thirties but, like many, was condemned to never grow up. Too expensive. There was no furniture aside from the grotty bed and a couple of old cardboard boxes. We hadn't talked about his occupation but he looked like he worked in a call centre. Not that I had anything against call centres – I'd worked in one myself years ago. He was also a bit like George, who still played Xbox and sent memes to his friends.

This was the problem with many of the men my age. They didn't want to be conventional. They didn't have the pressure of fathering children early on. They looked at Mick Jagger having kids and thought *why not wait?* But our eggs would only hold up to scrutiny for so long. I was still standing in the shower thinking about my eggs and worrying about their quality.

'Hey, baby!' a deep voice boomed from behind the curtain.

Now I found myself standing in a hairy stranger's shower. I could see Hairy's outline as I squeezed coconut shower gel into my palm. I'd last smelt something similar in the 80s – was he actually Tom Selleck? I lathered my arms, my legs, and my tummy, then the curtain opened and Hairy stood before me. *Who's been sleeping in my bed! Who's been eating my porridge?* He had an erection poking out from underneath a violently abundant nest of pubic hair.

What did I really know about him? What if he hadn't heard of my favourite singer - Gillian Welch? What if he watched *Top Gear* and thought Jeremy Clarkson was a positive representation of masculinity against a backdrop of crazy feminists trying to put men down all the time? Had he said this last night? What if he didn't like a fried cheese sandwich? That was basically the only dish I'd inherited from Mum and could make perfectly. Everyone who ate it said it was perfect. You basically fried it in butter and it was the bomb. Hairy was vomiting into the sink now but still had a semi-erection. It was *a sad, sad situation* as the famous Elton John song went. He groaned, wiped his mouth on a towel and shuffled out again. I put the curtain back where it was and aimed the showerhead below. Perhaps this had been a mistake…

Coming back to the bedroom, a small towel wrapped around my nether regions, I retrieved my clothes from where they were festooned on the bedside table beside a dying pot plant, like not-very-festive Christmas decorations.

Hairy groaned again. 'Why did I drink that green stuff?'

We had put away a bottle of red wine and a few cocktails. I was pretty good at handling alcohol but had stopped at the first cocktail and he'd continued, swaying as we got into an Uber. 'Can you show yourself out?' he said now, not even looking up from the bed. I could tell he would have one of those hangovers where he would try some toast in about ten minutes, and a large glass of water, and in another ten these would come back up again. Then he'd wait a bit, try again, this time with perhaps a packet of crisps and a Coke and again this would return and eventually, by three in the afternoon, he'd keep something down and feel normal or semi-normal. There was no talk of exchanging numbers or seeing one another again. It was better than all that *I'll call you, yes let's meet up, yes that was fun, we'll do it again,* etc. I left his flat with the sound of his retching echoing in my head. I was hungry. The hangover wasn't going to be too bad.

I put my headphones on and listened to Radiohead again. 'I'm so miserable I could die,' Carl used to sing whenever I put 'OK Computer' on. 'Jesus, Kate, can you please put something a bit chirpy on? It's Saturday night!' There were people who understood Thom Yorke and there were those who didn't. It was lazy to call it miserable. This was where Carl and I disagreed. We had bluegrass in common but I secretly knew I could never marry someone who didn't admire Thom and think him a true genius – he was also the kind of nerd that I fantasised about, but I didn't tell Carl that. He felt a million miles away now. It was six-thirty and the sun was coming up, the first few birds chirping away.

Worries:

1. Has it worked?
2. Will the baby be excessively hairy?
3. Will the butterflies in my stomach calm down now?

The first attempt. It was going to work. Or if it didn't, it was only the first step, so that was OK.

Chapter Two

'**R**ight, let's kick off our session today by going through your form. So, on a scale of one to ten, how bad has your low mood been this week?'

'I guess maybe a five.'

I looked down at my feet. In reality, it had been more like a nine but I wanted her to feel like I was progressing. I'd been paying for counselling for some time and even now I wanted to please her rather than truly think hard about whether I was improving or not.

'So you've medium anxiety too, I guess?'

'I just feel very little at the moment – is that good?'

'Well, we'll work on that.'

I could hear my counsellor, Sarah, tapping on her computer in the background. The bus was busy but today I was doing our session over the phone. I knew I'd not make it to the appointment in time and nobody really listened to you talking on the phone anymore (all too absorbed in their own entertainment/drama/admin).

'So how was your anxiety the previous week?'

'I'd say an eight. It's worse in the mornings. It starts as soon as I open my eyes.' This wasn't strictly true. Sometimes I had heart palpitations all day. Sometimes so bad it felt as though a heart attack was on the way. Sarah had explained during another session that my body was preparing for 'fight or flight'.

'It's perfectly normal for your body to react in this way.'

'But why do I get them when I'm getting ready for work?'

'Well, because, as we've discussed before, you're catastrophising about the day ahead and that gives your body the idea that something is badly wrong and that sets off the physical symptoms and *then* you worry about those symptoms. It's hard to break out of that cycle.'

She'd shown me a diagram that illustrated this particular point. A stick figure trapped in a circle of worry – physical symptoms – more worry. It made me feel giddy just looking at it.

The anxiety got much worse after Mum died. The thoughts were like grenades raining down on my brain, making me jittery and tense.

1. What if I never have a family?
2. What if I'm barren?
3. What if I get eaten alive by cats when I'm old?

Sarah had persuaded me to create a 'worry tree', classifying each negative thought into a 'practical' versus 'hypothetical' worry. The fact that the majority were hypothetical meant that there was nothing I could do about them so needed to forget them. That was the theory. It felt good to be tackling the anxiety but so far I wasn't seeing the benefits of the counselling yet. The thing was, I'd *always* had these feelings, they'd just intensified more recently.

Mum had called them the heebie-jeebies.

'Are you feeling bad, darling?' she'd ask as I cowered under the duvet, aged six, refusing to go to school.

'I have those feelings in my tummy, Mummy,' I'd reply.

'It's the heebie-jeebies, darling. We all get them. You just have to ignore them and get moving. They'll pass.'

Wikipedia entry:

Heebie-jeebies or **Heebie Jeebies** is a phrase meaning a feeling of anxiety, apprehension, depression or illness

So many choices! When I read that it really resonated.

I often found it hard to determine what *exactly* was making me feel the way I did.

Mum had died two months short of me turning thirty-six. Breast cancer. It had been discovered so late that nothing could be done. Her death was a catalyst for this current downward trajectory. It was also what sparked off thoughts of having my own family. I wanted to create my own unit and her death had made me realise just how short life could be if you didn't get a move on.

George and I now shared Mum's house with my friend Meg who I'd known since university. I'd met Meg on my first day at the University of Westminster (we were both studying media) and she'd stuck out because she had really flappy flared trousers on and hair down to her waist. She looked like someone from a 60s university campus. She came from an incredibly posh family – her uncle was a duke or something – but they'd fallen on hard times and now lived in a decrepit manor somewhere in the countryside with lots of dogs and fleas and mice everywhere.

I'd visited Meg's family once and the first thing her father had asked was, 'Where do you summer, then?' I hadn't understood what that meant and it was only afterwards that Meg explained that wealthy families went to specific places at key times of the year. It was his way of working out what kind of background I came from – very much lower-middle class, I guess.

Meg had no airs or graces and was a joy to be around. She was endlessly positive. She never seemed to wake up in a bad mood. She genuinely believed that life was getting better, despite the fact that she hated her job and had a pokey, crowded room in a house-share with George and me. Meg had been the one who'd persuaded me to start seeing a counsellor a few months before.

'Kate, it's not normal to wake up and feel dreadful. You don't need to live with that terrible feeling.'

I'd resisted, but then the symptoms had become so overwhelming – not just my heart going nuts but upset stomach and dizziness – that I'd had to do something. The problem was, once you were in the grip of an attack, there wasn't much you could do but hunker down and endure.

It was hard to let go.

My only other good pal was June. She was an eighty-five-year-old woman who came into the bookshop twice a week or so. We both had a mutual love of crime novels and I was always on the lookout for one she'd enjoy. That was another thing that had happened recently – I'd stopped reading. I just didn't have the concentration for it anymore. So I usually read the summary on the back of the book and then tried to figure out if June would like it or not. June didn't always help with the sense I had of panic and anxiety because she was constantly reminding me how life on Earth was getting worse, and that we were headed for catastrophe.

'It's all these mobile phones, Kate. They're turning us into zombies. Have you been on a tube and just looked around and thought how sad it all is?'

'Yes,' I replied and it was true. Everyone talked about how it didn't feel right to be addicted to their phone but no one was taking any steps to change their behaviour.

OK, you left it downstairs in the morning so it wasn't the first and last thing you looked at *but* you still spent your day desperately checking.

'We don't know enough about this stuff. Why do we trust it? Why? And why not watch a film at the cinema?' June said.

The truth was I loved watching stuff on my phone. I felt restless in the cinema, nowadays, and wanted to be able to google the actors and see who they were going out with and how old they were. I'd seen other people doing this too – unable to focus for an hour and a half because their social media feed was constantly updating and they were missing another baby-scan photo.

'Where's the popcorn and holding hands?' June had continued.

'It's more convenient, I suppose...' But I agreed with her – we were all in our own bubbles, barging into one another, not offering seats to old ladies, unable to tear our eyes away. June didn't have a smartphone. She had an old Nokia. I liked hanging out with her because she reminded me of Mum and there was something about her that calmed me.

'It's nonsense, all this anxiety stuff,' June had said. 'In my day we just said you were having a bad day. Does it make you feel better to have a name stamped on your head?'

'Mum used to call it the heebie-jeebies,' I'd said.

'Yes, exactly. Your mum sounds just like my kind of woman. Why label it with something that makes it feel even worse?'

'Well, I guess it means you're more likely to seek help.'

Was it better to dismiss the feelings? Had it been easier before everyone thought they had anxiety and it became a problem rather than a temporary discomfort?

Mum's house was still filled to the brim with her nicknacks. In the front room there were three shelves with antique royal-family mugs that she'd bought from junk shops. There was her collection of old French perfume bottles in the bathroom. She liked Indian embroidery and above each bedroom door was an ornate hanging or a beaded curtain or a macrame plant hanger. The truth was it was comforting with Mum's stuff around. The rooms still smelt of Shalimar, her favourite scent. And neither George nor I were interested in interior design so it was easier, as the years passed, to leave it. Besides, it looked like the house of someone who'd travelled, someone sophisticated, when in reality Mum had gleaned all her treasures from skips and charity shops. We'd always said that she'd be one of those people who ended up having to crawl into their home because they've hoarded so much.

'I love old things. They make me happy,' she'd said. 'Each thing reminds me of a happy time. That Indian carving I got two months after you were born. It was in a pawnshop on Brick Lane; and then the green Buddha? Well, I found him in a bin coming back from dropping you and George at school.'

I sometimes wondered whether her love of things had been brought about because Dad had left so she ended up channelling a lot of her love into inanimate objects. She always raged if one of her ornaments was broken by accident – as if she was losing a friend rather than an old china cocker spaniel.

People deal with grief in different ways. Some retreat from life, eat frozen ready meals, wear jogging pants, grow facial hair. They emerge 'cleansed' – so it feels like a grief detox. Others are more destructive, turning to hedonism, drinking, drugs, sex. Me, I worried. I found it impossible to live in the present. First thing in the morning, just as I was easing my way into consciousness, I'd remember Mum had died and I'd rush to the toilet and stand over the sink, retching. I'd crawl back into bed, my heart hammering a cornucopia of different images, freeze-framing the ones that made me miss her most, like the times when she'd sat in the bath and I'd rubbed her back and we'd talk about the day. Or when I'd been mean and hateful – like when she'd discovered my teenage diary, and the first page explained in detail how much I hated her. If a question popped into my head, any time of day or night, I'd automatically picked up the phone and called her.

'Who is the cheapest electricity supplier, Mum?'

'I've got a lump on my knee, should I go to the doctor?'

Then the bigger questions – 'When should I think about having kids? What if I don't have kids? I'm pretty sure I want to be a mum but it doesn't feel like the right time.'

That was the thing. It hadn't seemed the right time. Not early on with Carl. Then, in the middle, we simply didn't discuss it – and then he left because he said I was selfish and too introspective and no fun. He had a point. When had I last been fun?

In the beginning he'd seen me as quirky and quiet – someone he had to fathom out (or that was what he'd said) but then he'd realised that I was essentially a bit of a blank page. Yes, at uni I'd snogged lots of boys and danced all night but even while dancing I was secretly thinking, *when will this be over? When can I get under a nice comfy duvet? When will this lifestage end so I can just rest and put my feet up?* Carl also didn't respect the fact that I'd abandoned my ambition to be a documentary filmmaker early on; I'd applied for a couple of jobs as a runner but then realised they were so poorly paid that I'd never have any meaningful money of my own, so I'd worked in a clothes shop, then done some more retail work in John Lewis for four years before I'd got the job at Franklin's bookshop and stayed and that was that. My career had stalled.

Carl had initially been very understanding after Mum's death. I then quickly got the impression he wasn't listening. He started working late, making excuses as to why he wasn't coming home and going back to his house-share instead when he'd been living at Mum's with me. 'It's easier if I stay at mine,' he'd say. 'There's less of a commute and we've got a big pitch this week. I have to keep on top of it with all these whippersnappers at my feet.' Then he stopped coming over on weekends too. 'I need to work overtime and if we don't win this account then we won't get bonuses.' And then he stopped making excuses and just didn't turn up.

'What's going on with you two?' George asked one Saturday night as I sat on the sofa watching *Love Island*, a programme George and I both loved – until the contestants had sex, then it would get embarrassing and one of us would get up to make a cup of tea.

'He's busy at work,' I said, helping myself to a handful of cheese puffs.

'He's not been coming over at all, though,' George said.

I loved my brother but he wasn't always brilliant at being tactful or thinking through whether what he was saying was wise.

'He's busy,' I said irritably. 'They've got a big tampon client and he's had to work late.'

Carl had found my anxiety attacks irritating, so I'd stopped telling him when I felt ill. This was what happened when you started to move away from one another.

'What do you mean, your heart's hammering?' he'd say as I sat up in bed, a pained expression on my face. 'God, Kate, there are people out there who are *dying* and you're getting all worked up because you've got to work in a bookshop?'

'What if I get breast cancer?' I'd said.

'It's always about *you*,' he'd said. 'And yes, I understand that you miss your mum but all this anxious shit isn't going to bring her back. Your life is a walk in the park.'

And yes, Carl was right. I had a lot to be thankful for.

It was just very hard to see it when all you could focus on was what was missing.

Carl had detached himself – come to think of it, perhaps he'd never been attached in the first place. He'd always seemed slightly removed. He liked going out with friends and introducing me as his girlfriend; he liked it when we walked in the park holding hands; but when we were alone he spent his time scrolling through his phone. One night, when he got in at three in the morning and I suspected he'd been having it away with an intern he'd been talking rather a lot about – saying she was 'rather annoying' and 'very ambitious' but also saying she needed 'extra hours of mentoring after work' – I said it was all over and he hadn't put up a fight. I'd checked on Facebook a few times but he'd blocked me which was childish. I'd bumped into a mutual friend in a pub and she'd said he was seeing someone.

So this brought me back to executing my plan and standing outside Hairy's house and waiting for a bus home. The morning air felt exhilarating. The bus pulled up and I sat downstairs. There were already two or three old biddies with shopping trolleys setting out for their morning errands. Thom Yorke was still singing about alienation and how society was in meltdown, how we were all lonely people who would die soon. I put my 'upbeat' playlist on, and dance music started up. I'd had enough sad for now. A commuter got on and held his phone at eye height so he could continue watching his film. I thought how irked June would have been and saw the world through her eyes. In her youth, people would have chatted to one another and looked at the scenery. It made me feel sad, like we all knew we were heading in the wrong direction but nobody could figure out how to change course.

Right now, I visualised the sperm travelling up inside me, bumping up against my egg. 'Hello, I am here to fertilise you.' And my egg would say, 'Beggars can't be choosers at this stage in the game.'

I shook my head and tried to imagine what this baby growing inside would be like … perhaps they'd have soft, delicate skin covered in a fine down of hair. Already my memories of this man were fading. Perhaps I needed to take a photo next time, just so I could capture the physical characteristics properly. If there was a next time – hopefully there wouldn't be.

Dear Hairy,

I hope you are no longer vomiting. Thanks for the sex. If I have your baby I promise to shave it each morning.

I will also tell him about your love of Bob Marley and Xbox.

Love Kate x

T he event was called Fertility Fest, and was held in the gardens of Chiswick House. I'd booked the tickets a couple of months before and the blurb had promised 'The way to a fertile, happy body for wannabe Mums'. The queue to get in was long and everyone seemed to have turned up with their partner. They all looked younger than me and many were wearing exercise gear while I'd turned up in a flowery tea-dress and leggings. I tried not to stare too much; I was often prone to watching people and trying to figure out their couple dynamic, i.e., who was the dominant one, who was the one who decided what restaurant they'd eat in, who dressed whom, etc. The security man put a stamp on my hand and I walked in. There were a variety of yurts and tents and soft, soothing music playing in the background (whales, Indian chanting, panpipes). On the grass were a variety of comfy beanbags. Today there would be talks about fertility, and alternative treatments to help us be as fertile as possible. It was only a few days after my encounter with Hairy but I wanted to maximise my chances of being pregnant. I'd booked a pre-pregnancy stress-relief meditation session, and a fertility tarot reading.

I bought myself an almond and cashew sacred womb smoothie, and went in for my first appointment.

'So… when I make this noise with my lips,' the woman said, 'I'm sucking the bad energy out of your body, the *barren* energy, and I'm injecting you with good, strong, potential *baby* energy.'

I was lying on a bed and she was hovering over me, two hands over my pelvic area. Each time she touched my hips, she made this strange sucking noise that sounded, if you closed your eyes, like cicadas. I closed my eyes. If I looked at her I might laugh.

'You are hovering above the Earth and there is a gold cord that ties you to the centre; this gold cord is sucking up all the minerals, the energy, the fertility of the earth and it's travelling up your spine and into your womb and it's radiating positive feelings and your womb is receiving these feelings and it is relaxed and happy and receiving all the positive feelings and potential.'

I tried to focus on what the woman was saying, but I could feel my worrying brain taking over.

What if I'm not pregnant? What if it didn't work? What if there is something actually wrong with me? What if I don't have a gold cord? What if the core of the Earth is full of toxins because of global warming? I then thought about Sarah, my counsellor, and realised these were all hypothetical worries.

'It's hypothetical,' I whispered to myself, 'stop overthinking because it's all hypothetical.'

'What's that?' the masseuse asked, leaning in.

'Sorry, nothing.'

'Are you focusing on the gold cord and the positive energy flowing into your womb?'

'I'm trying.'

'Put your hand on your heart and the other hand on your womb. Feel the energy exchange. Feel the healing taking place. You are ready to receive your baby.'

'Am I?' I said, opening one eye and looking up at her. She had a kind face and was very young. I was worried that I would cry if she kept touching me. I couldn't remember when someone had last touched me with love. Hairy had been strictly functional.

'Are you OK? Do you want me to stop?' she asked, moving her hands onto my stomach and stroking up and down.

'I'm fine, thanks,' I said but I felt a little shaky. I found it sad that I was paying someone to be kind to me and wondered whether this was why so many alternative therapies were popular now. People essentially just wanted to be touched and reassured and it was something that was missing from our culture.

'Are you following a healthy diet?' the therapist asked.

'Oh yes, super healthy,' I said.

'Lots of seeds? Lots of nuts? Lots of orange fruits?'

'What, like oranges?'

'Well, anything orange, basically – it attracts fertility you see.'

I'd been eating lots of protein since I'd had sex with Hairy. I'd also cut out alcohol and was drinking water. It was boring but I wanted to give myself the best chance of it working. I was trying to switch off my heebie-jeebies.

'I'm putting a hot cloth on your pelvis and this hot cloth represents your future baby. The cloth is pushing through into your womb and making itself present. It's creating a safe space. You are radiating positive feelings of potential.'

What if it hadn't worked?

I started thinking about Russell Brand. Wasn't he a fan of this stuff? I was sure *he* was fertile. Unfortunately, he was no longer a womaniser and had settled down.

'Russell Brand,' I chanted in a sort of reverie.

The woman frowned. 'Why are you thinking about him?' she said.

I didn't answer as I was worried she'd find out I hadn't been focusing on her golden cord and hot cloth, etc.

'You have a lot of tension in your body,' she said. 'Do you ever relax?'

'I know. I'm an anxious person.'

'Anxiety isn't good for fertility.'

'No kidding. My mum called it the heebie-jeebies.'

'I feel like you're not taking this seriously. I'll work on your shoulders. If you want to be fertile then you need to loosen those shoulders right up.'

The treatment had cost seventy quid. I felt like this was quite expensive but definitely worth it (even though the woman had been a bit grumpy at times). I walked away feeling lighter and more optimistic. I might already be pregnant. Even if I wasn't, then I'd be pregnant soon. Perhaps I'd go out to a bar and Russell Brand would be hanging out, drinking some sort of kombucha concoction as he was sober now. I'd have to work hard to convince him to sleep with me. Who was I kidding? He would never sleep with me. I'd be lucky if he even *kissed* me.

The stalls were selling herbal supplements (to enhance conception potential) and special room sprays with essential oils (to create the optimum fertile environment at home) and a mobile that you hung over your bed (to inject more positive abundance into your abdomen while you sleep).

I sat on the grass and tried to ignore the fact that everyone around me was in a couple. I texted Meg. I hadn't told her about my plan, so I'd said I was going to a 'health and wellbeing event'. She'd been instantly suspicious as she knew I wasn't usually into being super healthy and looking after myself. Like I said, my favourite meal was fish and chips.

I texted:

I'm bored.

There were times when I wished I could talk to Meg about my baby plan. The problem was I knew she'd try to talk me out of it. I didn't want her to interrogate me either. If it worked then perhaps I'd tell her how it happened retrospectively. For now it was only June who knew the truth about what I was doing. I'd confided in her because I knew she wouldn't judge. We'd talked many times about my desire to be a mum and she understood how important it was to me.

She sent back:

Is it full of young people eating kale chips and bircher muesli?

42

There's no chips and no alcohol.

Well, what the hell are you doing there? Are there running leggings that cost eighty quid?

There were definitely expensive leggings. There were also matcha-infused eye masks, lavender balls to carry in your bra, crystals to push away bad infertile energy, and positive visualisation books. There was an entire book called *Monitor Your Mucus*, with close-up black and white visuals of different samples of vaginal mucus to help you monitor when you were at your most fertile. I preferred to use the tests. Yes, they were more expensive but they didn't require you to stare at the contents of your pants for long periods of time.

Worries:

1. Do I need to monitor mucus or are the ovulation tests just as effective?
2. Why are orange fruits recommended?
3. How do I remain calm and not go totally batshit?

I ate some dried chicken from a packet. It tasted a bit like cardboard. The slogan said *Wannabe-Mama Power Protein*. The problem was I didn't feel any *pregnancy* symptoms. When were they supposed to kick in? A few days after fertilisation? A week? Or was it longer than that? I googled again to check on some of the forums. It seemed that there was a whole thread dedicated to analysing symptoms day by day. I scrolled through and saw that the symptoms for pregnancy were often very similar to the symptoms for getting your period. Cramps, moodiness, sore breasts, insomnia, hunger ... well, I had none of these feelings right now.

I looked up to see a woman walk past with a baby in a sling. It was one of those very expensive slings that I'd looked at in John Lewis and decided I'd buy when the time came. It had a Liberty print on each strap and then a really cute sheepskin head cover. I was nodding happily to this woman when I realised that there was a *mother* at the fertility festival. A mother with a baby! I saw a few women staring at this baby with hungry looks in their eyes. I'd read stories about women who'd snatched babies because they couldn't have them themselves. What was this woman doing? She was parading her baby in front of us, apparently unaware that we were all frantically trying to eat up protein and have sex at the right times and avoid alcohol and not wear synthetic underwear and not stress and do positive manifestations, just so we could have the thing that was hanging off her chest with a little bit of brown hair poking out the top.

I looked away. I wasn't happy about the way I felt. I

was a feminist – or at least I tried to be. It wasn't this woman's fault she'd had a baby. It just felt rather mean for her to be so casual and unaware of where she was and how she was making the rest of us feel. One of the women sitting next to me leant forward.

'That's not right,' she said. 'It should be a policy not to allow babies. The last thing we need is seeing *one of those.*'

'I know,' I agreed, but I also thought our response was a tad extreme.

The thing was, it wasn't rational this envy. There weren't a finite number of babies. It didn't mean that just because this woman had had one there weren't any more to share out. The problem was this was exactly how it felt. With each pregnancy, each Facebook pregnancy update, it felt like the chances of it happening to you grew less and less. There weren't enough babies. There just weren't. With each baby that arrived I felt the urgency growing inside. *Another one that's not mine. And another. And Another. And another…*

To help a sperm travel up to the egg there are several things you can do.

- Stay in bed for twenty minutes after intercourse (or ideally an hour – I'd failed to do this with Hairy because I'd been too keen to get into the shower and away from him)

- Put your knees up or place your feet on the wall or put a small pillow under your hips to accentuate the angle of the pelvis and help sperm pool at the top of your vagina
- Lie down for three days (this was impractical, especially if you had to get to work like I did)

When I'd come home after my night with Hairy, Meg and George weren't up yet and it was quiet. I'd made myself some toast and lain on the sofa with a cushion under my knees. I'd studied one of the many embroidered cushions on the dusty leather chair opposite. There was an owl with a missing eye – there had once been a button there, years ago, but it had fallen off. Mum had been right about memories as I still remembered George and me whacking one another over the head with this owl and Mum rushing in and saying she didn't believe in physical violence but she had the strong urge to 'box our ears'.

'What's that mean?' George had asked.

We'd both been very young and she'd tried to demonstrate softly and then a bit too enthusiastically, putting both hands over George's ears and pushing.

'That hurts, Mummy!' he'd said.

'Yes, sorry, I got carried away,' Mum had replied and picked George up to console him.

She'd been nice as pie one minute and then an

erupted volcano the next. There was no middle ground. I would aim to be a more reasonable parent, for sure. Mum had been under a lot of pressure with the two of us. I was only aiming to have one child. It would be too ambitious to even entertain the idea of two.

The truth was the first night of the pregnancy plan had taken it out of me. I wasn't sure how many partners I'd have to sleep with before it worked. Carl had used condoms but then we'd had a few occasions when he hadn't bothered. This was another thing that contributed to my anxiety – I'd actually been to a fertility clinic in town and had been through a series of blood tests and a scan – the results had all been okay but they'd warned that I needed to get a move on.

'Your eggs aren't getting any younger,' the doctor had said. 'Your chance of falling pregnant naturally isn't very high, I'm afraid.'

Underneath it all I was wondering whether the plan would actually work – it sounded as if it was a very slim chance. However, I preferred to push this worry under the table. Sarah, the counsellor, was not a fan of pushing things under the table.

'You need to face your fears head on, Kate. Tackle the worries and don't just bottle it all up.'

I hadn't told her about the plan, of course. I knew she'd think I was certifiable otherwise.

'Have you been thinking about taking your own life?' she'd ask.

She asked this same question every week. It was a way of measuring my progress, despite the fact that I never felt suicidal, just full of panic or flat as a pancake. Why was it that things were considered OK as long as you didn't want to kill yourself? What if you woke up most mornings and wanted to vomit? Or woke up and felt like you were on a ship and it was spinning out of control?

Mum believed in control, had always been a big fan of 'Five Year Plans'. She'd put herself through an Open University course when my brother and I were little and then she'd started working for Oxfam part-time as an office manager. She'd learnt how to speak French in her free evenings, via those audio courses where you repeated key phrases over and over. She'd always been hellbent on self-improvement, always interrogated me on my long-term goals. Where did I want to be in a year? Two? Four?

'I have no idea,' I'd reply.

'That's not good enough,' she'd say. 'You'll still be in exactly the same place if you don't set yourself some objectives.'

'I think I'd like to make documentaries,' I'd said (which was true).

'Well, make a start. Do some research. Go back and study again.'

'I will … one day.'

That day had never come. It was as if I was infected with a horrible inertia and time was just steadily moving forward. Everyone else's life was taking shape and mine was just a horrible, shapeless blob of a thing. This baby idea was part of that. I could work in a bookshop, live with my brother and mate watching *Love Island*, or I could shake everything up and become a functioning adult. Without a baby, the future stretched into infinity, full of monotony and routine. I knew some mothers would say that having a family felt like this too, but I wanted to find this out for myself, thanks.

Of course I admired women who decided to remain childless, but I didn't want to travel, write a novel, climb a mountain – all the things you could do when you didn't have kids. I didn't particularly like spending time on my own. I didn't mind doing it (I didn't have much choice) but the prospect of being alone forever frightened me. I lived the life of someone who had kids – with more rest, of course. I liked to nest at home. I liked to eat carbs, especially bowls full of pasta. I preferred to drink wine in front of the TV and go to bed at about nine or ten.

I was living the life of a middle-aged mum and had been for some time.

After my first trip to a fertility clinic I'd looked another one up, hoping that I'd get more positive news. This one specialised in supplying donor sperm. The first consultation was £250. I found the amount stupendous, and when I leafed through the brochure and discovered that each and every appointment would be around the same, with £4-500 for scans, I realised that, in effect, it would eat up any savings I had and I'd have to put the rest on a credit card – and my salary wasn't enormous at Franklin's, though I was lucky enough not to have to pay rent.

'Have you looked at our database of donors?' the woman asked. 'It's all online if you want to scroll through. We don't provide photos but you can read about their physical characteristics and what their hobbies are.'

'Not yet,' I said.

After she'd taken some blood and sent it away to be tested she opened the database up on her screen.

'So … you just type in your criteria here – nationality, height, eye colour, hobbies – and then your selection comes up here. You order the sperm and put it in your basket and then we defrost that sample and that's that!'

Twenty different matches popped up. What did I really care about? Eye colour? Hair colour? Where the donor had been born? I'd not bothered to think about any of these things. I just wanted a baby, didn't I? I visualised all these different men standing in white-tiled rooms, furiously masturbating. What was their motivation? They were only paid a nominal amount, apparently.

'Some of our clients are in their mid-forties and we have quite high success rates.'

She handed me a price list of different options. It seemed expensive – too expensive for a small tube of sperm.

I couldn't stop thinking that there was a cheaper, more human way of doing this. With a one-night stand there was at least some kind of *connection*, wasn't there? A temporary relationship. Maybe even some mutual attraction – although this was hard to manufacture if you were desperate. I'd also have some sort of impression of the father – more than just eye colour and whether he liked playing tennis on the weekends. And there was the money thing, too. I'd rather spend my savings on the baby, if at all possible.

It wasn't entirely logical, but it made enough sense for me to create the plan rather than go down the conventional route to having a baby.

It was time for my next treatment with the Fertility Fest tarot reader. I got up off the grass and went to have my tarot reading (which was happening in a tepee decorated with painted hummingbirds). On the way I spent forty pounds on supplements, some of which were designed to help you get pregnant and others to be taken when you *knew* you were pregnant. I hoped that this would soon be the case.

'There's a baby trying to come into your life but you're blocking him out,' the tarot reader said. She had a mass of curly black hair piled up on top of her head and a cold, businesslike manner. I got the impression she found all these infertile women annoying, but they were also a good source of income for her so she had to put on a front of being sympathetic and kindly.

'This baby wants to stay with you, but there's just too much stress and anxiety in your world,' she said, turning over a card with a small child surrounded by sticks. 'He's trapped in the in-between world. He's fighting to get out.'

I felt a lump in my throat. This poor baby was fighting but my own anxiety was keeping him at bay. How selfish I was!

'You need to relax. It's only when you relax that you'll have a baby.'

This *relax* advice was the most common given when you did any research on having a baby. If you relaxed, then it would happen immediately, apparently. It only required staying calm and you'd be pregnant in no time. I didn't believe that this was the only factor at play. Otherwise, why were all these women at this festival? Were they all just too anxious for it to happen? Why were they paying so much money if it was just about staying calm and remaining stoical about it all?

'Do you think I could be pregnant right now?' I asked, on the verge of tears.

I was hoping she could sense something in my body – the beginnings of a tiny person growing. The massage had made me feel vulnerable and now this woman was making me feel awful, as if *I* was responsible for not being pregnant. And yes, I did feel responsible. It was my own fault. I'd never prioritised it at the right time. Why was that? That poor child trapped in the in-between world! Surrounded by sticks. Trying to get out! The anxiety was building inside me and my heart was hammering in my chest.

'You're not pregnant,' she said confidently, holding onto my palm. 'Your womb is vacant but a baby will come into it eventually … not until you relax, though, not until you open your world.'

I couldn't speak as I knew my voice would break.

'It's fifty-nine ninety-nine if you want another reading and I can give you more details on your future child if you like?' she said wearily. 'I do a prediction on what kind of personality they will have and what kind of parent you'll be.'

I hated this woman. I wanted bad things to happen to her. It was awful to take advantage of poor, sad people. I picked up my tote bag, with its Fertility Festival logo and a unicorn holding a baby on the front, and walked out. There was a couple waiting to go into the tent. They looked excited and were holding hands tenderly.

'Don't go in,' I said, my voice breaking, 'she's *horrible.*'

They looked at me with puzzled expressions. I didn't wait around. It was depressing to be on my own, without anyone to console me. I was anxious and a mess. I didn't deserve to be a parent. I needed a glass of wine.

I crumpled up the ticket and got the bus home. I refused to be taken advantage of. *I* was going to be the one directing my own destiny from now on.

Luckily, there was no one home. Was it true that I'd blocked this child out of my life through my anxiety? I would have to talk to Sarah, my counsellor, about this – not the plan, but how fertility and mental health were linked. The thing was, I'd never tried to get pregnant before, not properly, not until now, so the tarot-reading woman was crazy, talking nonsense. I wanted to contact the organisers and get my money back, but I also knew I was hormonal and that nobody had forced me to part with my money.

I spent the rest of the day in my room, scrolling through social media and watching Netflix. After three hours my eyes bulged and I had a headache. It was a massive waste of time but I'd switched off for a little while and it was possibly more effective than the festival.

I ate macaroni cheese from a can (the only thing that was left in the cupboard that looked unhealthy and didn't require lots of effort to prepare). Then I had a quick bath and went to bed early. I had a dream that I'd just given birth. The midwife handed me a perfect little baby wrapped in a muslin. I breathed a sigh of relief. How had this happened so quickly? The face looking back at me was that of Hairy man.

'Can I put my willy in your bum?' he asked.

I awoke in a cold sweat.

Chapter Four

Franklin's was not as big as Waterstones and positioned itself as a quirkier, left-field bookseller (though we stocked all the same writers and didn't have a lot of small, independent imprints). I'd fallen into the job while at university, then stayed when the realisation that I'd struggle to become an award-winning documentary maker became more apparent. And now I'd been there fifteen years, which was mad when you thought about it! Lesley, the manager, had offered me promotions over the years, and I'd risen to the lofty heights of her deputy but had never moved to another store or tried to get any higher up. The truth was I wasn't interested in rising to the top. It didn't look much fun, you see. Lesley always seemed to suffer from terrible headaches – each week brought pdf files full of our sales targets from head office and I was happy to have a job that just kept my brain ticking over. No stressful managing of people. No having to deal with head office. Some might call that a lack of ambition, but I was more comfortable that way. Mum had been disappointed that I hadn't aimed higher – she'd had a lot of frustrated ambition – but I wasn't sure that selling books was what I wanted to do all my life, although I was making a jolly good job of doing it all my life, regardless.

I could hear the radio blaring from Meg's room – she had one of those old, tinny radio alarms because she was trying to stop herself from checking her phone first thing. It didn't work and she could usually be found sitting up in bed with the radio on, scrolling through her social media and emails. Meg worked for a beauty company in Slough. It was French and sold premium skincare. Her job involved coming up with new ways to position poncey face cream to ageing women. We sometimes brainstormed things together – increasingly, as we both slid past our mid-thirties, ageing was becoming less abstract and something we noticed around our eyes, necks and chins.

Mum hadn't bothered to redecorate over the years, so some parts of the house were 70s in style – we had a peach bathroom, for instance, the kind you very rarely saw anymore unless in a Mike Leigh film. The location was good – just off the Harrow Road with a twenty-five-minute walk to Portobello Market – and the house was situated between two massive estates, both of which had a bad reputation. That I didn't mind, but I was always informed of it on the way home from a night out by taxi drivers. George had checked on house-price sites online and if we sold up we'd each be able to afford a small flat (nowhere in this area though).

The three of us got along well. We knew when one another needed space but equally when we needed company. Some evenings after work we'd make dinner together (taking it in turns) and then sit and watch TV. There was an old TV in the front room and we sometimes watched it together, but more often than not we went into our separate rooms and watched our laptops instead. Meg was in a relationship with an Australian guy called Tim, who stayed over more and more often. Tim annoyed me as he tended to see himself as the man of the house, even though George was around. He was also obsessed with exercise, especially Joe Wicks. He sent him messages on Instagram, and even tried to find out where he lived so he could 'accidentally' run with him one morning.

A typical conversation with Tim went like this:

Me: 'What's that?' (staring at repulsive green sludge in a plastic cup)

Tim: 'It's a probiotic smoothie with kale, wheatgrass, coconut oil and charcoal.'

Me (drinking tea with one sugar – my usual tipple): 'Sounds tasty.'

Tim: 'It means my body is burning energy from the moment I get up. Your tea will give you a little lift but in ten minutes you'll be feeling flat again. I bet you put sugar in it too, right?'

Me: 'Yes, just one though.'

Tim: 'Do you know how dangerous sugar is? It's the number one cause of death (I was pretty sure this wasn't true). If you eliminate sugar from your diet, you'll feel so much better.'

Me: 'Is one sugar really that bad?'

Tim (showing a diagram on his phone of how sugar kills you very quickly): 'Here, look at this. It kind of speaks for itself.'

There was now this lifestyle thing where everyone eliminated everything. No sugar. No wheat. No carbs. How come we'd lived all these years and not realised we were allergic to these things? Did medieval people suffer with IBS? Did they mush up greens and try and drink them before they went for a run? Where was the rock-and-roll spirit in jogging every single day and weighing chicken before you cooked it? As far as I could see, this health boastfulness was all about making yourself feel superior to other people. There was no mistaking, however, that Tim was thinner than me and way fitter – but for what purpose? Was it to avoid death? Or live a couple of years longer than me? Tim had turned so much attention to his diet that it left no space in his brain to tidy up after himself. He left tiny pairs of sweaty running shorts draped over the backs of chairs. He left towels on the bathroom floor. And he used my expensive Ren shower gel – I knew this because I smelt it on him when he'd come downstairs one night.

It was time for work so I pulled on a stripy T-shirt with my favourite black trousers and was ready. I checked my reflection as I got to the bottom of the stairs – there was no discernible bump. I'd had zero cramps (sometimes you apparently felt twinges when the embryo implanted into your womb lining). It was hard not to keep googling symptoms. I'd paid forty quid for the fertility massage and another fifty for the festival day pass. That didn't include the supplements I'd bought. This baby-making process was very expensive. I looked at my face – I'd put my usual flick of black eyeliner on and a bit of blusher and I'd treated myself to a great primer a few months back which basically turned my face from corpse-like to just about passable.

My job was ideal because I loved reading. Or at least, I *had* loved reading until Mum died and then I'd found that all the books seemed very trivial and I couldn't focus on the plot or characters. I was still trying to get back into reading because I knew it could offer a great escape, but my brain was too fragmented and my anxiety usually meant I had to keep turning back to the first few pages to remind myself what was happening, making it feel like a test rather than something enjoyable.

I often felt jealous of authors. I was someone who didn't have a creative bone in my body – even my fashion sense was uninspired. I had two or three key looks and I rotated these each week. I'd been put on Earth to absorb other people's content – I was the girl staring at everyone at the party with nothing to say. George was a massive fan of BBC4 music documentaries and we'd watched so many over the years that I could recite verbatim how the Rolling Stones had formed, and how punk had evolved from the clubs of NY to the Sex Pistols' iconic gig at the 100 Club (always the same grainy video was shown of a dark, cavernous nightclub with angry young people slamming against one another).

Worries:

1. Why don't I feel a sense of purpose?
2. Why does everyone else seem to know where they're headed?
3. Why can't I seem to have good days? But how do you make a good day?

Why were there no documentaries made about people who coasted all their lives? People who were average? I'd never excelled at anything aside from maybe swimming when I'd won first place in the 100 metres breaststroke at my school swimming gala at the age of twelve. I couldn't play an instrument. If I tried to draw a figure, it always looked like a scarecrow. I was rubbish at dancing. I'd never been cool.

It wouldn't matter once I was pregnant. Being pregnant would get me noticed. Or perhaps this wasn't strictly true. I'd seen plenty of pregnant women get ignored on tubes and not offered a seat. An image of Hairy vomiting into the toilet hit me between the eyes. The plan was a good one but it wouldn't be without fallout. I was aware that sleeping with people you didn't know wasn't particularly good for your self-esteem but I felt pretty low anyway, so how much worse could I really feel?

I knocked on Meg's door and told her I'd see her later. She didn't reply so was perhaps getting some early morning action with Tim. Out of spite, I took a pair of his running shorts off the back of one of the chairs and wiped the kitchen counter with them. I liked the thought of him running with toast crumbs stuck up his arse. On the Ealing Broadway tube on the way into work, I got my notebook out. It was good to write a few notes about Hairy in case it had worked and one day my child might ask about him.

1. Good and plentiful hair genes
2. Poor at holding drink
3. Bob Marley fan. Could be worse – i.e. old Dire Straits
4. Why does he own a skateboard in his late thirties?
5. Too much bong = sperm damage? Must google this!
6. Possibly brain damaged?

Mum had given me scanty knowledge about Dad ... a few phrases such as:

'A miserable sod.'

'Selfish.'

'Immature.'

'Unable to deal with real life and only happy when listening to music.'

I looked at the man sitting opposite. His legs were spread very wide and I could see the outline of his balls through his tight black polyester trousers. He had a penis the same size as his balls which was perhaps why he felt the need to take up lots of space. There had been an Instagram account set up with lots of photos with men like this, spreading their legs. I had immediately thought of Carl when I heard about it, because despite his relatively nerdy ways and his supposed feminism, he tended to take up lots of space. In bed he'd sprawl across diagonally and end up taking half of my pillow, covering it with drool. There were definitely advantages to not being in a couple – and having a whole bed to myself was one of them. This wouldn't be for long, though, because once the baby arrived I planned to try co-sleeping because it sounded lovely and an ideal way to stay close.

I came across an article on my phone that claimed marijuana made sperm 'swim in circles'. For a moment I felt panic; had I really gone through the whole debacle for nothing? Of course I'd had sex with people I didn't know very well at uni, but once you'd had sex with someone you cared about it was demoralising. Sex with Carl had been good, but then we'd just stopped. Three times a week ... once a week ... once every two weeks ... once a month and then ... nothing.

I went back to making some notes.

1. Would a fitness fanatic be better? (Healthier sperm?)
2. Avoid heavy drug users – drop into conversation early on to gauge drug habits and level of hedonism

Franklin's was quiet. Unfortunately, all too often people came in to look at books and then bought them on Amazon because it was cheaper. I'd caught people taking photos of new books and then leaving again. Lesley said it was so they could come back in and buy them another time but it was obvious that buying online was cheaper. Lesley was my boss. She had flame-red hair and was perpetually exhausted because she'd taken it upon herself to have four children. Nowadays it was rare to do this – the majority had two. I would be happy to have one. It felt unnecessarily greedy to have more.

Lesley didn't like her husband Toby and was always complaining about the fact that he locked himself up in his home office (he worked in IT consultancy) and used work as an excuse to never help her out. Lesley complained *a lot* about being a mum. It was tiring. Hard work. There was no 'me time'. I, on the other hand, had too much of the stuff. Lesley got on my nerves but I tried to be sympathetic. I had no idea why she'd needed to make her life difficult but there was no denying that working five days a week and raising that many children was a challenge. I tried to be as supportive as I could even though Lesley could be annoying at times as she assumed that my child-free life was perfect. She'd often say things like:

'At least you have lovely lie-ins.'

'You could backpack around Nepal if you fancied it.'

'God, I can't imagine being able to read a book with no interruptions.'

The thing was, I couldn't read a book with no

interruptions because a voice inside was always screaming *I want to be a mum!* And this voice made focusing on the narrative entirely impossible. Also, there are people who want to backpack around Nepal and others who really don't; I was in the latter category. Plus lie-ins lost their allure when you were in bed on your own with nothing to entertain you all day. If anything, I got up earlier these days just to give myself a sense of purpose.

'Can you start tackling those new arrivals downstairs?' Lesley said as I walked past the till. 'Nice stripy top. Is it Boden?'

I wasn't quite ready for Boden yet – I associated it with mumsiness. Lesley loved Boden. She was always telling me when they had money off and nice dresses in stock. Not that there really was such a thing as 'mumsy' any more as mums wore nice trainers and camo jackets and dungarees – these seemed to be a bit of a thing. But Boden was one of those brands I'd earmarked for when I was officially in the club. Then I'd be flouncing about in seagull-print dresses while I told everyone on Instagram how much wine I needed at the end of the day to get through the week. I glanced down at my phone. George had sent a GIF of Jim Carrey vomiting up half of what looked like a pumpkin.

Someone stopped out all night.

I texted back:

Luckily I don't suffer with hangovers.

This was true. I rarely felt bad the next day after drinking. I'd also drunk nowhere near as much as Hairy. He replied:

I've got another job interview

Good luck.

I sent him a GIF of Beyoncé twerking and then put my phone in my locker. George had been to a job interview roughly once a week. He wanted to work in film but he didn't have the connections that other people did to open the door. He was a bit like me in that he wasn't completely passionate about the idea so instead he just went on lots of job interviews. He'd tried lots of different things and had recently been fired from a market research position that he'd found too tedious (he'd luckily saved enough money during this time to tide him over for a while). My original plan after I finished uni was to make award-winning documentaries. By the time I got to my mid-twenties I realised that working for nothing was incredibly demoralising. If I'd been into the idea enough then I probably would have just chugged along, but when I saw the job advertised at Franklin's I'd gone for it.

The stockroom was a messy, disorganised space with stacked-up boxes in every corner. There was a poster of Martin Amis with two horns drawn on his head. It was a nice place, somewhere to get away from the customers. Most were OK, but some liked to come into the store and make your life more difficult. There were still people out there who thought shop workers were beneath them and they enjoyed lording it about – plucking an obscure book title out of the air and then making you sweat over the laptop for twenty minutes trying to order it in from a branch in Cardiff before telling you not to bother because, 'I'll get it from the library instead.'

However, many of our daytime customers were old and lonely. They just wanted to chat and tell you about their day. This was OK with me. It helped pass the time. June was different because she didn't feel like an old person. She still had a good sense of humour and embraced life. I'd come to the conclusion that I was more rigid and conservative than she was in many ways. She loved trying new things and embraced any opportunities to put herself outside her comfort zone – she'd taken a couple of Saga holidays to Italy even though she didn't know anyone. Her husband had died ten years ago and she had a daughter called Julia who she rarely saw because she lived in Australia and it was clear that she missed her a lot. I looked forward to seeing June when she came in – her presence was reassuring.

I'd also told her all about my need to become a parent.

'I worry that you think motherhood is going to change everything for the better,' she'd said as we sat sharing a piece of ginger cake in the M&S café, 'because it's tough.' She picked a crumb out of her teeth with one of her fingers. 'In fact, if I remember correctly, it's not always a bed of roses, you know.'

'But it gives your life more meaning,' I said. 'I mean, what is it all about, otherwise? You basically are born, live, and then die!'

This was the key thing. With no relationship, no meaningful career, no status, I was relying on motherhood to make me feel like my life was worthwhile. I also saw this kid as a project – a test to see if I could get One Thing Right.

'And when I hear people go on about how they have kids to "help me out when I'm old"? Well, let me tell you … you can't rely on *that* happening,' June said ignoring my comment.

'I feel like I'd enjoy it,' I said. 'I don't expect them to look after me when I'm old.'

This wasn't strictly true. Whenever I saw the vision of the old lady in the smelly kaftan being eaten by her cats as she lay comatose on the floor, it was usually the future without children. I imagined my kid would at least come and visit when I was old and possibly bring nice posh cat food so the cats wouldn't be tempted to eat me when I collapsed from old age.

'Essentially, motherhood is like being broken in like a horse, Kate. It takes every piece of your identity apart, smashes it up and then reassembles it again.'

'That sounds just the ticket,' I said, laughing.

And it did. People talked about it changing your life and how you couldn't go out anymore and had to sacrifice your freedom. But what if you had no life to begin with? I didn't like adventure. I didn't do drugs. I smoked occasionally but no longer enjoyed it and would usually rush to wash my hands right after because I hated the stench it left on my fingers.

'Anyway, you've got me. I'm kind of like a surrogate daughter,' I said. 'I mean, if you're lonely.'

'Yes, I'm lucky there's you who'll take me out for cake now and then.'

'And listen to your paranoias about technology. And recommend good books.'

'It's not paranoia. Did you hear about how they used data to manipulate voters in America? Do you know they can send you specific adverts so you don't know why you're buying a thing but just feel compelled to do it?'

I should have been worried about these things but the world had reached a stage where so much was going wrong that it was hard to prioritise what to worry about the most. I made a monthly donation to the WWF as the rainforests were being burned down but there was also sex trafficking, child abuse, war crimes, animal cruelty ... the list went on and on. Apparently, badgers were being culled in a very painful way. There was footage of a baby whale crying as its mum was dragged behind a whaling ship. Misery was everywhere and there were very few reasons to feel good about life. I didn't know what to do to change anything. I tried not to use plastic bags. I carried a bottle with me everywhere so I didn't have to buy plastic bottles. I didn't eat too much red meat. None of these things seemed to make much of a difference as we were on this course to oblivion and it was decided. In this context, having a baby seemed slightly foolhardy.

'So how is your plan coming along?' she said.

'Well, I've had my first attempt so now it's just about waiting.'

'It's modern,' she'd said. 'There's a girl on *EastEnders* who's going to a clinic in Copenhagen – you know, to find a donor, a sperm donor.'

'I want to try this first. It's cheaper and somehow feels less anonymous. I will at least be able to tell my child something about their dad.'

'It's not good for the soul, though,' she said. 'I mean, I had one fling when I was in my twenties, but I felt lousy after. I don't think we're programmed to just get our ends away and then never see one another again.'

June had gazed into the middle distance at the rows upon rows of linen trousers.

'I have always fancied linen,' June said wistfully, 'but it looks so unflattering on your bottom. I do have a few pairs of trousers but they never look quite right.'

Chapter Five

'On a scale of one to ten with ten being every day, how bad has your anxiety been this week?' Sarah asked.

This time we were sitting opposite one another in her office. There were no pictures on the walls, just a laptop on a desk and a box of tissues in case I started crying.

'I guess it's been not too bad this week. So, like a three?'

'That's progress,' Sarah said.

She had beautiful almond-shaped eyes and long black hair. I'd been seeing her for a few months now. It definitely helped. Or at least I thought it did. I had no idea how bad I'd feel without these sessions.

'Why do you think it's lower?'

I wanted to tell her that it was the thought of being

pregnant, the kick-off of my plan, because it had given me something to focus on ... but I also knew she wouldn't approve.

'And can you read me out some of the worries on your tree?'

I got my piece of paper out.

'I'm worried that I will never be happy.'

'Is that a hypothetical or a practical worry?' Sarah asked.

'Hypothetical?'

'Right, so there's nothing you can do about it right now, so forget it. Do you think you can do that?'

NO, I CAN'T! I wanted to scream but I nodded. I always thought things sounded easy when I was with Sarah. She had such a lovely, calm manner. I wanted to carry her around in my pocket – she could just whisper in my ear when I was in the midst of an anxiety attack and make me feel better.

'I'm worried that I'll be in the same job all my life.'

'OK, so that's more practical. Why don't you try and look for something else? What do you really want to do? What would be your dream job?'

'I have no idea. I thought I wanted to make TV documentaries.'

'And what happened?'

'I couldn't afford to work for nothing for years on end.'

'OK, so can we agree that by next week you'll have looked at some other careers that might suit you?'

I nodded but knew I couldn't be bothered. There was little point in trying to change direction at my age. Everyone was younger and had more energy. I was putting all my hopes on the baby thing.

'What else is on the tree?'

'I'm worried about my heart palpitations. I haven't had them this week but I know they'll come back and I'm worried about that.'

'OK ... well, that's hypothetical. So what do we do, Kate?'

'Forget it?' I wished it was so easy. I knew, in theory, it made sense. It helped to write it down though. It also helped to see that my thoughts were often the same. They all involved a future that was negative. I said goodbye to Sarah and went home. I never spoke to her about my desire to be a mum. I wasn't sure why this was.

Worries:

1. I'm not pregnant.
2. I'm not pregnant.
3. I'm not pregnant.

I experienced nothing unusual for two days. Online, it was hard to get a steer on what was normal. Some women felt cramping. Others felt nothing at all. I busied myself thinking about new candidates. If it hadn't worked this time, then focusing on someone who was very fit made more sense. The fitter the man, the better the sperm. It would also make the whole experience more pleasurable, perhaps, too – though fit men weren't necessarily good in bed as I'd discovered a couple of times before.

There were three gyms within walking distance from Franklin's. I wasn't a member of any of them because I preferred to go on the occasional jog rather than fork out sixty quid a month to attend once a year. I hated the way gyms smelt. It didn't matter how premium they were or how much expensive equipment they'd invested in, there was always a dire pong. I also hated the swimming pools in gyms, which usually had a small selection of old Band-Aids and balls of hair collected in the water vents. I'd once witnessed a guy blowing his nose directly into the pool and after that I decided I didn't want to pay money to swim in someone else's snot. Gyms weren't hygienic. It was better to go outside to exercise, though my trainers hadn't seen much action either because there was just so much good TV on these days.

June came into the store during the week.

'Have you read this yet?' she asked, gesturing at Lee Child's new book.

'I've not been reading recently,' I said. It was three years but I wasn't prepared to admit this to June who relied on my recommendations which were mostly gleaned from the reviews I'd read or things other customers had said to me.

'I forgot to ask you what this guy was like ... you know, the guy you had the fling with.'

'He was hairy.'

'That's no bad thing. A hairy man is nice and masculine. It's hard finding men that look like men these days. I like a good beard, as long as it's trimmed and kept clean. I hate those great big fisherman things. They make me feel queasy. Robert never had a beard. He always kept himself well and he always used a lovely aftershave too.'

'There's part of me that doesn't want to have his child,' I said.

There was a woman with an armful of books looking impatient as she waited for our conversation to wrap up. This was the part of working in a shop that I hated. Sometimes I forgot that there were customers and it was our job to please and placate them. I sometimes got the urge to tell them to shove the hell off. After I'd bagged up her books and she'd paid, June said, 'I won't tell anyone. I mean, who would I tell anyway? My own daughter doesn't bother keeping in touch. Like I said, there's no guarantee your kid will keep in touch with you.'

'It's not about that, June. I've said it before: I *need* this in my life. Once it's grown up I'll be like you and befriend a young worker and tell her all my woes.'

June laughed.

I downloaded an app on my phone and tried to visualise the baby growing. The app told me to think about my womb as an apple with a seed growing inside. The seed was a baby. Each day the seed got more robust. The walls of the apple thicker and more fertile. The voice was soothing. While I was often quite cynical about new-age stuff, I felt like it might just be maximising my chances.

On Friday I did a quick recce to see if there were any fitness fanatics that I could hit up for some sperm. I bought a Pret avocado wrap, and then walked to the first gym, which was upstairs from Boots. It was called MuscleMax, one of those old-school body-building gyms frequented by wrestler-types. These guys usually had massive arms and chests, inflated stomachs and twig-like legs. Was this healthy? This was what I liked about the plan. It gave me a mission, something to strive for that went beyond the usual lose weight/get a new haircut/redo my wardrobe fare that women were supposed to be interested in. Carl had always been naturally thin and hadn't had to exercise. It used to frustrate me that he could eat so much food and yet you could see his ribs sticking out. For a split second I wondered what he was doing. In an ideal world he'd be on his own, sitting in bed, feeling lonesome, and looking at photos of me on his phone. Instead, he was probably in a fun meeting with the pretty intern, creating strategy for a new deodorant. Why did I care? I didn't love him. It just made me feel better to think of him as being full of remorse and loss. *I had a perfect girlfriend,* he'd be saying. *She was quiet but really a person of substance. Not some daft flibbertigibbet.*

In the gym reception there were photos of people who looked normal in the 'before' photo and then scrawny and malnourished in the 'after' one. Underneath each was the length of time it had taken for them to 'shred' themselves down to a skeletal body mass. To turn themselves into strips of biltong in tight Lycra. The receptionist was bored and happy to let me look around the place (I told her I was considering a membership). In fact, it wasn't just men; there were lots of slim, blonde girls with high ponytails and Sweaty Betty leggings mooching about, staring at their phones.

The whole place made me sweat. The thing is, there's

a reason that your bum is on your back – the reason is so that you don't have to see it every day. The young men were so besotted with their reflections and taking photos of themselves in the mirror that they didn't notice me. Trying to get one of them to sleep with me (if I wasn't already pregnant) would be hard work. No booze to lower their standards. No dark lighting. I couldn't face working out here and didn't own any expensive workout gear. I only went jogging about twice a year and usually wore an old pair of pyjama bottoms and a Snoopy T-shirt. I had a veritable trouser suit of cellulite (life was too short to body brush every single day). I was too old to be a millennial, so had missed the whole body/health/wellbeing/give-up-every-food-group-one-at-a-time thing.

'I hate men with massive muscles,' Mum had said while we sat watching some reality show. 'Never trust a man who cares too much about what he looks like.'

'But everyone cares,' I'd said. 'We're all image obsessed.'

'But what are you going to talk about with such a man? The attraction always goes. And then you're just faced with a plonker who spends four hours in the bathroom shaving his chest and exfoliating his bottom.'

She was right. There was something unattractive about a man who was entirely obsessed with how he looked.

'It was better in the 60s. A quick bit of talcum down your pants and a bit of lavender oil behind your ears and that was it. We would have never got anything done if we'd spent all our time trying to get rid of our wrinkles and doing our nails and getting our hair done. It feels like we're going backwards. And the fact that men are doing it now doesn't make it any more equal.'

It was sad how we thought we were feminists but still bought into the idea that we had to look a certain way to be accepted. The feminists Mum had idolised all had hairy chins and dungarees. They had been the true revolutionaries. Now it was all these women on social media selling Mac lipsticks while they danced about in their expensive bikinis with no cellulite or body hair to be seen.

Worries:

1. Am I in danger of being irrelevant because I've never had a bikini wax and have always sorted my bits at home?
2. Am I the only woman allergic to exercise? Why don't I care enough about what I look like?

I was objectifying men too. Here I was in a man-market with different male bodies sliding past on a conveyer belt. Too big, too small, too fat, too thin, too stupid, too arrogant, too bald, bad teeth. It was repellent – but also quite liberating – to stop looking for love and just boil it down to functional characteristics. It was possibly what men had been doing for some time. On the way out, one of the men winked at me. He was wearing an all-in-one black Lycra suit and a black baseball cap. I was sort of flattered. Nowadays I snatched these tiny compliments up like a sparrow pecking up crumbs. Could I get a temporary membership and come along in the evenings? Then try and slip into the male changing room and hide in the shower?

'We have a three-month deal,' the receptionist said. 'Lose two stone and get two months' free membership,' she said, looking me up and down. 'It might take some time.'

'Thanks,' I said coldly. 'I'm actually looking to tone up and am quite happy with my size.' This wasn't true of course.

I forgave the receptionist. It would have driven me mad – techno blasting in your ears all day, people losing their passes, people stinking of BO, men in Lycra winking at you. She had those strange eyebrows that all the young women sported now. There's a thing: once you saw make-up on people and didn't understand it, you were old.

'What about the changing rooms?' I asked. 'Are they unisex?'

I was thinking about the plan and how easy it might be to shuffle up to someone in the shower, someone fond of winking and not too worried about an older woman with cellulite and sagging boobs.

'We have separate male and female changing rooms, madam,' she said.

'Aren't we supposed to be gender-neutral?' I asked.

I left without getting a membership. There had to be easier ways to meet men. There were pubs. Bars. Clubs. Dating apps.

Besides, I might even be pregnant. I just had to stay positive.

I thought about the donor-sperm man I'd read about. You could contact him and he drove to your house and brought fresh semen out. He only charged whatever it cost him in petrol. The only real downside was the fact he looked like Noel Edmonds, like he'd had his hair done at a barber's in the 80s. He was someone to keep in mind if all else failed, but that wasn't true. *Just* yet.

In four days I could take a test. *Four days.*

I sat on a bench in Ealing shopping centre watching all the people going by. There was a huge Primark that was three floors high. People emerged with giant paper bags full of things they didn't need but which made them feel better. Lesley always lectured me if I went in there and bought anything, usually a unicorn-shaped hand-sanitiser bottle.

'There's a reason the stuff is so cheap in there, Kate. You need to avoid it on principle. Did you know the clothing industry is the second biggest environmental polluter?'

I did. I also knew that the clothes were probably made by children and the dye was from baby monkeys with their juices squeezed out. Was it any wonder that we were anxious? That *I* was anxious? You couldn't even buy a unicorn-shaped hand sanitiser without fearing you'd brought about the end of the world.

I opened my notebook.

I am pregnant. I am fertile. I am optimistic. My womb is ripe and ready. I am powerful and loved.

Then I started thinking about sex parties. George and I had started to watch a programme about how they were rebranded now and were aspirational and not in the suburbs with Peter-Stringfellow-types gyrating in leopard-print thongs to Duran Duran records. Now the people that went were good-looking and the women could just snog or choose to go the whole hog. The key issue seemed to be that you had to be vetted before you could attend. I didn't know much about what actually happened as we'd had to turn it off before the couple profiled in the documentary actually went to the party, because George and I felt awkward watching it side by side. But just as with the gym plan, it was clear I'd never get voted into a sex party. I didn't even have any decent underwear. Whenever I had the choice to buy something I chose on-top clothes – who actually saw underwear? – and if you were having a one-night stand then you took your clothes off quickly so the underwear was redundant.

Carl had bought me some ludicrous pants from a sex shop once, which had two red strings on either side that cut into my hips. I never wore them. No, I wore them once. I think even he realised they weren't a good look on my body type. I wasn't mad keen on sex anyway, so the idea of a party where all you did was get your end away troubled me. Perhaps I'd never had the right lovers. Maybe I had a low libido. That seemed to be something that was happening to lots of people. Sex was tiring; it took a lot of effort. If you were trying to have a baby then it was worth it, but otherwise you were better off masturbating. Although, I didn't do this often, either. Masturbation was quick and you didn't need to have a conversation. You could watch a video and get it all wrapped up in five minutes. In the future, nobody would bother having sex. I was just slightly ahead of the curve.

I checked Tinder to see who might pop up. There was rarely someone I liked who liked me. It seemed to be older men who liked trout fishing who were attracted to a slightly overweight, pale, Goldie Hawn lookalike. I wasn't sure what I'd selected on my profile to attract these men. Carl was on there too. I had seen his profile flash past only a month after we'd split up. It made my heart stop for a minute to see him posing (and he *was* posing) in his flat, bookshelves of books he rarely read behind him (he never had time as his job took up his entire life) and an expression I'd only ever seen in the early weeks of our relationship (when he'd had lust in his eyes). I wondered if he'd looked at my profile.

I'd shown his photo to Meg. 'He looks quite fit in these – did he always have those glasses or are they new?' she'd asked.

'No idea and that's not what I want to hear, mate,' I'd said.

'Right, you're well shot of him. I mean, anyone who can leave their girlfriend just after their mum dies has to a psychopath.' I'd nodded but didn't agree. I knew I'd played a part in our break-up. Long before Mum's death I'd disengaged. Once the attraction waned, I grew less interested. I found it hard to show enthusiasm in his work because I didn't understand it. Carl was right that there was no politics at Franklin's – it was a fairly steady, monotonous place to be. He also seemed to snore more loudly than when we'd first met. I saw him picking dead skin off his feet and it made my stomach turn and he'd developed a very small bald spot on the back of his head. I knew he'd probably noticed similar things in me too.

Mum's death had sped things up but it would have happened eventually.

The following Monday it felt like my period was on its way. And so I visited another gym. My heart was sinking but I had to keep pressing on. If it hadn't worked – and let's face it, it would be a miracle if it had – I had to move on to the next donor.

'You're on a bit of a fitness drive!' Lesley exclaimed as I told her where I was going. 'You're lucky, going to the gym. When would I ever fit it in?' she said. 'I sometimes wish I could be single again and just magic wand those kids away … but don't tell anyone I said that.'

I grimaced. It was hard to listen to her being so blasé about being a mum.

'If I didn't have kids I'd swim every day before work and then do a lovely yoga class *after* work. You're a lucky girl, Kate,' she said as I left.

Yes, I'm very lucky. *If only she knew.*

Gym Dreams was far busier than the other gym I'd visited because it was the beginning of the week and everyone was detoxing from the weekend. The men were much younger and didn't even look up as I walked past. They looked like they didn't have sex very often or, if they did, it was mainly to burn off carbohydrates before they did another HIIT workout. They possibly had an app they ran over your body to analyse your BMI before they agreed to sleep with you. I'd have to wear a girdle. And get a spray tan. And get my teeth whitened and some Botox. The expectations of how a normal body should look had changed dramatically. It had to be hairless. It had to be absent of fat. It had to be tanned. A man in his early thirties was doing push-ups and caught me staring at him. He gave me a look that suggested he might not dismiss a woman in a size-sixteen boilersuit who was past her sell-by-date.

Finally, some eye contact!

The PMT symptoms were growing stronger – my period wasn't due for another two days now but it wasn't unusual for me to have cramps for days leading up to it, which were a reminder that I needed to get a move on with the baby-making thing or time would run out. I was trying hard to stay optimistic. I had the plan to hold onto. It was ridiculous to believe it would work *first* time. It was silly. I had to stay focused. Calm. There was no point letting myself cry and break down. At least I was only thirty-eight and not fifty.

So here was this man looking at me and he had shoulder-length brown hair and looked a bit like Christopher Lambert in the Tarzan film, *Greystoke*, one of Mum's all-time favourites. 'That Lambert is so dreamy,' she'd said. I walked towards him, trying to look seductive and breathing in so he wouldn't see my round tummy.

'Hi,' he said sitting up, 'are you joining the gym then?'

'I'm thinking about it,' I replied. 'I need to work out more regularly.'

'More regularly or just work out?' he said cheekily. 'It's really good here. Lots of classes too. Have you done Psycho-cycle?'

I shook my head.

'Hip-Hop HIIT?'

'No, sorry.'

'Suspension Elevation?'

I hadn't heard of any of these classes. The last fitness class I'd been to had been step aerobics and that had been ten years ago. I didn't like exercising with a group of people. I got self-conscious because my face always went very red and I looked as if I was about to have a heart attack. I hated getting changed with people and then having to shower and use a tiny towel to cover my massive arse. I was more of a swimming type of girl. Swimming pools often attracted people of all ages so you didn't feel so bad about your overweight body.

'Tuesday night is the 90s retro class,' he said. 'That might be more up your street.'

It gave me a chill when people referred to the 90s as

retro. It didn't feel retro to me. It only felt like a couple of years ago.

'I'd say you need to lose a stone, maybe two, right?' he said.

I looked at my feet. Had I asked for his opinion on my physique?

'I mean, I hope you don't take this the wrong way, but you're good-looking for someone your age. Losing a few pounds would definitely do you a favour. I'm actually one of the trainers here, you see.'

I walked away. I felt like I was about to cry. Back at school I'd always been slightly chubby. I walked around knowing I was certainly above my optimum weight but I'd never been one of those women who was prepared to diet and exercise like a loon. That didn't mean I was immune to the pressure to conform. Right now the cramps were growing in intensity. Was I so deluded that I believed that one of these gym zombies would fall for me?

God, I was stupid and pathetic and the plan was never going to work because I was unattractive and had no idea what was going on in the world of exercise – and by extension, the world of contemporary culture. I'd got a couple of tests in my bag so I went into the public toilet – the one toilet in the shopping centre that was relatively clean – hurried into a cubicle and ripped the test open.

After I'd peed on the stick, I sat on the toilet seat, not

daring to look at it. My heart was hammering in my chest and I thought of Sarah's advice to try and accept my anxiety symptoms rather than pretend they weren't happening.

It's just your heart hammering in your chest. You are feeling anxious. It's normal to feel anxious. It's your body's way to prepare to fight or flight. You want to be pregnant so your body is feeling anxious. You may be pregnant. This may be a hypothetical anxiety about nothing because you may in fact be pregnant.

None of this positive self-talk helped. The personal trainer thought I was old and fat. I was too inhibited to go to a sex party. I missed Mum but didn't dare to think about it too much. My job was OK but it wasn't what I really wanted to do. It felt lonely to realise that you were ploughing this path on your own. On the other hand, I was tapping into the zeitgeist. Women didn't have to settle for Sky Sports, man farts, and M&S ready meals. They could go it alone.

If I ignored the test, washed my hands, put the toilet seat down, it would be positive. If I gave it a very quick sideways glance it could go either way.

There was one line.

I wasn't pregnant.

I checked the pack instructions. Did one line perhaps mean I was? I held the test up to the light and studied it more closely. Was there a tiny line? I stared so long at the line that I thought I could see a second one. I thought about Hairy and how he'd vomited with an erection. I thought about how the man in the gym had told me I was overweight. It wasn't a good day. It really wasn't.

I visualised one of my eggs pinging down the toilet, never to be seen again.

Worries:

1. I am not pregnant – *This is not a worry. It is a reality.*

I put the test in the sanitary-towel bin. Staring at my face in the reflection I felt nothing. The hammering had stopped. I had managed somehow to switch off my feelings completely. I went back to the bookshop. I was fine as long as I didn't have to talk to anyone or see any babies or any pregnant women or listen to Lesley complain about being a mum.

The store was a little busier in the afternoon as we had a promotion on where you could get four books for the price of three. There were one or two regulars with piles of books under each arm. I spotted June but I couldn't speak to her now. I knew if I did I'd start crying. She was next to the crime/thriller table. I knew she found it hard to navigate these books as many of the covers looked similar – a shadowy female figure standing under a streetlamp at night. She didn't like anything grisly, which was hard as there was a trend for everything to be super-gory. I couldn't remember the last time I'd read a book. I needed to get back into it because it would offer up some sort of escape – escape from the voice in my head that kept screaming: *BABY! BABY! BABY!* I snuck behind the till and bent down so she wouldn't see me. It wasn't a day that we were due to have tea together so if I was lucky she wouldn't come over looking for me.

I kept feeling OK for a minute and then I'd remember that the test had been negative and I'd feel bad again and then OK and so it went on. I tried to block Hairy from my mind. If I dwelt on the fact that I'd not been attracted to him, that he'd been pretty repellent, then it only made the negative spiral even more pronounced.

'How are you doing, love?' June asked, and I looked up and realised Lesley had told her I was back from lunch.

'Fine,' I muttered and stared at the book she'd handed me – a new female author's tale of a prehistoric creature that came alive and lived in the drains.

My womb is empty. I have no child. Perhaps I will never be a mum. My life is basically just a series of the same things happening over and over. I go to work. I watch films with my brother. I chat to Meg. I eat sandwiches. I get anxiety. I have nothing to look forward to. I slept with a man just to get

*pregnant. I thought the plan was a good idea but perhaps it
really isn't…*

'You don't look fine, love,' June said trying to catch
my eye.

'I'm OK – just tired.'

I often found that the more people pushed to find out
how I was feeling, the cagier I became. I didn't like
opening up to other people. Even with Mum I'd been
reluctant to volunteer stuff unless she really worked at
getting it out of me, usually over a cup of tea, after an
hour of meaningless chitter-chatter, then, eventually, the
real cause of my anguish would emerge.

'Is it bad news? Is it the heebie-jeebies?' she
continued.

'Can you stop calling it that, please?'

I wished I hadn't told her about the anxiety now. Or
the plan. I wanted to be left alone to get on with my
suffering.

'Sorry, love. I thought it would make you laugh. You
know, lighten the mood a bit.'

'I don't want to talk today,' I said. 'Anyway, this book
looks great,' I went on, my voice breaking ever so slightly
and holding up the book she'd just handed me. 'It got
four stars in the *Guardian*. I'm not sure the plot is very
realistic, but what does that matter?'

If I kept talking about this easier stuff, then I wouldn't
break down. If I just pretended all was OK, then it would

be. Sarah sometimes told me that the best thing to do when I was suffering with anxiety was to just carry on as normal. This was the best course of action for now. I could either run out of the shop and knock my head against the marble statue outside Boots (which was of a mother and baby embracing) or I could stand here and recommend books and draw little black lines on this notepad and try not to notice the fact that a baby had just been wheeled into the store and had a tiny tuft of blonde hair and was waving in my direction.

'It's OK to talk,' June said. 'It's OK to break down and tell me things aren't going well.'

I didn't want to talk about it. It was too soon. I had just taken the test. There was nothing she could say to make me feel better.

'Remember, I'm always here for you, love.'

I could feel tears welling in my eyes, a scratchy feeling in my throat. I ran the book through the till and nodded. Luckily she didn't push and she left. I then felt guilty for being so cold with her. She'd only been trying to help. Why did I find it so hard to open up to people? Part of me was worried that once I did, I'd just dissolve into a big, emotional pile of jelly that could never be fixed again. It was better to hold it together. It was better to keep it inside.

Sometimes I wondered what June would think if she really knew me. If she knew that this baby wasn't just some flibbertigibbet flight-of-fancy thing. That it was all I could think about. That I'd developed such bad tunnel vision that sometimes all I saw when I walked around was babies and all I could think about was how my life would finally start once I became a mum. She thought I was happy, was totally unaware that I was a saucepan on a low boil, just simmering away with no ups or downs, just a steady temperature but no real happiness to speak of, or anger, or *any* strong emotion. No, this wasn't true because there was always the anxiety, and the fear that the anxiety would come … but even then it was all inside and never externalised.

I often had disagreements with George because he spent inordinate amounts of time playing computer games, but my existence was no more meaningful. I spent my days at work thinking about what I would eat for lunch. If I never had a baby, I would end up being one of those women who was seventy and still shopped in Topshop and had so much stuff injected into my face that I looked like I'd got giant pillows under my eyes.

Part of me wanted to run after June and scream *I'm dying, I'm actually dying.* Instead, I went to the back of the store and reorganised the health and wellbeing books. The books about greens. About how to make dinner in five minutes. The ones about how to bake everything in a kettle. It was all meaningless. You ate the food and then you shat it out and that was that.

Why did we obsess so much about it?

'Make a plan, Kate. Whenever you're having a bad time of it, *make that plan*,' Mum had always said.

I mulled things over in my head and started thinking about my next move, my next donor. It helped me breathe and focus. It helped quell some of the panic that was rising inside. In my brain there were two courses of action: I could grab this customer and scream in their face, *I need your baby now,* or I could just sit here, leafing through this book about edamame beans and how to prepare them for a healthy lunchtime snack, and hopefully nobody would notice the tears dropping onto the page or the fact I was compulsively sniffing.

Who were the potential candidates then?

1. University professors: smelly, too old, halitosis.
2. Writers: any author events coming up soon?
3. Musicians: sperm damage? Bad lifestyle? But what about Mick Jagger? No, only dates models and not plump ageing ladies with wobbly bits.

I felt weary thinking about doing the whole thing again. My vagina deserved better than this.

Chapter Six

'So I'm just massaging it into your heart chakra now that it's all burnt away,' the acupuncturist said. 'This will get rid of all the negative energy and help welcome the new baby in to your bodily field.'

'I can still feel a bit of a burning sensation,' I said, 'just above my knee.'

As part of the therapy she'd applied some black substance to strategically important parts of my body and then set it on fire – just for a few seconds and then she quickly blew it out. It was still unnerving and didn't feel very relaxing. The hour-long session cost £150 and I'd bought a course of four sessions. The Sacred Fertility website had promised immediate results though, and the words of the tarot reader were still ringing in my ears. What if I had some kind of block that was preventing a pregnancy from happening? The lady was sympathetic when I told her about my desire to have a baby.

'So you're having fertility treatment?' she asked.

'No, I'm going to try the natural route first,' I replied.

There were lots of thank-you cards on her mantlepiece which indicated that this particular kind of acupuncture obviously had a high success rate.

'So has your partner's sperm been checked?' she asked.

'Which one?'

'The partner that you're having a baby with?'

'Oh, I don't know him yet,' I said.

She looked slightly aghast, as if I might be suffering from a delusional mental illness; nonetheless, it didn't stop her from booking in my sessions. I didn't have the will to go into the details of my plan. It wasn't really her business. The only thing that concerned me was that I hadn't been more preoccupied with the quality of the sperm. Yes, I'd started thinking about people who were into fitness and wellbeing – men who went to gyms – but were these people actually healthy? Did they have good sperm? Certainly, someone like Tim who ran every day seemed to have more potential than Hairy, who looked like the only exercise he got was standing up from his bed to switch off his Xbox, but was that actually true?

'How do you feel?' the lady asked after we'd finished the forty-five-minute session.

'I feel really good,' I said, which was true.

The therapy itself had had no discernible impact, but the fact that I was doing something that might help me get pregnant in the future had calmed me down. I was starting to deal with the disappointment that it hadn't worked. I realised it was naïve to think it would work right away, anyway. I hadn't even minded having the black stuff set on fire and the needles hadn't been painful either. The point was, I was *doing* something. I wasn't wallowing in the *what ifs*.

'Try and eat as much orange fruit as you can,' the lady said. 'It'll cleanse out your womb and ensure you attract more harmony into your life.'

'Do you mean oranges?' I said.

'Well, yes,' she said briskly, now that the time was up and she was readying herself for the next infertile person. 'Or mango. Or pumpkin.'

'Mango is green, isn't it?'

'You know what I mean,' she said irritably, her manner switching.

She turned off the whale music that had been playing in the background and forced a smile at me.

'So, Kate, I'll see you in a couple of weeks' time. Remember to have intercourse when you're ovulating – but I think you know that already. And do some meditation every day if you can.'

'I keep a worry diary,' I said.

'Good.'

On the way out I saw a nervous-looking woman, about my age, gazing at the floor. I wanted to reach out my hand and give her a squeeze. 'We'll get there in the end, mate,' I wanted to say. She looked up and smiled but it was a sad smile – the smile of someone who's last to be picked for the netball team. It was an expression I'd carried many times myself.

'Good luck,' I said.

'Yes, good luck to you too,' she replied.

I wanted her to be successful, but ideally I wanted it to work for me first. Was that bad?

On the way home, my mood of calm and relative optimism quickly collapsed. I kept thinking about the week after Mum died. I'd been standing in her room and had found a box full of photos under the bed. They were photos of George and me as kids and she'd written notes on the back of each one – where we were, the date, etc. I found one of the three of us eating ice creams on a park bench. I didn't remember who'd taken it; perhaps Mum had asked a stranger who was passing. We looked happy. Mum had one hand on my shoulder and George was looking down, trying to pick up a bit of ice cream that had landed on his dungarees which were decorated with

Wombles. I'd stood staring at this photo for some time and the enormity of Mum's death hit me head on. I would never see her again. I would never feel her hand in mine. Or hear her laughing at some crap TV sitcom. I'd never have to help her schlep some piece of junk back from a secondhand shop and then listen while she described how she was going to turn it into a plant stand or a TV table. I'd never have her come to me at night and pat my knee and say, 'You're the best – just remember that.' She'd done this even when I was an adult, which was weird but comforting.

In that moment, that moment of thinking about how hard life would be without her, I'd felt a presence in the room, a weight pressing down on my shoulder. 'Mum!' I'd said out loud. 'Are you there?' But the presence had gone. I knew she'd been watching. Was she watching me now? As I'd slept with a stranger? As I'd had weird, black stuff burnt on my body and paid a fortune because I thought it might help me have a baby?

'I think it's rotten how these people take advantage of women who want children,' Meg had said to me one day.

She'd been reading an article in the *Evening Standard* about a 'fertility retreat' which was held in France and promised women it would 'heal past stress and depression within the womb and create the optimum balanced environment for a baby.'.

'Do they really expect us to believe that a massage and a healthy salad will help fix infertility?'

'Well, it probably helps,' I'd said.

Meg wasn't keen on children. 'Too much mess. Too expensive,' she'd said. 'I can't be bothered with them. And besides, it's not good for the climate.'

Her sister had two kids and Meg said that was enough. 'I get to be the funny aunt who swoops in, does cool stuff, and then leaves again. It's ideal.'

'You'd make a good mum,' she'd said. She knew it was something I wanted to happen more than anything else.

'I don't believe in relationships, though,' I'd said.

'Carl just wasn't the right one.'

But even before Carl, my love life had been a giant mess.

My list of past conquests consisted of Jody, a fat boy who enjoyed burping. I'd snogged him when I was fourteen. There'd been a house party; someone's parents were away on holiday. The Beastie Boys played very loudly. We'd snogged on the bottom bunk and then he'd pushed me to the floor and rubbed himself up and down. I later learned this was called 'dry humping' and it seemed slightly pointless. Eventually, Jody had got my home number (no mobiles then, so much easier, now I think back), and we'd gone out. We'd dry humped three times a week in his loft room. His mum was downstairs, but she was cool and smoked spliffs while listening to *The Archers*. It was before the days of porn everywhere. He hadn't seen a vagina except for one in *Razzle* (it was super-hairy, he said). Was Jody a dad? I wondered if he had fond memories of me whenever 'Fight for Your Right to Party', came on and he was driving his kids to football.

Then there was Dan. He was intense. He liked The Smiths. He drove a Morris Minor and he never did up the laces of his DM boots so he kept falling over – but I found it endearing. He was great. If I wasn't home when he called, then he kept leaving messages. The problem was, the keener *he* was, the more *I* withdrew.

And there'd been a string of one-offs. I couldn't remember their faces or bodies. A whiff of Aramis aftershave here, a hairy armpit there, one that screwed up his face and made a noise like a chicken when he had an orgasm. One called Juan. *Juan*! He was a holiday romance. He'd had a tight, curly perm and wore dungarees with no top, but he'd been a good dancer and if you're a good dancer you can get away with anything. The more I thought about Juan, the more I realised that he was probably the one to make great children. Great, dancing children … It was a shame I'd never got his number when I'd left Alicante that summer.

Then there was Carl.

I'd finally felt as if I'd reached the end of the road,

relationship-wise. Here was a man who shared my taste in music, who didn't sneer when I made ratatouille more than twice a month and who thought I was cool despite the fact I'd worked in a bookshop for a very long time. When we'd first met he'd said he thought bookshops were 'sexy'.

Since splitting with Carl I'd noticed there were certain types of men that flashed up on Tinder. Certain typologies, so to speak.

Top Gear fanatics
This type wore navy fleece sweatshirts, liked to fish on the weekends, and was good around kids, listened to Radio Two and nodded his head to The Lighthouse Family. His specialist subjects were loft conversions, the time and effort they took, how builders let you down at the last minute, and how boundary-wall agreements could be frightfully tricky. These men probably made good dads but would bore you to death.

Ageing skateboarders
There were also men who didn't want to grow old and went to festivals even in their forties and wore trainers (it seemed everyone wore trainers these days) and some of them even skateboarded to work. No one pointed out that this was silly as

ageing was fluid and there were no distinctive boundaries any more. These men could also be dads, but often tried to make it look cooler than it was through investing in very expensive buggies and slings and naming their kid 'Iggy' or 'Bowie' and then playing them alternative music from an early age and joking about how their kid's favourite song was 'Where's Your Head At?' by Basement Jaxx.

Business Robots

Then there were men, like Lesley's husband Toby, who worked long hours and were never home. They wore fitness monitors all the time and were constantly checking their phones and shouting, *'Can you hear me, New York?'* into their mouthpiece. These were the workaholics but they didn't necessarily need to be working.

Strange Ones

And then there were the oddballs, the ones who were strange, rejected, lived on their own and ate Pot Noodles, watched porn all day, didn't interact with anyone unless it was online, secretly hated women, and had fetishes that involved dressing up as babies.

Fitness Bores/Cycling Fanatics
This was Tim, Meg's boyfriend, and anyone who
yawned on about their race times or how to make
a linseed-oil smoothie. These men were incredibly
proud of their abs. They thought their abs made
up for the fact that they had no personality at all.

'You haven't met someone because you haven't
prioritised it,' Meg had said, and this was true.

I avoided men. I was only interested in their ability to
father my child. Yes, I still checked Facebook now and
then to see if there was any news on Carl, but this was
just a mechanism to torture myself, like when you stick a
pin underneath your fingernail and watch a small bubble
of blood rise to the surface.

That night, George and I sat on the sofa. We had spent
fifteen minutes scrolling through all the different options
on Netflix. This was the modern problem – too much to
watch, too much good quality TV, not enough time.
Every night I promised myself I would do something
more edifying, but I wasn't sure what that might be. I
was tired after a day spent on the shop floor.

'Do you want to watch something funny? This had
the woman from *Parks and Recreation* in it,' George said.

'I'm not in the mood for that,' I said.

I wasn't in the mood for anything. I was feeling
worried about the amount of money I'd spent on the

acupuncture and how I'd signed up for three sessions. I was going to cancel the other two as soon as possible. I wasn't convinced it would make much difference, plus I now had small burns where she'd put the black stuff on and set it on fire. I had paid her to do this to me, which seemed sadistic.

'What about the new crime drama with Nicole Kidman?'

'I can't be bothered. She looks strange now.'

I hated the fact that Hollywood actresses were all succumbing to the pillow face. It made me feel uneasy that women I'd grown up watching in films now looked younger than I did. Would there be any old women left? Or would it become compulsory, because you were the only one that had a wrinkled face and actually looked your age?

'How about a documentary about how the ice caps are melting?'

'Are you trying to make me feel even more depressed?'

'Or how Trump won the election? Or how about this – all about how the Japanese have started whaling again?'

I had a hot water bottle resting on my belly. My period was finishing but it had been particularly punishing this time. Each twinge and irritable mood reminded me of failure.

'What about *One Born Every Minute*?'

The truth was I usually loved watching this programme, but now it was too close to the bone. I felt no sympathy with the women crying for mercy and begging for the midwife to give them an epidural. They just didn't realise how lucky they were. We settled on a documentary about the rise of veganism, which was sort of interesting. And wasn't as depressing as the other options.

'I haven't heard anything back from that job interview,' George said as we switched over to a documentary about a famous serial killer. 'Can you think of anywhere that's looking for people?'

'Franklin's needs people,' I said flatly.

It was true. We'd had two members of part-time staff leave recently and Lesley was just about to advertise. I wasn't sure why I hadn't thought of George as a good candidate. Perhaps it was the fact that he rarely read books and often pointed out that my work was 'dull and boring'.

'Lesley needs another sales assistant because Paula is going back to New Zealand,' I said.

The more I thought about it, the more I realised George was pretty capable. He'd probably be a good addition to the Franklin's team. Ideally, he'd be good but not too good. Truth was, I was insecure about work. The people who'd joined were usually fairly transitory and didn't make an effort. Lesley liked me and trusted that

I'd do what was required, and not much more. I was good with customers in an understated, quiet way. I had a comprehensive knowledge of our stock and knew exactly where to find everything. I never proffered any new ideas and I rarely showed much enthusiasm but Lesley seemed to be OK with that.

'Would you be OK if I worked there?' George said.

'Of course. I mean, you'd have to do everything I told you to and not get big ideas or show me up. And not be too impressive.'

'Look at me,' he said, shrugging his shoulders.

He was wearing a dirty sweatshirt with *The Goonies* on the front. I realised that I rarely looked at him anymore. I just took him for granted. How was he even feeling? The problem with my obsession with getting pregnant was I had switched everything else off. I could only focus my energy on this one thing. That would change once I was successful and had the baby – and got over the first bit which was apparently quite overwhelming.

'You'd have to smarten up and shave more often,' I said.

The Franklin's uniform was a maroon polo shirt with the company logo on the pocket. You could wear it with anything black. I promised to mention it to Lesley. It made me feel slightly better. I slept OK. I had something else to focus on for a bit. Perhaps this was what I needed.

'Oh, that'll be nice,' Lesley said when I told her about George, 'but is he super-reliable? I need someone who turns up on time, takes instructions, and doesn't expect to progress every five minutes to the next level.'

She often complained that younger people came in and wanted to manage the store after their first week. I told her that yes, George was reliable. There was nothing to suggest he wouldn't make an effort at Franklin's. He was unlikely to set the book retail world on fire, but he wouldn't embarrass me either. I took an application form to pass on. I felt a momentary worry, thinking about working with George every day. The thing was, we already spent a lot of time together. We rarely argued, but there were certainly times when he got on my nerves. His excessive chattiness. The memes he forwarded to me every day.

June came in. She was looking for a new recommendation but was also worried about me. I could tell that she wanted to see how I was doing after her recent visit and my evasiveness.

'That book was so scary,' she said. 'First off, I thought it must be the teacher who'd stabbed the school nurse, but then I thought it might have been the strange boy who didn't get on with his mum. And how are you feeling?' she whispered.

'I was hoping it would happen first time but it didn't, unfortunately. I went to see this specialist acupuncturist in Harley Street, so maybe that'll help.'

'I bet they're charging an arm and a leg.'

'It's expensive and she left these big burns on my chest,' I said, 'so I've cancelled the rest of the sessions.'

'You have to have sex too, though, right? And it takes more than having sex *once* to get pregnant.'

'I know, I know. But I haven't found another candidate. I have an idea and I have a week or two to get organised.'

'That might just be the flaw in this plan,' June said. 'I mean, wouldn't it make sense to have a *proper* relationship?'

'It all takes too long – meeting someone, liking them, them liking you, going out, going out again, then having sex, then talking about kids but not doing it too soon, then finding out they don't want them or are dating someone else or only want to mess about. I could be two years down the line by then.'

There were times when I wished I hadn't told June. I didn't want to talk about it while I was in the midst of it. I hadn't said anything to the counsellor. I only really wanted to tell people when I was actually pregnant – then I'd tell them it had been a nice surprise, a one-night stand. I'd construct a narrative that worked and then, when the child grew up, I'd tell them as much as I could about their dad but also how *I'd* grown up with an amazing mum and had never missed out – even though I'd never really had my dad around.

'Did you read that thing about how men are getting infertile because of all the plastic in the water supply?' June said, picking up a bookmark with a polar bear on the front. 'Here, give me one of these too if the proceeds are for charity. It was in the paper yesterday and *we* are eating plastic because it's in the fish. The world is going to hell in a handbasket! Oh, I see there's a new Jack Reacher.' She reached out and picked it up. 'And these damned mobile phone waves? They're making our brains disintegrate. We need to protect ourselves, my dear.' Then she was off again.

———————

Lesley appeared after lunch.

'It was fucking "green hair day" at school today! I mean, why don't they tell us these things in advance? I get in and all the other kids have sprayed their hair green for "ethical world climate change day" or some such, and of course my kids are all wailing because I've forgotten.'

'What a nuisance,' I said.

'It's basically a massive ball ache. Some days I wish I'd never become a mum. You never get a thank you and

I spend ninety percent of my life picking up stuff off the floor.'

She had kids. She had a respectable job. She looked OK – rocking too much Boden, but it had changed and was acceptable now. She had friends. She basically had pretty much everything the modern woman was supposed to have. And *still* she complained. She was exhausted. She had too much on her plate. She had no 'me time'. She couldn't do a wee on her own. She never got enough sleep. The domestic chores all fell to her. She had picky eaters…

I let her vent. It depressed me that she couldn't see how lucky she was.

I went back to tidying. It seemed that, nowadays, even the most mundane of things were seen to be significant.

1. 'How to Organise Your Drawers so You Don't Feel Depressed Anymore.'
2. 'What Your Kitchen Is Telling You About Your Relationship.'
3. 'The Joy of Handwashing: How washing your smalls can reinvigorate your life.'

At least if your drawers looked OK then you had a semblance of order, perhaps.

George met me after work. He was wearing long,

frayed, flared jeans, 90s style, and a bright yellow T-shirt. Facially, my brother was attractive – he had good bone structure but, like many men his age, he chose to cover his entire lower face with thick fuzz. He also wore a topknot which had become such a cliché look now that you could go into the hairdressers and they would do an artfully mussed-up version for you. When Mum had found out she was dying, she'd made me promise I'd always look out for him. She knew this was the wrong way round because, in reality, George looked out for me. He was the positive one, the one who brought me a cup of tea when I'd been hidden away in my room for too long, the one who sent me a stupid joke when he hadn't heard from me all day. After Carl left, he cooked every night for me. I went off food and actually managed to lose twelve pounds in a month, which was pretty good going but then I put it back on when I started to feel normal again. I didn't appreciate him enough. It was rare that we did stuff together. This was the problem with living with someone: you took them for granted because they were always hanging about. Having him working in the store with me would be a good thing – a way to pay him back a bit.

I handed the application form over. He always had the ability to pull me out of the dumps. Why couldn't I talk to him about my longing to have a family? Why had I only confided in June? We walked to the local sushi bar together. I got salmon sushi and he got ramen.

'I think Mum spoke to me last night,' he said. 'You'll think I'm being a Russell Brand wanker, but she told me that my life was going to come together. She looked exactly how she looked in the hospital – you know, tired and hardly able to stand up. In fact, she even had her hospital gown on.'

'Are you sure it was Mum?' I said, pouring soya sauce into one of the plastic compartments in my tray.

'Of course I'm sure.'

'I told you about the time, just after she died, when I felt her in the room with me.'

'Yes, I remember you saying that. It's nice to think she's around, that she's still part of our lives. I think about her all the time, don't you?'

'Yes,' I said, 'I don't think I'll ever really get over it.'

'You will. I mean … eventually you will.'

Part of me didn't want to get over it. It felt like we weren't being fair to her if we recovered and continued on with our lives.

For so long we'd been this tight family unit. The three of us. Not perfect – George and I had argued like all brothers and sisters do, but we'd been self-contained. We'd not ever had playdates with other kids or gone away with other families. We had no extended family nearby as Mum's family lived in Wales. It was just us against the world, dragging crap furniture out of skips and making it into something new.

'So Lesley will ask you what kind of books you're passionate about,' I said, changing the subject.

'Mmm...' George said, wiping his mouth with a napkin, '*Harry Potter* – I read all of those.'

'OK, and what about more recent stuff?'

'Manga? Does that count?'

It would help George if he peppered his answers with some more up-to-date literature too. I gave him the names of some of the top authors' titles that year, books he could mention that would illustrate that yes, he did read, and he was in the know in terms of what the public was reading too. This year there was a trend for misery memoirs, so I gave him the names of some of those too.

'I have a good feeling that you'll get the job,' I said. 'You need to be able to use the computer system and Lesley wants to start running more in-store events to get a wider, more diverse demographic in.' This was something Lesley had talked about a lot, yet I'd done nothing to help.

'I'm good with tech,' George said, 'and I like the idea of running events. I'll try and come up with some clever ideas before the interview.'

Perhaps if I'd been more determined I'd have been working in TV rather than at Franklin's. Perhaps I'd given up too easily. I knew there were women who were changing their lives in their late thirties but there wasn't enough bandwidth right now for me to embrace motherhood and a whole new challenging career. I was jealous of people who were more determined than I was to create their ideal life. I'd floated through life for so long now. I went back to the shop feeling my anxiety levels rising.

Worries:

1. What if my life never has any sense of direction?
2. What if George is actually much better than I am at Franklin's?
3. What if I'm never good at anything and go to my grave just being average?

Perhaps George would be rubbish and Lesley would have to let him go. If he was good, he'd make me feel inadequate – or even more inadequate. If he flopped, he'd be mooching about at home again with nothing much to do. Neither option was optimum.

Chapter Seven

The plan was going ahead. I would keep going. I just needed to find my next candidate. Meanwhile, I definitely had some solid advice for my future child…

1. If you wake up in the morning with your heart hammering and an upset stomach, this is called anxiety.
2. The more you say the word *anxiety*, the more *anxious* you will feel, so try to avoid this.
3. It helps to put your worries into two categories – hypothetical or practical. It is not always clear-cut which category they belong in.

But what if the anxiety felt monumental? What if 'only anxiety' really meant that your heart was going to stop? For a few months after Mum's death I'd started suffering with heart palpitations. These happened in the morning while I waited for the kettle to boil and on my way into work. It was as if my heart was missing a beat every now and then. I knew it was anxiety, I'd googled it many times, but the more I fixated on what was going on – *These are only heart palpitations, they are heart palpitations!* – the worse it became.

I worried that I'd inherited some of this from Mum. She'd often had trouble sleeping and leapt from one bout of worry to the next. She worried that we had mice living under the floorboards, that there were crows nesting in the roof, that the damp in the kitchen was spreading and we couldn't afford to get it fixed. The house became a representation of her fears. Each time she discovered another problem, the shakier her foundation became. What was this anxiety about for me? It was multifaceted, it seemed. Anxiety that I would never have a baby. That I would remain fixed in the same job, in the same situation, in the same routine for the rest of my life. That there was nothing on the horizon to look forward to. That my body wouldn't be fully equipped to get pregnant, that I was probably infertile even though the tests had shown everything wasn't too bad for someone my age. That I would never learn to love anyone again. That Mum's death had damaged me irrevocably. That I was too quiet. That I never 'joined in'. That I was locked into being an observer for the rest of my life.

It was Saturday morning. I went downstairs where Meg was clanking pots and pans around. Cooking a big breakfast meant she was suffering in some way. It was her method of working things through. If she was thinking about stuff, then she'd construct delicious breakfasts with expertly chopped mushrooms and tomatoes and egg-white omelettes (for Tim, of course).

'Spinach, kale, and broccoli smoothie,' she said looking up at me, then poured it back into the machine to blend it up some more.

She switched the blender on and then poured the sludge back into a glass.

'Do you want to try some?'

I sipped a bit but it was very thick and tasted like I'd faceplanted in a ditch.

'Tim's doing a Tough Mudder in Putney today,' she said.

'Didn't you want to watch him?'

'It's so boring. I mean, I love him, but I sometimes go

mad with all the times and the weights and the food he's eaten each day.'

'Are you still working on that snail serum concept?'

Meg nodded her head. The latest concept she was working on was for a product that contained sixty percent snail extract. She'd brought some of the prototypes home and we'd trialled it for a week. My skin definitely seemed smoother, but the consistency was horrible. It was shiny and sticky – exactly like the stuff that came out of a snail's arse. Her boss was very stressed and set very high standards.

We ate mushrooms and tomatoes on toast. It felt nice that the boys weren't around. George had gone shopping for new clothes. He'd got the job at Franklin's and was over the moon.

'It feels like we haven't talked properly in ages,' Meg said running her plate under the tap and putting the kettle on. 'How are things?'

'OK,' I said, though of course they weren't really OK.

'Well, I'm just questioning my relationship with Tim,' Meg confided. 'I feel like we get on fine but have nothing in common. That's the bit you need when the sex fades away. What do I actually talk to him about?'

'What music does he like?'

'U2?

'That's all right. What about films?'

'He doesn't watch films. He likes those history documentaries about wars and stuff. He doesn't read books. Or if he does, it has to be the biography of Nick Faldo or a football manager. It's not like you and Carl were.'

We sat in our pyjamas and worked on a mood board for her snail-extract concept. We needed to pull images out of magazines and stick them to a board. These images would help shape the positioning for the product. It was relaxing, and I'd helped Meg before.

'Is this good?' I said holding up a bright green plant that I'd cut out of *Red* magazine.

'Yes, that works – the cream has these plant extracts in it so anything you can find that looks green and fresh.'

We eventually created a board with lots of good-looking, shiny-skinned women looking enthusiastic about their faces. We drew a giant snail and wrote some adjectives in felt-tip pen around its shell. Youthful. Glowing. Radiating. Invigorating. Meg would show the idea to her boss next week. Afterwards we flicked through the magazines and dissected the models as we went along. I'd always been a glossy fan. I knew they were loathsome but I also found it remarkably calming to imagine an existence where all you worried about was how frizzy your hair was and what shade of lipstick was most on-trend. Magazines spoke to women as if they were children constantly learning the ropes, unable to look after even the simplest parts of their existence.

'Jane Fonda – look at her *face!*' Meg said. 'It's strange how everyone ends up looking the same, though, don't you think?'

'If I've got enough money, I'll be doing *everything*. I don't want to be the only one that looks like an eighty-year-old's nut sack.'

We had more toast (we'd eaten almost an entire loaf), drank tea, and stood on the balcony and smoked (ageing, bad for fertility, but you had to be reckless sometimes.)

We were in the midst of a heatwave and it was blisteringly humid – like a hairdryer blowing directly into your face. I was enjoying this time; it was a bit of escape and reminded me of our lives at university – hungover mornings spent lazing about and chatting and eating endless rounds of toast. I was thinking about the next candidate, how I already knew a runner (Tim) and how he'd know lots of other runners potentially.

'Shall we do Parkrun next week?' I asked.

'But you *hate* running!' Meg said, astonished. 'You said it was the most boring thing on Earth.'

'I mean, it releases endorphins. So it would make us both feel better.'

'You said runners were boring.'

They were also *fertile*. As long as their shorts weren't

too tight and they weren't excessively sweaty. After all, too much heat around the ball area wasn't good for fertility.

In seven days, I would be about to ovulate so it was time to put the plan into action once more.

Chapter Eight

I t was ambitious, perhaps, to run 5km without stopping when you'd only done two practice runs of ten minutes. On the first, I'd had to stop after two minutes because I couldn't breathe, and on the second, I'd been chased by a small but frightening dog and had to head home and have a lie-down. Meg was a natural runner, even though she hated to admit it.

We arrived at Parkrun and Meg and I worked our way to the back of the crowd. Everyone at the front looked like a professional athlete and I'd invested in some nice running gear which had cost me seventy quid. The leggings had a special bum corset so they lifted you up and stopped your arse flopping up and down. I'd designed a special playlist with all my favourite rousing tunes – Nirvana, Hole, Dr Dre, Goldfrapp, Justin

Timberlake – and for the first five minutes I enjoyed it. Even my anxiety subsided. After ten minutes I felt uncomfortable and out of breath. My face felt like it was on fire. I had a stitch. I was trying to look around while I ran to size up the men who were taking part. Who would my next candidate be? Was anyone checking me out? It seemed not. By 3km I forced myself to run again. By the end I could barely move one foot in front of the other and I felt as if I might be sick any minute. Tim was waiting at the finish with his phone and took a photo as I crossed the line and got the ticket which would record my time – forty minutes, according to my phone. Meg had finished five minutes ahead of me and I suspected she'd been training in secret and hadn't told me.

'Look, here's a great shot of you,' Tim said, holding out his phone as we queued to get a coffee in the park café afterwards.

I saw an ageing woman in a sweaty headband with a bright red face and a body squashed into leggings that were too tight so all her fat was pushed up around her midriff.

'Can you delete that, please?' I said.

'Don't you want to keep a record of your first run?'

I could tell he was enjoying my discomfort and the fact my face was still flaming red and wouldn't seem to return to its normal colour. It wasn't a very erotic backdrop. *Everyone* was sweaty and the smells weren't great. I'd taken an ovulation test that morning and was just entering my fertile period.

'Could you get me a coffee?' I asked Meg, who looked perfectly calm and the same normal colour she always was.

I went into the loo. It was one of the ones that you get at festivals with blue toilet water and what looked like a gear stick to flush afterwards.

1. I am preparing my body for pregnancy.
2. I am ready and welcoming my baby.
3. I am full of potential and opportunity.

These positive statements were from a stack of Fertility Motivational Cards I'd purchased on Amazon. They made your mindset more positive and helped drown out the screaming in your head which said over and over: *you are an unhealthy, stupid person. You will never have a baby. You will die on your own and the last thing you will see will be the broken stairlift that you're lying underneath with the realisation that nobody is coming to rescue you.*

_____

When I came back, there was a guy in the tent wearing a tight red Adidas tracksuit. He was probably being ironic. I was sweating profusely and felt like my face was still ablaze but I had to seize the moment. There was no room in the plan for cowardly acts or backing out.

'Your body will adapt,' Tim said as he handed me my coffee. 'You're out of shape but eventually you will get fitter and be able to do a better time.'

He typed into his wrist fitness monitor and smiled. I found it maddening that he was acting so superior but had to remind myself he had quite a small brain – there was always a compromise somewhere along the line. He grabbed his foot and pulled it up to his bottom to stretch out his thighs. Meg rolled her eyes. I could tell she was embarrassed at how much he was showing off.

Why hadn't I just gone on Tinder and found me a fitness fanatic? Possibly because none of them would like me or message me as I seemed to mainly attract trout fishers from Staines.

There were two women at the front of the queue who were discussing Davina McCall and how fit she was, then debating whether she had a personal trainer or organised her workouts herself, and whether she was too thin or actually just perfect for a woman her age. The parched grass around us amplified the sense that we were in Africa. The rain would never arrive and all the flowers would die. My skin was falling off.

'Look, there's Ben,' Tim said, pointing to the guy in the Adidas tracksuit that I'd been planning to approach – once my face went back to normal.

'Hey, mate!' Tim called and then Ben was coming over.

He had red hair and was quite pale, making me look even more out of shape because of the heat radiating off every cell of my body.

'How's it going?' Tim asked, slapping him on the back. 'Did you do the interval hill training last week? Didn't see you, mate.'

'No, I had a cold so just stayed in with ginger and turmeric,' Ben answered.

I noticed he had a tattoo on his calf. *Without you to hold I'll be freezing.* A quote from an Ed Sheeran song. I wasn't sure I could sleep with someone who liked Ed Sheeran. Then again, who was I kidding? I was ovulating. It didn't matter. I needed to get a donation. I needed it soon and I didn't even care if this guy had verrucas and toenails that curled over the tops of his feet.

'How was your time?' Ben asked, looking me up and down.

I tried to breathe in to camouflage all the flesh that had worked its way up around my girdle leggings.

'I'd say it was thirty minutes,' I said.

'More like fifty,' Tim laughed.

'Tim, don't be rude,' Meg said, nudging him. 'It was great for a first run. Well done, Kate.'

'So you've never run before then, Kate?' Ben asked.

He had a nice face. I could tell that he liked me a tiny

bit. I wasn't sure why this was as I looked bloody awful, but perhaps he liked the fact I wasn't a regular, that I didn't own a fancy fitness monitor, that I could talk about other stuff (like what, though?) that wasn't carbohydrates, matcha lattes and vegan burgers. I figured he was maybe thirty-three. What normal, functioning, healthy man would turn down a proposition from a normal (borderline), functioning (in the most basic sense), young (ish), healthy (well, I only smoked a couple of times a week and had definitely curbed my booze intake) woman?

'And did you enjoy it?' he asked. 'It was a bit hot, so not ideal conditions for a first timer.'

'Oh, I run quite often,' I lied. 'I just don't come to this one.'

'What was that?' Tim said craning his neck to hear what I was saying.

'Nothing,' I said. 'Thanks for the coffee, Tim.'

'Which Parkrun do you do then?' he said.

'Oh, you know. The one in Northala fields.'

'That's a long way to go if you're in Kensal Rise.'

'I love Ealing. Such a pretty place to run.'

I only knew about Northala because Lesley did that one sometimes and had mentioned it a few times.

'I love Ed Sheeran,' I said gesturing at his tattoo.

'Oh God, I can't stand him but my ex loved that song so I did it for her. I'm getting it lasered off.'

I felt a wave of relief. Maybe this wouldn't be a one-night stand. Maybe there was more potential… But why was I even *thinking* about a relationship? It was just because I was ovulating. It had turned me into a hormone-crazed, loved-up mess.

'So, do you want to take up running or are you just here to meet guys?' Ben said.

'Oh, both,' I said being bolder than normal.

If I wanted to have sex with this guy then there was no time for playing games or pretending I wasn't interested. Meg and Tim were looking over and I felt like Ben was slowly gaining more interest. I had to strike. If he wasn't interested that still gave me some time to seduce someone else, maybe in a bar, maybe scrolling Tinder, maybe even opting for a trout fanatic.

'Fancy going out for dinner tonight?' I said.

He looked taken aback but smiled.

'You don't waste time,' he said.

There was something slightly creepy about him but I couldn't put my finger on it.

Besides, I was a total creep too. Who was I kidding? I had to stay positive and not interrogate the whole thing too much. I could feel in my bones that this was going to work. When the baby was older I'd tell an amusing story about how I went to Parkrun and met their dad and my face had been bright red and he'd had an Ed Sheeran tattoo. Or maybe I'd tell them none of that.

'Watch out, Kate,' Tim said on the drive home, 'he's worked his way through most of the women in the Queen's Park Runners Club.'

'What makes you think I want a serious relationship?' I said.

Men always assumed that women wanted to settle down. I'd tried that already. It hadn't worked. Carl was gone. He was going out with an intern. He was probably making her my favourite pancake recipe, where he threw chocolate chips into the batter before he fried them in a pan. The intern would be very funny and would wear her hair in a high bun. She would be adventurous and like travelling. She'd be very, very *fun*. It was time to move on.

'I just thought you might like someone to hang out with on the weekend,' Tim said, 'so you don't have to spend time on your own.'

'Maybe Kate likes her own company,' Meg said.

Tim was driving Meg's old Golf, which she rarely used, and I was sitting in the back feeling like an unsuccessful child being driven home after a bad school report.

'Nobody likes to spend *that* much time on their own,' Tim said.

'Anyway, I'm not on my own. I'm with George,' I said.

'But don't you think that's weird? That the two of you

hang out and you're siblings?'

'Shut up, Tim. Why are you going on about this?' Meg said before I could explain that no, I didn't think it was odd to spend time in my dead mum's house with my younger brother, though I could see from the outside looking in that it was perhaps slightly eccentric. No, of course it was weird and this was why I wanted to start a family of my own – to get away from the weirdness of my life.

———

Back at home I had a hot bath, shaved my legs, tidied up my bikini line, washed and conditioned my hair, and applied a full face of make-up. I used an expensive primer that I'd bought online after watching a woman my age complaining about how old she looked. It had light reflecting stuff in it and seemed to shave at least five years off. Did men notice your skin? I'd also bought a new bra recently because most of mine were grey and the wrong size – my boobs seemed to be getting smaller as I aged. Once I'd made all this effort I actually looked good. I went through my wardrobe. What did fitness fanatics like their girls to wear? I was aware that my usual casual wear (dungarees/jeans) wouldn't cut it. An old floral tea-dress from the Topshop Kate Moss collection? Borrow one of Meg's work blazers and look like a boss? No, too intimidating. In the end I opted for a pleated skirt and a sweatshirt with *C'est La Vie* on the front. And trainers (so a bit sporty).

I peed on another ovulation stick just to be sure. I had the smiley face. This meant the next forty-eight hours were good for baby-making. Perhaps, if I was lucky, I could convince Ben to have sex more than once, maybe appeal to his competitive/fitness side?

'You look nice,' Meg said.

'Don't judge,' I replied, 'I know you think this has been a bit fast but I just thought it would be good to have a date. You know, get out of the house, not spend another night watching TV, listening to you two shagging.'

'Oh God, can you hear us?' Meg said blushing.

'Well … sometimes.'

I headed out – we were meeting in Notting Hill at an old Italian place that looked a bit tacky but had really nice food. I'd been surprised when he'd suggested it as I'd expected he'd want to go to some macrobiotic, mung bean, kimchi, sporty kind of restaurant. I made a few notes in my book, just to keep my head straight. I was ovulating. I really couldn't afford to be too fussy but it was helpful to think through this chap's relative pros and cons.

Ben (AKA Running Man)

<u>Positives</u>

- Decisive.
- Good cardiovascular function.
- Won't want to settle down as is very promiscuous.

<u>Cons</u>

- Arrogant?
- Will be appalled at my unfit, unexercised physique.
- May be boring like Tim.

George texted me.

Good luck!

I felt like a fraud. The people who cared for me thought I was looking for love but all I really wanted was sperm. Why hadn't I confided in them? *Because they'll think you're weird, Kate. Because it's a strange way to go about getting pregnant, Kate. Because once you tell someone you love something you can't untell them again.*

141

The restaurant would have been Mum's idea of a 'nice classy place'. The tables were festooned with gingham tablecloths and there were candles inside Mateus Rosé bottles.

'I love pasta,' Ben said, sitting down. 'It's exactly what you need after a long run. I did fourteen miles last week which is a short sprint for me but the heat made it unbearable.'

I nodded. There were really only a limited number of things people could talk about. House prices. Food. Crime. Brexit – which I didn't really understand so tried not to bring it up. Then there was work. Family (I tried to avoid this too). Books (but it wasn't often that you liked the same thing and besides, I'd not read anything in a long time now). Then there was your exercise regime. In terms of interest this sat next to 'The time I wired a plug correctly' and 'I once saw a family of ducks crossing the road.' Ben had made a real effort with his appearance, which implied he cared, which implied he'd sleep with me, which implied I might get pregnant. He was wearing a pale blue fitted suit with a striped T-shirt underneath and looked like one of those models from a *Guardian* fashion spread, trendy but casual. He'd slicked his hair and put some kind of pomade in his beard that made it very shiny. I couldn't stop staring. It was true that I fancied Ben. I was even quite looking forward to sleeping with him. I hadn't had enjoyable sex in a long time. With Carl, in fact. But with Carl in the early days, not when things had got stale and we both couldn't be bothered any more.

'Did you know Omega-3 fatty acids are perfect for reducing inflammation in your muscles after you've been exercising?' he said, looking at the menu.

'No,' I said, 'but my mum always made us swallow cod liver oil when we were growing up. She said it was good for our brains or something.'

Why had I brought Mum up? She was off limits. Mum = too much explanation = sad girl = no sex = end of plan. Luckily, we went straight back to health and wellness which was safer.

'I try and eat at least four avocados a week,' he said. 'They're super-high in antioxidants and healthy fats. They can also be incredibly fattening, though, so you have to watch out.' Was he talking to me now? 'I mean, people think an avocado is like a shortcut to good health but you have to put the physical effort in. I see so many people shovelling down avocados and I think, mate, you don't need a smashed avocado! You need a good workout!'

One of the things I enjoyed about old music documentaries was the fact that the men were reckless and hedonistic. That idea of a man who swigged JD from his cowboy boots, his butt squeezed into tight leather trousers, was so appealing. Iggy Pop covered in peanut butter. Iggy Pop didn't eat avocados! Or maybe he did now, but not back then when he'd been mad and dangerous. He'd wanted to be a sex slave, he'd taken drugs, he wouldn't have checked on his Fitbit every ten minutes to be told how many calories he'd burned. Men who ate avocados were not sexy. Didn't they realise this? I wished I could actually meet someone and enjoy their company, flirt with them, be genuinely attracted to them, but it felt like the last attractive man – to me anyway – had climbed onto the tour bus (a cliché, but yes, it was sexy) and hit Route 66 to chain-smoke and take drugs next to a dying cactus. Now we were left with Ben...

Ode to the Sexy, Dangerous Man

Where did you go?
Why does everyone play it so safe?
Can you come back in your leather trousers and show all these
bores how it's done?

The waiter came over to take our orders. He'd got sunburn on his nose and it had started to peel. I opted for a chicken salad as knew this was high-protein and low GI and would earn extra brownie points with Mr Runner.

'You can't come to a pasta restaurant and not order pasta!' Ben said, disapproving of my choice.

'Oh, OK then,' I said (truth was I far preferred pasta), 'I'll get the spaghetti vongole, please, and a glass of red wine.'

'Let's make it a bottle – and let's make it white – it goes better with seafood, right?' he said.

Ben ordered a lasagne.

'So I find it fascinating that you *don't* exercise regularly,' he said, licking his lips.

'Well, I do sort of, just not all the time,' I said sheepishly.

'But it's just everywhere. Like, how do you feel when you go on Instagram and see all the fit young women? Doesn't it bum you out?'

'I try not to follow those people.'

'But then there's all the TV shows and stuff. I find it kind of refreshing that you just don't give a shit about how you look.'

This comment stung somewhat. I'd spent a long time getting ready and didn't quite feel like I was an old fat slob, but Ben obviously hadn't noticed. In fact, he hadn't even commented on my appearance. I was worried that his motives were strange, that he wanted to experience a 'normal girl', one that wasn't obsessive about her food and weight and so was trialling me out so he could tell his friends about it. My motives weren't very wholesome either, though. I drank the wine too quickly because I was feeling nervous. Ben was boring but he was also attractive. It also had something to do with the fact that I was ovulating. I would have found a lamppost sexy. My ovaries were clicking together like those little silver balls that stressed executives had on their desks many years ago. They were reminding me that time was of the essence.

'I bet you've never set foot in a gym,' he said, tucking in to his lasagne. 'I don't see *you* doing spin workouts or HIIT training.'

'I did a spin class once,' I lied. 'Or at least, I think I did.'

'So what do you do instead of exercise?' he asked, wiping tomato sauce from his mouth.

'I watch TV. I read sometimes. I think. Actually no, I worry. I spend an inordinate amount of time worrying.'

He laughed.

'You're funny.'

'No, seriously, there's a lot to worry about, don't you think?'

'But if you're not worrying about your fitness and taking care of your body, what do you worry about?'

He was starting to get on my nerves now. Was it true that his entire universe revolved around himself?

'There's climate change. There's right-wing politics. There's terrorism. There's the fact that there's no decent affordable housing available anywhere or that we only want to shop and can't think of anything else to do with our time.'

None of these things were things that worried me. I was actually no different from Ben. I worried about myself too. We'd all become so self-absorbed and narcissistic that we pretended we were concerned with other stuff but actually weren't.

'So many girls I meet are obsessed with diet and exercise,' he continued. 'I could tell that you wanted the pasta when we walked in. No low-calorie shit. It's good that you're worrying about the world. Perhaps I need to do that too, but it's not good for you to worry. It gives you wrinkles.'

Was I really so desperate for a baby that I'd put myself through this shit?

But there was a voice inside chanting: *it will be worth it. You can forget about this douche bag. You'll have a connection. You'll have a purpose. Don't forget, this is the tricky part.*

This was easier than fertility treatment. If it worked, it would be cheaper too. And at least I knew more about this guy – he wasn't just a short description on a computer screen. Although in this case I wasn't sure that knowing more was particularly beneficial.

Ben's leg brushed mine under the table and his eyes studied me with intensity. He wanted me to riff on how much I loved fatty foods. I wasn't going to play this game. I was ovulating, yes, but you had to draw a line somewhere.

We finished another bottle of wine and things were slightly more fun. He ordered an Uber and we went back to his house in Willesden. He lived in a house-share but his housemates were all out. His bedroom was tidy and I went into his bathroom and poured water into his tooth mug and drank it. I came back out and he was lying on the bed. Behind him was a motivational quote against a black and white photo of a mountain. *Go hard or Go Home*, it said. There were stacks of sports magazines on the floor and his duvet cover had a faded Manchester United logo on the front. I just wanted to get it over with now.

'Come here,' he said, pulling me towards him.

We started kissing. He wasn't a bad kisser but I wasn't used to the beard and it scratched my face. He put his hand down my shirt and twisted my nipple. It was a bit too hard. I realised that many men copied what they saw in porn films now and you had to remind them that these were not real life or things that women enjoyed. I moved his hand and he shoved it down my pants inside.

'Urgh! What's that?' he said, pulling away suddenly.

'What?' I said horrified.

Was there something strange in my pants? Did I have

discharge? Had I got all my calculations wrong and started my period again?

'What's that stuff in your pants?'

I put my hand down there.

'It's all hairy,' he said, looking appalled.

I'd tended to my bikini line but had left hair on my fanny. I'd always done this, apart from one occasion when I'd taken everything off. Carl had said he'd liked it, but when it grew back again it was maddeningly itchy so I'd never tried it again. Was it *so* unusual to have pubic hair nowadays? I felt horribly gauche. Like I'd got spinach between my teeth but a million times worse.

'Sorry I overreacted,' Ben said moving towards me again. 'I just never met a girl who was natural down there.'

'I'm hardly a wildebeest,' I said, feeling hurt.

There wasn't anything much worse than someone making you feel insecure about your body at this stage in the proceedings. If he thought being hairy was a problem, what would he think of my unfit body? My wobbly tummy?

I tried to tune out and just focus on the baby. I visualised what we would do each day. I'd get it up, dressed, and then we'd go for a walk in the park. We'd go out for lunch and I'd sit breastfeeding and gaze out at the passers-by feeling very blessed. I would go back to the park and push it in the swing. Hang on, that actually sounded very boring. Ben's hand was stroking my boob more tenderly now but I was in a panic because I wasn't entirely sure what you did with a baby all day. Was it, in fact, interesting? I had assumed that it was because everyone always said how amazing being a mum was, on social media at least, but was it really? Yes, of course it was. When the baby got bigger, it would be more interesting. Then we could chat together and I'd encourage them to be more daring than I was and not to play it safe. I didn't, in fact, notice when Ben climbed on top and his penis went in. He wasn't particularly well-endowed but I didn't point this out, despite the fact he'd made me feel bad about being too hairy. He thrust away and I stared at the ceiling.

'Aren't you having a good time?' he said.

'Oh, I am,' I said, closing my eyes.

The baby would have red hair and green eyes. If it was a girl I'd call it Clover. Mum's name had been Ann so I'd call it Clover-Ann. I didn't have any boy names yet.

'Are you close?' he asked.

'Very,' I muttered, and then let out a long moan.

It was rare that I climaxed through penetration. Men didn't seem to realise – or the men I'd been with anyway – that there was a thing called a *clitoris* and it was this thing that was key to making a woman come. Not pulling her nipples off – which felt nice but not if it was too aggressive – or shoving your fingers up and down her vagina, as if you were trying to retrieve something you'd lost up there, or biting her earlobes.

'I've never had sex with a girl who's a size sixteen,' Ben said rolling off again.

'Well, I'm glad I could be of service,' I said.

'Oh, I didn't even ask about contraception?' he said looking slightly worried.

'No, it's fine. I'm on the pill,' I said.

I did feel slightly bad about lying about this, but not bad enough not to go through with the plan.

'I'm not a sixteen. I'm a fourteen,' I whispered.

I rolled onto the floor and realised he'd fallen asleep already. I pushed my pelvis up so the sperm could swim to where it was supposed to.

I am welcoming my baby into my life.

There is no resistance.

I am fertile and my womb is readying itself for new beginnings.

I masturbated, as orgasming made it more likely that you'd get pregnant. I thought about Iggy Pop smeared in peanut butter. Not as he was today, but as he was in the late 60s in the famous black and white photograph.

'You're very hot,' he said, going down on me.

It didn't take very long…

Chapter Nine

'So, how have you been this week?'

'I think I've forgotten to be anxious,' I said, which was partly true.

'Are you still writing down your worries? And did you get the "worry management" file I sent through?'

I nodded. The truth was I *wasn't* feeling as bad as normal. I was optimistic that this time it had worked. I had done everything right. Ben was fit. He was fertile, as far as I knew. We'd actually had sex twice – he'd woken up with an erection and we'd had a quick shag before I left. I'd been at peak fertility. The stars were aligned.

'Can you read out some of your worries then?' Sarah said.

There was nothing there because I'd forgotten to write anything. Did this mean an improvement?

'I'm worried that I'll look ugly when I get older,' I said making it up as I went along.

'OK, hypothetical, so let's forget that one.'

'I'm also worried about mobile phones, that we can't seem to do nothing with our time anymore.'

'Also not proven, so let's forget that too.'

Sarah was looking a little bored. There were some weeks when I didn't have the heart for these sessions.

'We're making great progress,' Sarah said as I walked out the door. 'Remember, this is a condition that you live with. It'll never disappear altogether, right?'

I was making progress. I would soon be a mum and all the anxiety would go. I would be a natural. Motherhood would come easily to me. I'd been a flop at just about everything so far, or not even a flop but just *average*. This time I'd turn a corner. I felt as though there were two versions of me in the weeks that followed. One worked in a bookshop and smiled and chatted to customers and had lunch with June and discussed thrillers and the another one had successfully executed this plan and was about to find out she was pregnant. I didn't talk to June about it because I was worried I'd jinx it and at night I found it impossible to sleep because I felt so excited, which I sometimes allowed myself to believe could have also been the new hormones whizzing around my body. I was aware that I had an idealised vision of motherhood. This was despite the stories both Lesley and June had given me, first-hand accounts from the coalface of parenting, and for Lesley it was obviously fresher as she was right in the midst of it all.

Lesley's list of motherhood woes:

1. I can't remember what it feels like to sleep.
2. I keep repeating the same things over and over and nobody listens.
3. I can't pee on my own.
4. I never have clean clothes on.
5. I'm the only one who replaces the toilet roll.

All kids were different, so it was pointless to generalise. I had been a quiet kid who liked to sit on her bunk bed and read. George was chatty and liked to be around other people. I'd read a few parenting manuals already and it seemed pretty straightforward. You basically fed the baby and put it to bed and then you started giving it food. How tricky could it be? To me it all seemed like a lot of fuss.

'Well, it can't be that hard, can it?' I'd said to June one day when we were lunching. 'I mean, women have been doing it for thousands of years.'

'I hate to shatter your illusions, love, but having a baby was one of the most confusing times of my life.

Suddenly your whole identity changes. You don't feel the same. And the worry!'

'But at least I'll no longer be worrying about myself – it'll be refreshing!'

'It's probably the hardest thing you'll ever do *and* you're planning on doing it without a dad in the picture.'

'I have friends. I have *you*.'

'They have no idea what you're up to, Kate. Don't you think you should check how ready they are to be supportive of you if you do succeed?'

When June was sensible. It made me question everything. Sometimes I thought the plan was the best thing I'd dreamt up and other times I thought it was sad and depraved. I knew June was trying to help me, but I didn't need any doubt thrown in to the equation.

———————————

'So, I'm burning this onto your heart chakra again and then we'll put some sage around your pelvic area to clear bad thoughts.'

I was back at the acupuncturist for my second session, having re-booked. How could I afford to miss any trick? I'd told her that I was, hopefully, in the very early stages of pregnancy.

'Let's remain optimistic,' she said without asking further questions about how I'd got to this stage.

The black stuff smelt bad and the fumes filled the room. I closed my eyes. I tried to stay positive. I could feel something inside was forming, a group of cells. I had to believe it had worked this time.

'Think of a white light exiting the top of your head and heading up into the universe, then picture this white light coming back down your spine and into your pelvic area, filling you with energy and positivity.'

I was lying on my back and trying to fixate on this light but invasive thoughts kept coming into my brain.

'Your spine is a golden cord pulling into the centre of the earth, keeping you rooted and grounded at all times.'

It hasn't worked. You are a flop. Your plan is flawed. You need to give up.

'Let's book in some pregnancy enhancing sessions if you get good news,' the therapist said, 'I'm really hoping for you – and remember, you've given yourself the best chance.'

She was right. I was taking three different vitamin supplements (one had cost sixty quid from Amazon); I was trying not to get anxious and analyse my symptoms too hard (this was hard); and then there was the special fertility acupuncture. And the positive visualisation. It was hard to see how it couldn't work this time.

When I left I felt lighter than I had in years. It was something close to happiness. It helped that I had zero expectations about Ben so there was none of that 'will he ring me or not?' nonsense going on. I was happy for it to remain a one-night thing. It made life so much easier.

———————

Franklin's was relatively busy that week

'George'll be here soon,' Lesley said. 'I thought he'd come in with you this morning?'

'He was spending too long ironing his trousers so he'll be another ten minutes,' I said.

George had been so nervous about starting work that he hadn't slept properly all night. I hadn't slept either, but for entirely different reasons.

I was finding it hard to stay in this happy/calm place. My anxiety kept swelling up like a tide. I was doing everything I could to fight it. Anxiety was bad for the baby. The more I thought about this, the more anxious I felt.

'And just before he arrives can I point out that the new Zadie Smith definitely isn't half price? I've had to take all the stickers off,' Lesley said as I got the till ready and tidied up the desk.

'Sorry,' I said, 'I must have made a mistake.'

I wasn't quite on the ball. I felt a bit like a zombie. I wondered if this was early pregnancy or just the fact that I was super-focused on not being anxious.

'Are you all right?'

I nodded, but the truth was that the shop, Lesley, George, the entire world felt very far away, like I was up floating in space and looking down on them all.

'I was woken up three times last night by a child with an abnormally high temperature.'

I want to be woken up by a child with a high temperature! I felt like screaming, but how could I expect people to be sensitive around me when I hadn't told anyone what I was doing?

I was thinking about Mum as I organised all the new arrivals. There seemed to be a lot of books about people who were dying (and had realised what the meaning of life was) or had died (and their family had realised what the meaning of life was). I felt like Mum and I had never had the proper *end of life* chat. The one where the parent offers up all their wisdom on how to be happy. One minute, Mum had been conscious and talking about how she hated Aloe Vera Vaseline, which I'd been rubbing on her lips to keep them moist, and the next minute she'd fallen asleep and she never woke up. The doctor came in and said she only had a few hours left at most. George and I stood on either side of the bed. Every time I looked at him I thought how he still looked like a little boy. So many different subjects we hadn't covered…

George arrived at work. He'd brushed his hair and trimmed his beard and he'd got his work polo shirt on –

not some stupid, ironic one. I felt proud at the effort he'd made.

'I've been studying Richard Branson's style,' George said. 'Is this my locker?' He pointed at the one next to mine.

I'd stuck a sticker on the front of Homer Simpson. We'd both been avid fans of *The Simpsons* as kids and I thought it would make him feel more at home.

'You're basing your style on Richard Branson?' I said. 'You're the first person I've heard mention him as a style icon.'

'I saw Lesley just now and didn't know what to say. Did you tell her I was some sort of book fan?'

'I told her that you like science fiction.'

'Harry Potter isn't science fiction.'

'It's the one category that Lesley doesn't read, so she won't know if you're not clued up about it.'

I talked him through some of the store procedures. Then I showed him where all the stock was kept and how we went about prioritising what to put where. I was trying to feel happy for him, seeing him enthusiastic about something for the first time in a long while, but the dragging sensation inside, the fact that I hadn't succeeded in getting pregnant, kept playing on my mind.

I was also getting butterflies. I knew these butterflies weren't good ones. They were the ones I got when I was feeling anxious. Anxiety is not good for the baby. I needed to stop with the anxiety.

'Unfortunately, I think you're a lot like me,' Mum had said. 'I mean, you worry a lot. I look at George and he seems so carefree and happy. Then I see you and the way you tend to fret about everything.'

I watched George zipping about, tidying, talking to customers. He then sorted out all the mess in the front window under the display stand, which had become a repository for anything that didn't have a home, and freshened up the kids' area, dusting off the table with the colouring pens and books and plumping up the bean bags. George, at home, was a slob and a mess. In fact, George had often got enthused once he found 'the thing' he was passionate about. In secondary school, there'd been a group of friends who'd all gone to these manga conventions where they dressed up as characters. George had spent hours in his room, assembling the most perfect dressing-up garb, borrowing old clothes from Mum, applying face paint, the works. He'd always been the most impressive – all the details present and correct.

'He's doing so well,' Lesley said at five o'clock. 'I thought you said it would take him time to settle in?'

'I thought it would,' I said.

I was happy he was doing so well. I was happy. I was *happy*. I was *not* anxious.

I took the supplements. Two more days passed. I felt no different. This was OK as it was too early to get any symptoms anyway.

The next few days went quickly. There was always some mundane task that needed to be done, some new arrivals to be unpacked and labelled downstairs, some promotions that needed to checked, some new shelf design that needed to be implemented. Sitting in the stockroom with the radio on felt cosy, like a retreat. I went through each box, unpacking and pricing, checking each book against the list we had. A celebrity had launched a baby-weaning book. She'd got famous on TV for heavy drinking and partying but had turned over a new leaf. Now the photos showed her gazing adoringly at her baby. There was no chaos in this scene, not the chaos Lesley talked about every day: the fact that the floor was covered in food and Playdoh, and there was constant bedlam. I'd once bumped into Lesley in a local café one Sunday morning. Her kids were opening packets of sugar and emptying them on the floor. Another had wiped ketchup on the wall. Lesley had also told me about the Mumsnet forums and how mums went on en masse if there was a café that wasn't open to having kids running around creating chaos. I'd seen some of these uber mums in the store, like the ones who wheeled their buggies into the backs of your shins or assumed it was OK for their kids to open a book, tear a page out and put it back again. It was extreme motherism. Mothers given privileges that nobody else got.

I pulled another two books out. There seemed to be a lot of feminism in the air right now. These feminist books were more attractive than the ones that had stood on Mum's shelf with serious fonts and academic-looking covers. Now it was more appetising. In my mind, there were four waves of feminism.

First wave: women with big hats who ran in front of horses and were very cool – the suffragettes.

Second wave: women who wore dungarees, didn't shave and liked to look at their vaginas with mirrors and go to all-women swimming nights.

Third wave: Ladettes? Women drinking beer and ordering pints and going to gigs and smoking. What was this one about? Sara Cox and Zoe Ball – but also including lap dancing as this was 'empowering'.

Fourth wave: more positive and jauntier. Women

allowed to look however they want. Lots of
slogans like *You got this, girl! Go for it, woman!* etc.

I leant my back against the stockroom cupboard. I was feeling deflated. I was thinking about Ben and how this encounter had taken a heavy toll on my self-esteem. I was thinking how it would be nice to go out with someone who liked me and didn't see me as some sort of novelty because I wasn't a size zero. It would also be nice not to be thinking about what day it was in my cycle.

'June's on the phone,' Lesley said. 'She doesn't sound good. Can you come to the till?'

When I picked up the phone. It was quiet.

'You OK, June?' I asked.

'What?'

'You phoned?'

'Hey? Oh yeah, Julia was supposed to call yesterday but she didn't. I'm worried something's happened.'

'Did you text her?'

'Yes – and she still didn't reply yet.'

'Remember there's a time delay, right?'

'Oh yes, I forgot the time thing. That must be it. Thanks, Kate. I don't feel like I can go out now in case she calls.'

'But she'll call on your mobile, yes? So you can take it with you,' I said.

This was the kind of thing I'd have had to explain to

Mum. She'd had a mobile but had always left it switched off 'to save the battery life'. She'd never understood that you couldn't receive a call when it was off and she'd complain bitterly that no one had been in touch all day.

'Oh yes, of course. She can call me on my mobile. In fact, she said she wanted to do a FaceTime so maybe she'll do that.'

'I'm not sure your phone does that, June.'

I decided to pop over. I left work and got to June's at four. She lived in a council block in Ladbroke Grove on the second floor. When I got into the flat, the curtains were drawn and June was still in her dressing gown – it was a Per Una one that I'd bought her as a Christmas present and had lots of miniature reindeers on it. She sat down on her La-Z-Boy chair and flicked the TV on, not really acknowledging my presence.

'She still hasn't called and I've left several messages. I hope she's OK.'

'I'm sure she is,' I said feeling angrier.

Was it really so hard to give your mum a call when you said you would? I put the kettle on. The kitchen was messy and there was a big bowl of salad out on the counter which was steadily going brown.

'I didn't want to eat lunch, but there's some nice salad there,' June shouted from the front room.

June shook her head sadly when I came back in with two cups of tea. 'She shouldn't say things and then not do them,' she said. 'And why on earth is she so far away? I mean, could you even get any further away?'

She started to cry.

'I haven't slept. I headed out to the Co-op to get some food and I remembered how much she used to like iceberg lettuce and that made me sad.'

I sat with her and I tried to turn the conversation around to books. I wanted to tell her about Ben, but I was convinced if I sounded too positive I'd be jinxing myself.

June and I talked for a while and I think I made her feel better. I missed the gentle banter that Mum and I had always shared, usually while the TV was on, discussing an actress and whether she'd had Botox or not and then googling her age and checking what other films she'd been in. Julia had no idea what she was putting her mum through.

On the other hand, being with June had distracted me from the repetitive thoughts about whether I was pregnant or not. This was the good thing about focusing on someone else.

I'd heard people say that one of the reasons they'd had kids was because they thought it was more likely they'd have someone to look after them when they got old. Looking at the customers in the bookshop, many very old, many living on their own, it was clear there was no guarantee this would happen if you had kids. You could just as easily end up on your own. It was good that

I had this realistic vision of parenthood and didn't expect too much; my child wouldn't be expected to look after me – but I'd definitely expect him/her to speak to me every other day.

Worries:

1. Will my child abandon me when I'm old?
2. If so, will I still end up alone, in a baggy kaftan, surrounded by cats?

That evening I tried to stay busy and not think too much. But the more you tried not to think about it, the more you thought about it. On top of that, everywhere you looked there seemed to be pregnant women: on the TV soaps, on the bus, on your social media feed. I tried not to go on Instagram too often as it usually left me depressed but there was suddenly a glut of babies – tiny ones that looked like walnuts. Bigger ones with massive grins. Toddlers waving toast at the camera. I studied these photos – they all had one thing in common: happiness. Connection. A life worth living. Without a baby it seemed that life just jogged along until you died. No, that wasn't true, of course, but the tug inside grew more intense with each passing day.

My womb is fertile and receptive.

One more week and I could do a test.

Meg was having a shit time at work. The snail mood board hadn't gone down well. Her boss demanded that she go back to the drawing board and think of a more attractive set of visuals to bring the product to life. The company were worried because they'd invested a lot of money in this product. They'd bought two snail farms in rural France and spent a fortune on packaging the white ceramic pot in the shape of a snail that held the gunk. Tim was running every night and Meg retreated to her room and pretended to work, but I knew she was actually watching TV on her laptop. My life was in limbo. I was watching everyone else moving along and I was stuck in this hamster wheel of wanting to be pregnant and counting the days till it happened.

My tummy was a little rounder. I felt more moody than usual.

I felt a twinge of excitement. Perhaps it had actually worked. The night with Ben had been worth it.

Meg's boss issued her an ultimatum: come up with a winning positioning for the new snail product or potentially lose her job. She didn't say that exactly, but basically said, 'Things will get very unpleasant around here.'

I bought a manual called *Natural Pregnancy and Birth*

with my staff discount. Lesley raised an eyebrow when I paid for it.

'Have you got some news?' she said.

'No,' I said, 'but it doesn't hurt to be prepared, does it?'

'Two words are all you need when it comes to pregnancy and birth,' she said. '*Total shit-show.*'

It was easy for women with children to joke about how awful being a parent was. They didn't realise how lucky they were. They didn't realise there were women out there who would give their left arm (and all their dignity and self-respect) in order to become a mum. Sometimes it got on my nerves that Lesley was so fertile and so ungrateful. No one had forced her to have four children.

I intensified the positive visualisations.

I am pregnant.

I am growing a beautiful child inside my body.

All is well with my growing baby.

I will make a lovely mother.

All is well.

One lunchtime, I went to the shopping centre and sat on a bench. All I could think about was babies. It was worse than ever. I was developing tunnel vision. Every cell inside was chanting *baby, baby, baby*.

'Your first?' the woman next to me asked as I ate the spinach salad with my hands.

I'd forgotten to bring a fork out with me. She was pushing a buggy back and forth. It was one of those double ones with room for a small one below and a bigger one on top. I'd been rubbing my tummy in a contemplative way, trying to send good energy down there.

'Yes,' I said, smiling. It was nice to have someone mistake me for being pregnant.

'Oh, I've got three,' she said, 'and it's hard work but I love being a mum. It's the best job.'

'The best,' I said dreamily.

'Pardon?'

'Sorry, I thought you were still talking about how great being a mum was.'

'Do you have more children, then?'

'Oh no, sorry, but I mean I can tell it'll be great.'

'It's hard, of course.'

'Oh yes, I'm sure it is.'

But I was thinking: is it hard? Is it really? Is it as hard as losing your mum? Or having your boyfriend leave you? Or getting up each morning and groaning at the thought of the day ahead? Was it as bad as having to rewrite a concept about snail serum over and over because you were worried you would lose your job otherwise? Was it as bad as having a man you didn't like thrusting away on top of you?

'So how was the birth the first time?' I asked

'Great,' she said smiling. 'I enjoyed it. I mean, it was life-changing. It was completely natural. I gave birth at home with no pain relief. And, in fact, the midwife said my daughter was actually mouthing the word *Mama* when she emerged. I don't know whether you'll believe me, but it was true. I heard it.'

'OK ... I've heard it can be pretty awful so you're lucky it went so well,' I said.

What did women without children boast about? Of course you could run a marathon but you could never really outdo a woman with a birth story. It trumped everything.

I had a hard time believing this woman's birth had been exactly as she said it had. Lesley had had an awful time of it and made no secret of the fact that she'd almost died each time because she'd lost so much blood. It seemed that some women liked to be competitive in terms of how bad their birth had been and others took it the other way and wanted to talk about how amazing and transformative it had been.

One of her children started crying in the buggy and she handed it a large wafer which looked like a Quaver but was probably an organic pineapple crisp. She stared as I walked away. I should have been depressed that I'd been mistaken for a pregnant woman, but instead I felt flattered and couldn't help thinking it was a good-luck charm. This woman probably had a pregnancy radar and she'd picked it up.

My womb was a warm, pulsating red light, surrounded in love and good energy.

The night before my test date I dreamt I was inside a cartoon; it was like those mini fire-fighters in the indigestion adverts, the ones that are highly effective and get rid of acid indigestion. These firefighters were dashing about with hose pipes and they were inside my womb, trying to find the egg.

'Look here, it's here!' shouted one.

'No, I think I've got it here,' another replied, running.

One fireman had fallen asleep in the corner.

'It's still in the tube up there,' I said, but my voice was too soft for them to hear. I pointed upwards.

'Have you got acid indigestion?' the first fireman said.

I shook my head. 'I want a baby.'

'Well, we're the indigestion team. You're wasting our time.'

'Come on guys, let's go,' another said.

The next day, I delayed taking the test until lunchtime. I was playing this game in my head: if I test first thing it will be negative, if I pretend I don't care and test later it will be positive. All morning I could feel a humming in my ears like I was about to pass out: the world around me disappeared – I think it's commonly known as disassociation – and all I could think about was the pregnancy test that was sitting in my bag and how I would go downstairs into the staff toilets and test before I had my lunch. Or perhaps I should do it *after* I'd had my lunch as that might be better. If it was negative, I'd never be able to finish eating but then again, if I tried to eat first, I'd be too nervous anyway. I had barely spoken to Meg before leaving the flat, and my hands were shaking.

'Are you OK?' she'd asked as I pushed past her towards the door.

'I'm just late for work,' I said.

'This bloody snail serum shit is taking over my life.'

I gave her a brief hug but could feel a lump rising in my throat. If I hugged her a second longer I'd dissolve. Two lines and my life would be complete...

It was quiet in the store and I threw myself into rearranging our biography section. I tried to breathe but I could feel the anxiety taking over. Again, the moment I thought of the word *anxiety*, the more the feeling grew. Perhaps Mum had been right in calling it the *heebie-jeebies* instead. It made it sound like a big, floppy cloth-cat that danced about, a bit like Bagpuss, rather than a jagged flash of bad feelings that stuck in your belly.

I had an app on my phone that helped with breathing and so I popped downstairs and tried it out. It was only two minutes long, but I realised that the more I focused on my breathing, the worse I felt. In fact, I became very aware that I wasn't breathing. I was gasping. I went into the toilet with the test. The image on the pack stared back at me. A chubby, happy baby crawling. I headed straight for the loo, pulled my pants down, and peed. I waited. The test was balanced on the cistern.

There was a bit of blood on my pants. It was implantation bleeding. It had to be. I wiped again and the blood was red, not a pinkish tinge like the pregnancy forums said it should be if it was a sign that I was pregnant. I sat with my head between my legs and waited, but there was the unmistakable period-cramp feeling. There was no point even looking at the test now.

It hadn't worked.

I wanted to lie on the floor and never move again. A sense of hopelessness. There was no point. No point in locking my rucksack back in my locker. No point climbing the stairs. No point in books. What the fuck did books matter?

I had a sanitary towel in my bag which I took back into the toilet and stuck in my pants. I thought about the acupuncture I'd had and the supplements and even the tarot reader at the Fertility Festival. What if she'd been right all along? What if I was preventing the baby from entering my life in some way? I'd held my pelvis in the air after sex with Ben. I'd been ovulating. I'd chosen a fitness fanatic. Where was the missing element here? I knew it was also about frequency, yes, but surely if you were at peak fertility and you'd chosen a good candidate...?

When I got upstairs, Lesley was talking to a customer about a new fiction book that had just been released by a young female writer who was already being lauded as the 'best new voice in female fiction'. I hated this writer. I hated the customer. I hated Lesley. I just wanted to get through the day and then figure out how to end it all.

'Can I run some of the upcoming events past you?' Lesley said as I came up to the till after the customer had gone. I really just wanted to go home but there were another four hours to go unless I said I was sick. I didn't want to answer any questions right now because I knew I'd start crying again. 'I think it would be great if you could give me some of your ideas too,' she went on. 'Remember, we discussed how we could collaborate more on events rather than it just being me on my own.'

I nodded. At the moment my head was foggy and I had zero ideas. I was moving in this tiny little hemisphere that I'd constructed for myself and couldn't break free.

I never really had formal appraisals anymore, but Lesley had said that I needed to get more involved in any new initiatives to attract customers. Other branches of Franklin's had been running events – getting local authors in to read bits from their latest books, or fitness gurus coming in and running sessions on wellness or meditation. These events got new customers in, apparently, and also attracted a different demographic, maybe more working professionals. I'd promised to come up with some ideas but my mind hadn't been on it. Besides, what else could you really offer? I knew that George would come up with something. When he arrived, I saw him talking excitedly with Lesley and I felt a pang; I needed to make more of an effort but just couldn't get any energy in my body to go over and join them. I kept getting anxiety descending on me and I felt like I was on my own miserable, butterfly-tummy island.

What next?

Was I going to start frequenting sex parties? Was I going to shoehorn my fat, dumpy legs into stockings and suspenders and my trotters into high heels and then hope, just hope, that a few of the leopard-painted, mask-wearing freaks would take pity on me? Was I losing my mind?

Back at home, there was music playing upstairs. I wasn't in the mood to talk to anyone and wanted to just make myself a piece of toast and then maybe watch some Netflix. I would have to avoid any content with babies in it. Tim came down in his tracksuit bottoms and a T-shirt with *Cotswolds Mud Challenge* emblazoned on the front. This was the one night when I needed Meg to myself. I wanted to go back to the cosy Morecombe-and-Wise-style relationship we'd had before he'd moved in. Maybe leafing through some magazines. Maybe a cigarette. Meg came down after him.

'We're celebrating,' she said, holding up a mood board. 'The boss bought my concept and loves it. I've positioned it as "nature's secret ingredient that has lain undiscovered for centuries".'

'I told her to put some of that olde-worlde shit in there – people love that – like the idea that it's been around for thousands of years,' Tim said.

I tried to smile but it was tough. Meg raised a glass of wine and winked at me.

'I finally feel like I can relax for a bit. The last few weeks have been awful,' she said.

'Well done,' I said.

'Do you fancy a glass?' she asked.

Truth was I did, but I wasn't feeling celebratory.

'I'm a bit knackered, to be honest, so I'll have an early night,' I said.

I thought I saw Tim roll his eyes as I wondered who I would seduce next. The fitness fanatic hadn't worked and besides, statistically, the odds were slim. You didn't sleep with someone *once* and get pregnant. I'd thought that the fact that they were a stranger perhaps made it more likely as I'd read somewhere some sort of myth about that. I couldn't remember where and it was probably one of those internet fictions that went round all the forums. I wanted to confide in someone. I'd told June about the plan but why hadn't I said anything to Meg? For a moment I considered telling her. I thought about how she'd react. How horrified she'd be. How worried. How she'd say I was humiliating and hurting myself. How I was desperate and needed to go and see a doctor. Go through the proper channels. I didn't need this chat right now.

'You know you said you didn't want to be a mum?' I said when Tim had gone to the toilet.

'Yes?'

'How could you be so sure?'

'I've always felt that way.'

'I thought I was pregnant,' I said eventually.

'Oh, Kate. How do you feel?'

'I would have liked to be pregnant,' I said.

Meg came over and hugged me.

'So how come you thought you were pregnant? Was it Ben?'

'Perhaps.'

'God, you can do so much better than him. I want you to meet someone special who really deserves you.'

'I'm thirty-eight,' I said.

The hugging was dangerous. It brought my emotions straight to the fore. This was why I didn't want a relationship. You laid yourself bare. Tim was standing next to her now, waiting to be filled in, but Meg didn't say anything.

'You going to be OK?' Meg asked. 'I can cancel the cinema if you want someone to stay with you.'

'But it's only on tonight,' Tim protested.

I didn't want company. I didn't feel any better having told Meg the news. Probably because it wasn't anywhere near the truth.

I tried to get stuck in to a book that had been sitting on my bedside table but the plot seemed ludicrous – the writer expected me to believe that a mum would murder her own child rather than give it up for adoption. But what did I know? Would I ever know what it was really like to be a mum? I tried to watch TV for a bit but it seemed that there were even more babies than usual. There was a programme about a woman who had nineteen kids. She'd been pregnant for about twenty years and was now in her forties and pregnant again. The house was chaos and yet she had no intention of stopping.

How often did *she* have sex? The amount of kids suggested it was all the time and this made me feel even more hopeless about the plan. I thought again about the donor man. Did he just give you a sample and you inserted it yourself? I was pretty sure that was the deal. And did he give you more than one sample if you paid more cash? Did he just sit in his van, outside your house, masturbating while you ran back and forth with your turkey baster? At this point the idea didn't seem so terrible. It was better than being patronised by a man who only wanted to sleep with you because you were fat. Or a hairy man that you weren't attracted to in any shape or form?

Worries:

1. Does the kind of man you choose to father your kid really matter if they're never going to see them?

I browsed through some of the forums on my laptop. One was where women shared negative pregnancy results. Crying emojis. Screaming emojis. These were women going through IVF treatment. It was an option, of course. I had money – money tied up in the house – but for some reason the thought of IVF made me feel drained. I knew it would be more effective, though, but all that money? On average, it took three cycles for it to work, if you were lucky. I would potentially pay £10,000, or three times that for a clinic in Harley Street, which is where you should go if you wanted the best results. The money in the house was for the baby – but there would perhaps be no baby if I didn't pay for IVF.

And it would mean convincing George to sell the house and Meg would have to move out and in the end if might not work anyway. It seemed that for many women it didn't. And babies were expensive what with the buggy (£600), the cot (£400), the sheep that made the noise of a mother's heartbeat (£30), the clothes (£100 and that didn't take into account the poncey shops in Notting Hill), then there was the steriliser in case the breastfeeding didn't work and the breast pump if you wanted to express and the toys, the developmental toys, and the books that were black and white because apparently babies struggled to see colours in those early weeks. There was *so much* to spend money on. And then Lesley had taken her babies to classes when she was on her maternity leave. The baby signing. Baby swimming. Baby Mandarin. Puppet shows. Baby sensory. Baby yoga. The list went on and on. I'd waited so long to have a baby that I wanted to do everything properly.

I went onto the *Daily Mail* website. I browsed photos

of Angelina Jolie with her kids. She had so many. She looked well-rested, although perhaps a bit skinny, but that was the ideal if you were an actress. Then there was Jennifer Aniston and she was desperate and sad because she was childless.

I knew it was possible to be happy like this, but it just wouldn't be possible for me.

I tried to remember at what stage having a baby had become such an obsession. During my university years I'd not given it a second thought. Then, in my twenties, it was something that zoomed onto my radar now and then, a 'that'd be nice one day' thought here and there. But then it started to come into focus with Carl. Whenever we were drunk we'd talk about children, how we'd be cool parents – not too strict but also have clear boundaries, how we'd like to find a name that was different but not so out there it made you cringe to say it (Carl had loved Zelda). We'd talked about how we'd be happy to have one child (it was obviously easier) but two would be ideal. How we'd perhaps move out of London to somewhere that still had a bit of culture but also some cheaper housing so we could afford a garden. The irony was that I now had a garden, but none of the other things I'd planned for.

Then, when Mum had gone, I saw life just stretching ahead with nothing at all to look forward to. Carl had gone. I had a job that was OK but not something I looked forward to doing for the rest of my life. I could live in Mum's house for the rest of my life, relatively content, as I loved my brother, and Meg would no doubt move out and start her own proper life eventually, but we'd be like a weird couple, my brother and me. In fact, there was nothing to say that George would stick around; it was highly likely he'd settle down with someone and then we'd have to sell the house and I'd end up in a flat on my own.

And on top of all of this was the biological thing. It was an actual feeling, an absence, a *pang* whenever I saw a baby or someone handed me a baby and I smelt that sour/sweet scent.

The house was quiet. George had gone to bed early – he had suddenly taken up reading, which felt strange as it had always been my thing.

'I'm so honoured to have fathered all these children,' the donor man had bragged in the interview in the newspaper. 'It helps me sleep at night knowing I've made so many women happy.'

I fell asleep and only awoke briefly when I heard Tim and Meg coming in. I dreamt of the donor man and his van. He knocked on the door and I opened it.

'Let me impregnate you lady,' he sneered.

His toupee fell onto the doormat and I screamed. I woke up and my pad was soaked with blood. I got up, changed it and fell back to sleep.

Chapter Ten

'You seem very quiet,' Sarah said as I sat on the black leather chair staring up at the watercolour of a seascape she'd got on her wall.

Mum's death taught me that your insides could turn black and yet you'd still wake up to Heart FM blasting out of your neighbour's balcony, the milk would have run out, and the newspaper would be full of stories that made your heart ache. When someone died you still had to eat. You still had to pee. And still had to murmur over and over *I'm fine, I'm fine, I'm fine.* You said this even though the pain in your chest threatened to push you under.

The problem was that if you admitted you had a big problem, an obstacle, wanted something to happen very badly indeed, then people were programmed to come up with a whole bunch of solutions. Give it time. Try and do some exercise. Get out more. Focus on something positive. You'll get over it eventually. Things will improve. They usually do. I had offered this advice myself. But pregnancy … you couldn't make it happen, no matter how much green stuff you ate or how many early nights you had.

Still the stomach churn continued. It wasn't a full-blown panic attack but it was like the feeling you have just before you get on a fairground ride, not the waltzers perhaps, something a bit tamer.

'So how is the worry diary going?' Sarah said.

I hadn't even been listening. I'd stopped writing down the worries for the past few days. They were too large to comprehend. Looking at them written down on paper didn't make them any more manageable.

'You need to do the work,' Sarah said. 'We've almost finished all our sessions now.'

'I do it most of the time but this week is particularly trying,' I said.

I thought about wandering into that sea, moving up to my waist and just leaving my dungarees and a pair of trainers behind. Who would miss me? George? Well, June would definitely miss me. Oh, and Meg. And what sort of mark would I have left behind? Some mislabelled books in a bookshop and an ex-boyfriend who thought I wasn't fun enough.

'What's on your mind right now?' Sarah said.

'That my life is basically a big fat flop,' I answered.

'Let's break it down,' she said, standing up at the flipchart that she used to write diagrams and notes. 'So what's the thought that crops up behind this big thought?'

'That my life isn't how I wanted it to be.'

'Is this a practical or hypothetical problem?'

'God knows.'

'Kate, I need you to focus right now. It's hypothetical *unless* you can do something about it right now. So we forget about it.'

'*But how do I forget about it?*' I shouted.

I'd never shouted aloud before and it felt quite good.

'Set yourself a time. Say 4pm, and you can worry about it *then*.'

Sarah had suggested this before and it hadn't worked. I'd set a time and then sat down and worried and worried and worried. It hadn't stopped the anxiety at all. I had still been worrying fourteen hours later when the sun started to come up. The session finished. I only had three left and then I'd be thrust out on the world, supposedly 'healed' and normal again.

Work was the same as always. I shuffled about not doing much, observing how well George was doing, how he always had good ideas and lots of enthusiasm, how despite the fact that he never read books, he came across as someone fairly learned. If I'd not been so self-absorbed, I would have felt happy for him. June came in after lunch.

'How are you?' she asked, looking concerned.

I was stacking up some recipe books behind the till. It was a book called *Big Fry Joy* where you threw everything into one frying pan but it hadn't been selling well.

'Not very great,' I said, afraid I might cry again.

I didn't have the energy to even think about another candidate. The plan relied on the idea that I kept going and remained optimistic, but the process itself was draining me completely.

'Is it the plan?'

I nodded.

'Did you find out you weren't pregnant, darling?'

I nodded again and felt a lump rising in my throat.

'Oh, I'm sorry, love. So sorry…' She paused. 'So this comes at the ideal time then.' She waved a piece of paper in front of my face.

'What is it?' I asked, grabbing a tissue from my pocket and wiping my eyes.

Luckily George and Lesley were having an impromptu meeting at the back of the store, planning an event that would take place in a few weeks' time.

'A holiday for the two of us,' June said. 'You need to get away, love. This plan thing is messing with your head. I remember asking you weeks ago about whether you'd been away and you told me that you'd not done anything since your mum died. Well, that's not right. You need some headspace. A breather. A bit of perspective.'

'But—'

'No, don't say anything. You can give me a bit of money towards it but I was planning on going away and I looked into holidays for two and it really didn't cost much extra because the schools are going back next week.'

I wasn't sure why June had done this. Yes, we were friends, but not the kind of friends who went on holiday together. In fact, I'd never been on holiday with Carl either. We'd had the odd weekend break in the Cotswolds, but that was it.

'You shouldn't have done that,' I said, trying not to get angry.

It was sweet that June had done this but now wasn't the time. Going away was just a distraction from the mission. I needed to forge ahead, meet my next candidate, plan it around my ovulation, which would be in ten days, and then, if that didn't work, I needed to do it again and again until it *did* work.

'Corfu is one of the nicest Greek islands and because it's September it shouldn't be too hot. We can sit on the beach and read our books and then have some delicious food in the evening.'

Would it be good for me to get away? What if I missed another month of ovulation? What if that was the month that I was destined to get pregnant? Before I could refuse, I thanked June and agreed. There were lots of things that were good for fertility and one of them was relaxation. And it was well-known that people were less fussy on holiday, that you were more likely to have a one-night stand. Already I was more optimistic. There was something positive to look forward to. That's all it took to turn things around. OK, it hadn't worked last time but there was no reason why it wouldn't work next time. I'd get in another acupuncture session, take my supplements, try not to drink too much, cut out the cigarettes, and Bob's my uncle!

'Wow! Well, that's a generous offer,' George said when I told him later on. 'And there's nothing weird about going on holiday with an eighty-something woman either.'

'Age doesn't matter, does it? I just know that I need a break. It feels like I've had nothing that's fun for ages.'

'Will it be fun, though?'

'I'm going with an open mind. And I love Greece – well, I've never been but I'm sure it will be *amazing*. Lots of sea air. Sunshine. I can't wait, actually, the more I think about it.'

Secretly, I was having a couple of doubts already but no, no, this was a good thing. A distraction and an opportunity to take stock. It did seem uncanny however that the holiday was booked for two weeks' time. Two weeks and I'd be just at the tail end of my fertile period. It was within the window.

Yes, it was a sign. I would spend each day with June, do a bit of swimming (I loved swimming) and maybe I'd even be able to focus on a book without having to go back to the beginning time and time again, and we'd go to a taverna at night and I'd hunt down some desperado and that would be that. I imagined a barman, a barman like Juan Juo who I'd met on holiday so many years ago now, someone who worshipped me and thought I was fun and was also very fertile and so I'd only need to sleep with him once and it would work. It was funny how one minute your life was a bucket of horse manure, and the next, things were shiny like a spangling, golden door knob.

I was now impatient for the time to pass.

'You're going on holiday with an old lady?' Tim said, laughing, later that night.

'There's nothing wrong with that,' Meg said, rolling her eyes.

Was it just me or was she rolling her eyes a lot more now?

'Well, it should be lively,' Tim said, blowing on his noodles.

He had a drop on the end of his nose but I didn't tell him. Meg noticed and I saw her shudder ever so slightly. Were there rumblings of discord in the Meg-Tim love nest?

I tried not to get annoyed. I thought of Carl, how safe I'd felt with my head resting on his chest at night. How we'd walked holding hands and it felt so natural and comfortable. Then I remembered how that had all changed. This was simply what happened. All that love and awe eroded eventually. You shaved your legs in front of them. You didn't close the door when you were peeing anymore. You took your smart clothes off when you got in and put some old, stained jogging bottoms on. You didn't bother jumping out of bed and brushing your teeth before you kissed them. You noticed they'd left skidmarks in the toilet. It all ended up in the same place.

I went for my acupuncture appointment and didn't even care that the black stuff she burnt smelt so terrible.

'You seem really relaxed,' she said. 'I'd thought you might be a bit disheartened that you hadn't had good news this month.'

'There's no point being pessimistic,' I said, looking right up her nose. She was wearing a mohair turban that looked incredibly itchy. I realised that I rarely looked at her. It was like Sarah – these people who helped me but I didn't even notice them, not really. Another sign that I lived too much in my own head and was incapable of reaching out to my fellow human beings.

June and I went to M&S and bought new swimming costumes. I was careful to select mine from the Limited Edition range and she went for the Classic one. We both chose costumes with 'secret slender technology', though; I also got a black coverup to wear by the pool.

'Stand right next to me so I can get the coverage right,' the beautician said, spraying the tan all over my chest.

I was possibly the only woman in the UK not to have had a spray tan. I was shocked at how intimate it felt.

'The lighting isn't very flattering in here,' I said, catching a glimpse of myself in the mirror.

'Don't worry, love. I see all body types in here. You're nowhere near the biggest lady I've seen.'

I had my legs and bikini line waxed and, remembering how horrified Ben had been, I asked for a 'bit extra off the sides'. I bought some shorts. I always struggled to find any that suited my fat legs but opted for some that came to my knees. This would be an experiment as I'd never worn them before. In a way, it was beneficial to go on holiday with an older woman because, hopefully, nobody would notice my cellulite or thread veins. A very uncharitable thought, yes? Meanwhile, George went from strength to strength.

While I was happy that he was doing well, there was also a small part of me that was worried. He'd reorganised an entire section so that self-help was now ranged under different mindsets, i.e. low mood, confidence, meditative, grief management. He'd put all the books for stressed people in one bit, all those for the overwhelmed in another and all those for people who believed in angels and manifesting in a third. He'd also written a motivational quote on a blackboard.

'I thought we could change it each week,' he said. 'You know, it gives people a reason to come in and check out what we're saying each day. Like they do in the tube.'

'I love it,' Lesley said smiling.

He was proving to be too efficient. Making me look shit. I also felt guilty. He was happy. How could I begrudge him that?

'I love the fact that George is trying something different,' Lesley said. 'I mean, we've struggled to come up with new ideas, don't you think?'

I nodded.

'Thanks for suggesting him, Kate,' she continued, 'it'll be good to have his help when you're on holiday too.'

One of the mumbloggers with a zillion followers on Instagram had written a book about how to be a great mum and George had arranged for her to come in for a book signing.

'We don't really tap into that market, do we?' George had told Lesley.

Why had I never come up with this idea myself? Lesley had wanted me to deliver more – more engaged customers, more ideas – and now George was bringing all this new stuff and making me look ... well, real shit, yes.

'You hate Instagram,' I said. 'You said only saps went on it – in fact, you said I was a sap, didn't you.'

'I'm not a massive fan,' he said, 'but this mum has got two hundred and fifty thousand followers and her own range of baby clothing. She's also an ambassador for Save the Children.'

OK, George was coming up with the goods. But I had other things to pursue. I would soon be pregnant and Lesley was worried that we weren't getting enough sales. She felt that Franklin's was a bit stagnant and boring. George was actually doing me a favour. He was taking the attention off me and making the business more successful – if his ideas worked out, that is. The shop was ghostly at times. Today there had been three people at most.

Instead of dreaming up new ideas for work, I was wondering what the men would be like on holiday. Would there be stag parties, perhaps? I thought probably not. June had booked us into a hotel which was on a quiet bit of the coast called Kaminaki.

Later that night I heard Meg and Tim bonking and had to shove my headphones on. It wasn't actually the sex I felt jealous of, it was just the wasted sperm. I thought about Tim more earnestly.

Pros:

- Fits profile of being healthy and athletic.
- Seems to have a very healthy sex drive – hints at good sperm production?
- Rarely drinks alcohol.

Cons:

- Very curly hair which looks like an 80s perm.
- Out of bounds, so forget about it.
- Bloody pain in the arse and very arrogant.

I ventured downstairs later on. Tim was eating a bowl of pasta on the sofa. He was looking at his phone and showed me a video of a cat who'd fallen into a swimming pool and was making an awful, shrieking noise. I scanned him up and down. His physique was positive. He was very muscular and skinny and he had bright eyes which implied good health. His sperm would be good quality, no doubt. Once the idea had popped into my head, it was hard to ignore.

I went back upstairs. It was out of the question.

I came down again at about eleven. Meg was on the balcony, smoking.

'Don't let Tim see me smoking,' she said turning around and handing me one which I refused – I was trying to be healthy, after all. 'I've said I'll try a 10km in a month. Do you want to start running with me?'

I'd be pregnant soon and unable to run.

'I'm not so keen on running,' I said, 'I think I'll just take it easy for a while.'

'I assumed, after Carl, that you'd given up on having children,' Meg said eventually. 'I won't mention it again, but if you ever want to talk about it then you know I'm here, right?'

I gave her arm a squeeze. I felt we were drifting apart. It wasn't her fault but our priorities were changing. She was ambitious and wanted to get ahead in her career. I had no idea what I wanted to do and it felt as though it was too late to start again. I also felt that Tim was more and more unbearable to be around. The more relaxed he became, the more obnoxious he was.

Chapter Eleven

I t was only once we'd left for our holiday that it occurred to me that I'd never spent more than an hour with June at a time, and even that was usually while eating cake in M&S.

I knew a handful of things about her...

1. She hated smartphones.
2. She loved crime fiction.
3. She liked a classic Victoria sponge.
4. She only liked a drop of milk in her tea: if you got it wrong, you had to start all over again.

We'd flown into Corfu airport early in the morning. The back of the taxi was unbearably hot. My bum was stuck to the seat. It was day twelve of my cycle and I was feeling butterflies at the thought that I needed to find a partner in the next forty-eight hours. This didn't make me feel relaxed. June was sweating profusely and she kept bringing her compact out of her green beach bag and patting her nose. She was immaculately made up and had a straw sunhat which had *Out of Office*, embroidered on the side. (I'd seen them in Primark and considered getting one myself.) The taxi driver had a thick head of brown curly hair and a cigarette dangling from his lips. He seemed to have two pairs of glasses on, which made me slightly nervous in terms of how good he'd be at negotiating the curvy road that went up the side of the mountain we were rapidly ascending. As he went around each corner, he pressed hard on his horn, letting the oncoming traffic know that we were on our way. My vertigo was kicking in and I tried not to look over the side at the sheer drop that we'd fall down if we came up against a lorry or coach going too fast in the other direction.

What if my life came to an end now? I held on to the inside door handle. Corfu Airport had not been inspiring, and as we drove out of the town, bypassing completely the old town which was apparently very pretty, we passed lots of retail outlets selling swimming pools and giant plant pots. Then we came to small pink and yellow cottages dotted by the roadside with bright red and purple bougainvillea drooping down from the balconies and an old lady, all in black, sitting on a battered chair. The sea came into sight as we rounded the corner, deep blue with patches of clear light turquoise and white sailing boats on the horizon. I closed my eyes and took a deep breath. I hadn't had a worry in a few minutes, apart from the fact that we might drive off the side of the cliff.

'Bees,' June said.

She pointed to the other side of the road where several beehives stood underneath some olive trees.

'This area is famous for delicious honey,' the taxi driver shouted.

'I can't wait to get my first Greek salad,' June said. 'There is something about tomatoes on holiday – you can't get tomatoes like it at home. So juicy, and then the feta cheese. God, I could eat it all day long.'

As kids we'd been on holiday but never abroad. Mum hadn't had the funds to take us away. We'd usually stayed in Uncle David's caravan in Cromer (he was my mum's half-brother and was kind enough to let us spend two weeks there every summer). I was keen to take this all in.

Maybe I did like travelling but just hadn't done it enough?

The Nikolas apartment was on the top floor of a small complex next to a generous swimming pool. Inside the apartment there was no furniture aside from a luridly patterned sofa and a couple of plastic chairs and table on the balcony. In the bedroom there were two single beds and a piece of flypaper dangling above the light switch (with several flies struggling to escape). June whistled as she took her clothes out of her suitcase and hung them up in the wardrobe. Her wardrobe was impeccable as usual – co-ordinated scarves, sandals, and cardies. I'd struggled to pack as I didn't like wearing summer clothes because I hated my legs.

'Why have you packed so many pairs of leggings?' she asked.

I planned to wear them on the beach to alternate with my coverup. There was no way I was wandering about just in a swimming costume. A kaftan and leggings was my go-to on holiday – even if it was forty degrees outside.

'Where are your shorts?'

I hadn't brought them with me, in the end. I'd put them on and come downstairs and Tim had burst out laughing.

'Sorry, but I just wasn't expecting to see you in summer clothes,' he sniggered as Meg scowled at him.

I knew in that moment that the shorts had been a mistake.

'You're not going to swim?' June asked.

'Yes, but I just prefer to be covered up.'

'You're young, Kate. Get your legs out!' she protested.

I knew I'd never be comfortable with my body. I'd been slightly overweight as a child and one comment from a boy at school called Lee Barclay had stuck in my mind forever.

'You've got legs like a rugby player,' he'd said.

Everyone had laughed. I wasn't quite sure what a rugby player's legs looked like, but I was pretty sure they weren't like Cindy Crawford's. I'd then bought Cindy Crawford's workout video and spent every evening desperately doing lunges. The exercises just seemed to make my legs harder and thicker. How was it even possible?

'Where did I get these legs from?' I'd asked Mum.

'They're lovely, why are you asking?' Mum had said.

'They're short and fat,' I'd said, starting to cry.

'I think maybe you take after your dad a bit … not that I think there's anything wrong with your legs, darling.'

The leg thing had been another reason why I didn't fancy travelling in hot countries. It sounded absurd, but the fact that I knew I'd have to be covered up all the time meant I'd avoided exotic countries all my life – and I realised, aged thirty-eight, that this was pretty absurd.

A noise startled me and I turned around to see a mangy-looking cat wandering into the kitchen. It had a scab on the end of its nose and was brown and white.

'Don't touch it, Kate. They have a lot of strays here.

That one has been in the wars,' June said, bending down to stroke it.

I could identify with the weary expression of this moggy. When June wasn't looking I bent down and stroked it.

'I see you, cat,' I said.

The cat purred and walked off.

———————————

There were a couple of nice tavernas. One small pebbly beach. A boat rental company called Spiro's Boats, a small supermarket, and a few upmarket holiday rental cottages. We immediately walked down to the beach and selected two loungers under parasols. I listened to music for a bit, and June got on with her book. At lunch we walked up to the nearest taverna and ordered beer and Greek salads.

'I've been listening to *Woman's Hour* recently,' June said, 'and they had this whole special on women having fertility treatment and how stressful it can be. It made me think that maybe your plan isn't so crazy after all.'

'I haven't ruled it out,' I said, drinking my lemonade – I was still off booze, of course. 'I just want to try this first. It feels more natural in some way. I know that's mad, but if it works then at least I've seen the guy and know something about him.'

'A bit like your dad, right? I mean, he wasn't around but you knew what he looked like and had some basic information about him?'

'I guess so,' I said.

I had very sketchy memories of Dad. Mum had kept a photo of us on the beach together. I was about eight months old. His hair was long and he was wearing white shorts and a headband, so looked like he was in a rock band. He was dangling me over the shallows and looked about to fall over. I had a vague recollection that he smelt of cigarettes – he'd smoked roll-ups. He'd apparently sung me to sleep a couple of times but I didn't remember his voice. I'd seen Mum bring up two kids without a man. I knew dads played more of a role these days, but I also knew I would be OK on my own. She'd been a great parent and we'd rarely missed Dad. She'd helped with school projects, practised our spellings and times tables, come to the sports days, shown us how to wire a plug (she'd been great at DIY and had been adamant we should have the basics).

'Well, I think Carl would have made a terrible father. He was very self-absorbed,' June said.

'You only met him a couple of times,' I said. 'How could you tell what he was like?'

'He never once asked me a question about myself. He just talked about his job and how busy he was. That's never a good sign. You will be happy, Kate, I know you will. I'm so old that I know that, after a dip, comes an up again. That's just what life's like.'

We sat in silence, staring out at the sea. I felt remarkably calm. I couldn't remember having felt this calm before. There was no desire to check my phone or torment myself with updates from my peers who were all having babies. There was just the sea and the scent of salt and cypress…

Worries:

1. I have no worries today.
2. What is wrong with me?

That night we went to bed early. I slept fitfully and kept opening one eye and not quite realising where I was. The green polyester curtains flapped in the breeze and there was the sound of the waves propelling pebbles onto the beach, the sound of June snoring softly in the next bed. The curtain, when it flapped open, revealed more stars than you ever saw in London. I tried to identify some of them but there were so many it was hard to distinguish any patterns. Mum had had a special round piece of card which you moved around depending on which month it was and it told you what stars you'd see every night. Was that the three bears I could see? Mum had always described it as 'you, me, and George' when she'd pointed it out at night. For a moment I recalled her scent, Shalimar, and it felt as if it was wafting through the open window. I knew she was around me, then. She was always around, but I chose sometimes to ignore her.

I went back to sleep and awoke with a start to see an outline of a small figure standing at the bottom of the bed. I screamed.

'Don't worry, love, it's only me,' a voice said.

I sat up, pulling the sheet around my body. The light came on.

'The best time to swim is at night. Especially if you can't sleep. The pool was deserted,' June said.

'What time is it?' I asked shakily – for a moment I'd thought it was a ghost, the ghost of Mum coming to tell me to sort my life out.

'It's so nice and cooling and the lights are on so your body goes all shiny under the water.'

Her bedside lamp was on and the clock said it was three. She pushed her feet into her plastic flip-flops and squelched across the tiled floor towards the door which was hanging open. A small triangle of moonlight was reflected in the puddle she'd left behind.

'You only live once, Kate,' she said. 'Are you going to join me? I'm going back in again.'

I shook my head. I didn't like the idea of swimming at night. Besides, it wasn't allowed. There was clearly a sign by the pool which said it shut at 6pm and then no swimming should happen till eight in the morning. We'd probably get complaints tomorrow.

She padded back out, her plastic swimming cap which was decorated in giant daisies on her head. I went out onto the balcony and watched her. She didn't hesitate and just walked in to the shallow end. She swam a few lengths of breast stroke and then turned onto her back. Her expression was pure joy. Why could I never access that feeling?

'You'll wake people up,' I whispered and then realised it didn't matter, really, as there was only one other couple in the hotel and they were on honeymoon and probably having sex or recovering from having sex.

When was the last time I'd done something spontaneous?

The thing is, it was cold. My swimsuit hadn't dried completely from my swim earlier in the day. If I swam now then I'd have to go to bed with wet hair which would make my pillow all damp. I would then have a wet swimsuit in the morning as I'd only brought one with me. Then another side of my brain kicked in, the joy-seeking side which I'd supressed for so long.

But it doesn't matter if you have wet hair.

You could really let go and enjoy yourself if you just tried.

Nobody would see you swimming apart from June.

You could even take off your leggings and swim with just your suit on.

I looked down at June and she seemed to be staring up at me but I realised she was looking beyond, at the stars above my head. I looked up and yes, it *was* the three bears, and I realised that this was the proper ratio for happiness – me, Mum, George. The current dynamic of me, George, Meg, and Tim didn't work. And maybe the new ratio was me, June, and the baby? Although, I wasn't convinced.

Why couldn't I just throw caution to the wind and swim? In the summers in Cromer Mum would pour cold water into a washing-up bowl and I'd sit dangling my feet in there on hot days. I'd always loved water. I was drawn to it. This was something I'd forgotten, though.

———————————

We had a small kitchen and June had boiled two eggs and we were eating them with some sliced bread which was a bit stale.

'Aren't you tired?' I asked, slathering some local honey on my bread to make it a bit more appetising.

'The older you get, the less you sleep. It's ironic, really. You spend your whole life rushing about with no time and then you get old and you've got bags and bags of time and you can't sleep.'

'I look forward to being old,' I said, 'just letting it all hang out and not worrying about what I look like and doing what I want when I want.'

'It's not an invitation to let yourself go, love,' June said. 'We don't all grow beards and have warts on our noses. I like to keep up appearances.'

'Julia would love this place,' June said sadly as we sat on the beach together later that day. 'We always went to a little town called Olivia in Spain when she was little. My husband, Stanley, had a relative with a time share.'

'It's probably the right time now in Australia if you wanted to call.'

I was watching a family sitting together under a parasol nearby. The small kids hadn't stopped whining since we'd arrived – *I'm too hot, I want an ice lolly, I want to make a sandcastle, I want a new lilo*. It was exhausting. The parents didn't seem to have any energy to tell them off so each of them just took it in turns to traipse up to the small supermarket to fulfil another one of their demands. I hoped I wouldn't be one of these laissez-faire parents. Mum had always been quite strict – we were allowed one ice lolly as a treat but we didn't get spoilt. She was also very fond of telling us that 'only boring people get bored' and we were sent to our rooms to entertain ourselves.

This was when I'd taken up reading in earnest. Now I saw kids in restaurants and the parents were almost scared of them getting bored, so they immediately set them up with headphones and an iPad. What did they think would happen? That the kids would start talking to them? That they'd demand answers to questions? Lesley never gave her kids screens but said she couldn't go to restaurants anymore because they were too unruly. The thing was, life had a lot of incredibly boring bits and it was good if you realised this early on. I would let my kids be bored. I would give them a screen now and then but they'd definitely be exposed to boredom.

I would also:

1. Teach them to read as early as possible (certainly before they started school).
2. Make sure they wore gender-neutral clothing.
3. Teach them self-defence and how to whack a man in his Adam's apple with a newspaper. This was useful if you were male *or* female and Mum had taught me as soon as I started school.
4. Make sure they never whined. If they whined, I'd make them do ten push-ups
5. Breastfeed, if possible – but not beat myself up if it didn't work. I had lost count of the number of mums who'd come into Franklin's in tears,

looking for breastfeeding manuals. It was
obvious it didn't come naturally to everyone.

'She hates it if I ring out of the blue,' June said and I
snapped back into our conversation. She was talking
about Julia. 'She has no time to talk – the kids play
football and so she's constantly ferrying them about she
says and so she prefers it when we text. I know it's great
for keeping in touch, but call me old-fashioned, I prefer a
chat.'

I thought about Mum and how often we'd talked on
the phone. Usually every day if we hadn't seen one
another, although once I moved back into the house, this
was less frequent. Many of the conversations were
hugely meandering and covered all life admin – things
we had to do, how difficult it was to get through to
organisations when you had to do stuff, then deeper stuff
like the regrets she'd had about our childhoods. 'We
never had enough money to do stuff,' and then there was
the impact growing up without a dad had had on us.

'I think it impacted more on George than it did on
you. I mean, he's cheery enough, but I worry that he's
hiding his feelings.'

When Mum died, it was like all these words were
building up inside so that each day I got more and more
anxious because there was no outlet anymore. I felt that
Julia would regret the way she'd treated June – she was

taking her for granted and she wouldn't be around forever.

I closed my eyes and felt tears well up. When would it get easier? I hoped that having a child would be the catalyst for me to move on. Surely that would help me heal and get on with life?

June was tired that night and decided she wanted to stay in. She'd had too much sun and wasn't feeling great. It was peak ovulation time for me, however, so I looked on my phone and discovered there was a local nightclub that would be the ideal place to scout for candidates. The tavernas were full of families and I needed someone single, ideally someone on a stag night – or just drunk enough that they'd consider a quick bunk up with me.

'Have fun,' June called as I left. 'Just go up and say hello. Men like a woman who knows her own mind.' She chuckled. 'I'm going to sleep for a while and then I might swim. Join me if you're back by then. Good luck.'

The nightclub was very small and was essentially just one floor down from the taverna. It was extremely sticky inside and relatively empty. It was only eleven o'clock and people didn't tend to go out late but I was also aware that I hadn't seen any singleton under thirty-five so far. This was a family resort. Then I spotted a man sitting at a small table on his own. He had a small bowl of olives and was nursing a beer. He didn't look drunk but he did look up as I sat down at the bar and ordered a Coke. I'd made an effort and was wearing a new maxi dress and I'd blow-dried my hair so it looked nice and straight.

I really couldn't be bothered with all the chat and the what do you do and where do you live and have you been to Glastonbury? But there would need to be some of this. The music was very loud and a small group of women came in. They looked like mums who'd been let off the leash. They threw themselves onto the tiny dance floor and started dancing like mad, acting out the lyrics to each song, hugging each other, jumping up and down.

I secretly felt jealous. It had been a long time since I'd had a good night out. Like a night where I let myself go completely. The last time had probably been at university. The man looked at me as I walked over to the group – I was hoping they'd accept me into it (they were all incredibly drunk so I was hopeful). This was holiday rules. On holiday you hung out with strangers and danced to songs that were naff and got off with strangers. The man would be more likely to consider me if I was part of this group. Men would be suspicious of women who were on their own because it reeked of desperation.

'What's your name?' one of the women shouted in my ear.

'Kate,' I replied. 'Are you here with your family, then?'

'Yes, but we've got the night off. The dads are looking after the kids tonight.'

She whooped in celebration.

'Do you fancy a shot? We're doing sambuca. It's lethal!'

I could have one shot and it'd have no impact on my fertility. In fact, it would only help give me more courage to chat to the man at the table, who was definitely watching us now and appeared interested.

It was rare to see a man on his own who wasn't looking at his phone.

Two hours later and I was standing in the middle of these four women and waving my arms in the air. One was called Becky and she had two kids and she'd told me their names but I couldn't remember now; then there was Samantha, and she had a boy and a girl – or it might have been two boys or twins; and then there was Gina, who had one kid who was a teenager, I think, and last there was Faye who had three kids, but one of them was badly behaved and very challenging and she wasn't sure what to do about it because it was 'driving her up the wall.' I'd had no food since lunchtime and had, in fact, had several shots, reasoning that I needed to loosen up in order to get in the mood to get busy and the guy was still sitting at the table and he'd got up several times to get drinks and he was now reading a book.

'Do you have kids?' Becky asked as we took a break for five minutes and stood near the bar.

The music was actually pretty good, lots of dance music from the early 00s – my university years.

I told her I didn't, but was hoping to have them soon.

'Don't bother,' she said putting her arm around me. 'I mean, I love them. Of course I love them, but do you know, I have no time to myself? I mean, I often hide in the toilet just to get away and even then they knock on the door to ask me if they can have a snack or to tell me they've broken something or that they're bored.'

'I know, but it's rewarding too, right?' I said.

'I haven't got to that part yet,' she said. 'I'm just at the painful bit. I mean, I love them, don't get me wrong. Of course I *love* them.'

'What are you talking about?' Faye said, swaying slightly as she steadied herself on the bar. 'I just asked if they had that song that went *La la la la too too dee* – you know – the one we used to go mad to at Ben Bennies all those years ago.'

'Charlie just texted me to say Finn's been crying and so he wants me to go home.'

'Bollocks!' Faye said aggressively. 'When do you get the chance to go out? And *he's the father*,' she yelled. 'He's not doing you a favour, you know. *He's the father*!'

'I know, it's ridiculous,' Becky said. 'Kate here hasn't had kids yet so she's probably bored with our conversation now.'

'Well, when you do have them, *don't* let the father make you feel like they're doing you a favour because they're actually looking after their own kids. They always keep a running tab of how long they've had them and how many hours and they expect to get all those hours plus another ten hours in return.'

'And then there's all the stuff that they don't even think about, the kids' parties, the dress-up days at school, the fact that they've got a slight temperature or an upset stomach or that they need new uniforms or nit shampoo,' Becky said. 'Sorry, I'll stop now.'

'No, no, I find it really interesting,' I lied. I didn't really, but I liked these women and it was nice to see them letting their hair down and I was also letting down mine and felt that lovely, warm feeling of solidarity that you got with groups of women sometimes when you were all very drunk.

'No, seriously, Faye ... would you bother if you knew how bad it was?'

'Well, I mean I love my kids. Obviously I *love* them – but do I sometimes wish they weren't there?' Faye said raising her eyebrows theatrically. 'Yes! And do I wish I had more time to myself? Yes! And do I sometimes wonder what it would be like to be on my own and do exactly what I want? Yes!'

Each time she said *yes* she punched the air.

'It's bloody hard,' Becky said. 'It's the hardest job you'll ever do.'

'And make sure your other half is up for it. Mine is useless. He just walks out the door with his sunglasses and leaves me to pack the bag with all the kids' stuff. I do pretty much everything.'

'And you never have sex anymore. It just stops and you don't care because you're tired and you just want to sleep. I can't remember the last time we had sex. Probably my birthday two years ago,' Becky concluded.

They ordered another round of drinks and I noticed that the 'not-so-bad-looking' man was walking towards us. I was relieved that they'd not queried who I was partnered up with. It was fine listening to them complain about motherhood but I didn't want them poking their noses into my business.

I was drunk enough not to care if this man rejected me. I had a bit of a tan and had covered my body in Nuxe Shimmery Oil which made me look a bit glam and I was feeling confident and good. The girls (no, they weren't girls, they were grown women) had moved back onto the dancefloor, the classic CeCe Peniston song had come on and they were acting out all the lyrics with their hands like drunk women everywhere did. The man was now standing next to me. He was wearing exactly the same fragrance Carl had worn, Le Labo and it seemed like a strange coincidence. Was this a sign? A sign that it was meant to be *and* that this time I might be successful?

'Do you think you could help me?' I asked, gesturing in the direction of the cubicle.

'With what?' he asked, looking curious and leaning in.

He looked a bit like the kind of newsreader you get on the BBC when it's not peak time. Someone who's never going to be on *Desert Island Discs* but is reliable and has a decent enough amount of charisma for people to listen to him for ten minutes at three in the afternoon.

'Can I show you something?'

He nodded.

'OK. Sure,' he said. 'I've been watching you with your friends and was hoping we could chat.'

'Well, you'll have to come into the loo with me,' I said pulling him towards the toilet.

'You want to talk to me in the loo?' he asked, laughing, but he was still moving towards the toilets with me.

I realised this was seedy. A quick bunk-up in a bedroom was one thing, but a toilet in a nightclub was another. If we were in Studio 54 and he was Mick Jagger and I was Bianca Jagger and it was 1978 or something, and I had just ridden in on a white horse with my hair looking perfect and Mick was wearing tight leather trousers and Andy Warhol was smoking a cigarette... Well, that wasn't seedy but this – well, this was different. The thing was, I just needed to *get on with it!* I was ovulating. As each month passed I was less and less likely to get pregnant naturally, the desire to have a baby wasn't lessening any, and I was convinced it was the one thing that was going to tip my life from shitsville to brilliantsville. Then, before I knew what was happening, we were both in one of the women's toilets – there were four in a row – and then we were kissing.

'I knew you were up for it,' he said. 'Suck my cock.'

I didn't want to do this for two reasons:

a) if he came in my mouth it was a complete waste of time and also pretty disgusting.

b) I didn't enjoy blow jobs and didn't know many women who did – only women in porn films who seemed to be able to orgasm just from having a man shove their willy in their mouth. Did this man just sit in crappy Greek bars waiting for desperate women to pop up and was it really obvious that I was looking for a man? Was it my hormones?

'I prefer not to,' I said as saucily as I could. 'I am right up for it, though.'

He sniggered. I was aware that I wasn't particularly good at talking dirty. I sounded like a *Carry On Camping* actress.

'You said you needed some help?' he asked pulling me closer. 'What kind of help?'

The smell of Carl was confusing when I looked up and saw this not-so-charming newsreader face staring back at me. Carl and I had always opted for the traditional venues when we had sex … like beds, or once we'd had sex in a tent when we'd been staying with friends and they'd had no space and asked us to camp in their garden for two days. But that was certainly the most adventurous thing we'd ever done. He'd once asked if we could have bum sex but I didn't fancy it and he never brought it up again. I knew I should say something sexy to this man. What would Bianca say to Mick if we were in that iconic 1970s nightclub in New York?

'My knickers,' I said. 'I need help because they're too tight so I need help taking them off.'

'Suck my cock,' he repeated.

Was he a robot? Was he a *deaf* robot?

'Every man just wants his willy sucked,' Carl had said years ago. 'They don't even care who does it. It could be a dog as far as they're concerned.'

I knew he was right, but I had no intention of giving this man a blow job right now.

I was on holiday. I was ovulating. His breath was very boozy and I wondered what his story was. Was he single? He was wearing holiday clothes, an old Nirvana

T-shirt, and a pair of camouflage shorts with beaten up Converse shoes. He looked like he worked in IT or was a computer science lecturer trying to be hip – or he was a husband pretending to be single. He had a London accent.

I tried to remember these details, just in case it actually worked. I wanted my child to have at least some outline of who their father had been. Our teeth clashed awkwardly and I put my hands on his back and tried to feel sexy but realised that things were spinning and there was nowhere to sit down and I was too heavy to be lifted up and shagged against the wall; besides, this was something you only saw in films. It didn't happen in real life, did it? He put his hand down my dress but struggled because it was too tight (I'd always found Zara sizing unpredictable). And instead of getting lost in the moment, I started thinking about sizing and how difficult it was when you weren't sure what the European size was and had to google it in the store and that was what had happened when I'd bought this thing and I obviously had the wrong size.

I was overwhelmed by the smell of the bleach in the toilet and I didn't even know this man's name – wasn't this a fantasy for some people, though? – and then I kept thinking about Carl because this man smelt the same and it was alarming to see his face pressed up against mine and his hand down my pants when it wasn't Carl. I tried to push these thoughts away and just focus on the fact that I was about to be fertilised by this man. The flippin' timing was *ideal*.

Things moved quickly. After some very perfunctory tweaking of my nipples I was bent over the sink and he was entering me from behind. He had stopped going on incessantly about the cock-sucking and I felt relieved. Unfortunately, I now had a visual of a dog sucking his penis. The stranger thrust into me and it hurt. He was one of those who thought the harder he thrust, the better lover he was. There was also a pack of toilet paper on top of the loo and it was called *Nicky* and I kept thinking about whether that was a good name for a toilet paper and that perhaps *Johnny* would be better, and by the time I'd thought about other good names for toilet paper, he was pulling his trousers up.

'Well, that was nice,' he said, washing his hands as I pulled up my pants and turned to study my smudged mascara in the mirror.

He left.

'I enjoyed it too,' I said to myself, then started to cry.

I looked like Courtney Love but not the triumphant Courtney Love when she was having lots of hits with Hole; no, the Courtney Love that rolled out of a nightclub in the 00s looking like she'd been dragged through a hedge backwards.

As a child, whenever I'd got the heebie-jeebies, Mum

had sung 'Leaving on a Jet Plane,' by John Denver. I pictured her now, standing over me, stroking my hair, maybe taking a tissue and rubbing the grub out from under my eyes. I was ashamed at the stupid lengths I was going to in order to have a baby and concerned there was some sort of damage in my brain that drove me to hurt myself.

I left the club without saying goodbye to any of the women. I wasn't sure whether they'd seen me go into the toilet or not, but no doubt they'd judge. It was permissible as a woman to go bonkers on the dancefloor and moan about your husband but not to try and fertilise yourself in a toilet with a stranger. Luckily the man had already left. I had no notes to write down about him; I could barely remember his face. If the whole reason for doing the plan was to give me more of a connection with the father, then what had just happened?

'You all right, pet?' June said as I crept into our apartment.

I was feeling very sick.

'Are you still awake?' I said lying on top of my bed, unable to move.

'I was waiting. I was a bit worried, to be honest. What happened, where have you been?'

'I went to a club,' I said and then ran to the bathroom to be sick.

My head was throbbing. I knew I'd be sick again and that this would continue for some time. I'd only had shots a couple of times before but they always had this effect. I felt a hand on my back as I retched over the toilet and the light had come on.

'God, switch it off! I feel dreadful,' I said, then threw up again.

I hadn't had any food so it was just liquid, then more liquid, then bile. My body was punishing me for the stupid plan. It was trying to turn my insides out. It wanted to draw the whole thing to a close.

'I'll get you a Coca-Cola from the fridge,' June said. 'That will settle your stomach.'

Later, I sat up in bed, sipping tentatively from the can. I felt as if at any minute I was going to vomit again. I couldn't focus on whether I'd been successful or not.

'So what happened?' June asked, sitting up in bed. 'I'm not going to judge, but I'm pretty sure you didn't just get drunk.'

'I can't talk about it now.'

My throat was sore from all the retching. There was something about this encounter which made me want to die. People had sex all the time. *Not in toilets with strangers, Kate,* a voice said. I put my hands over my ears for a moment. It was Mum's voice. No, it wasn't, because

Mum wouldn't have been angry, she'd have been sad. And that was why I was drawn to June. June hadn't judged. She *cared*. She didn't want me to keep hurting myself.

'You want a baby,' June said, 'and I know it's hard, darling, but you can't go about it like this. It's not healthy. You must know it's not healthy…'

'I don't want to talk about it *now*,' I repeated.

I switched my bedside light off and tried to sleep. I heard June get up and go outside. She was probably swimming. What kind of loon went swimming at night? Her and her appreciating the small things and enjoying the moment and being mindful… She was so annoying!

My worries fell out of the sky and landed on my head.

1. I will never be a mother.
2. I will never be happy.
3. I will never be anything.

Eventually I visualised my 'safe place', sitting under an oak tree looking up at a blue sky. I woke to hear June clambering into the bed. She snored after two minutes. The air-conditioner unit didn't work and was blasting hot air into the room. I got up and stood on the balcony. My head was pounding and I stared at the sea, wondering what was wrong with me. I was torturing myself, undoing myself, making myself into a nothing.

I must have fallen asleep, as soon the sun started coming up and June was bringing me a hot coffee that she'd got downstairs from the buffet.

'What's this?' she said holding up my worry diary.

She started reading aloud.

'Should I try and be famous on Instagram? Will I ever be part of the exclusive Mum club? How will I react if I'm not pregnant?'

'Hey, can you stop please?' I said, sitting up and rubbing my head which felt like someone had taken a shovel to it.

'Will I find a man who can make me pregnant? Will I get pregnant? Will I ever be happy? Can I cope with motherhood?' she continued softly.

'That's my worry diary,' I said. 'My counsellor says it helps if I write them all down.'

I wasn't annoyed that June was reading them – in fact, the worries seemed to lose their power as she read them out.

'Will I ever become a mum? Will I lose my job? Will I be an old lady with cats and a Findus roast dinner? Why don't I feel a sense of purpose?' she continued, walking around the room.

'This makes heavy reading, love.' She read on, 'Why does everyone else seem to know where they're headed? Why can't I seem to have good days? But how do you make a good day?

'Like I said, it helps me vent, I guess. Then I'm supposed to categorise them and it helps sort out what I can do about each one and what just needs to be forgotten.'

'Am I in danger of being irrelevant because I've never had a bikini wax and have always sorted my bits at home? Am I the only woman allergic to exercise? Why don't I care enough about what I look like? What if my life never has any sense of direction? What if George is actually much better than I am at Franklin's?'

'All right you can stop now – God, I can't actually believe I've written all those things down,' I said, growing irritable.

'See if listening to them makes you feel any different,' June said. 'Don't move and just listen.

'What if I'm never good at anything and go to my grave just being average? Will my child abandon me when I'm old? If so, will I still end up alone, in a baggy kaftan surrounded by cats? Does the kind of man you choose to father your kid really matter if they're never going to see them? What is wrong with me?'

She paused then continued again, 'I will never be a mother. I will never be happy.'

I started to cry. My head felt like it was going to explode and my mouth was dry. The sex with the stranger had finished me off. I wasn't cut out for having sex with people I didn't know.

'I'm broken,' I said shaking my head. 'I can't keep doing this.'

'You're hungover,' June said. 'So let's get some breakfast downstairs. And Kate, I'm not sure how useful this worry diary thing really is. It seems you just add more and more worries each day. When are you supposed to stop?'

'You can't stop,' I said, sniffing. 'The world is coming to an end. Nobody is talking to one another anymore. Everyone has their eyes glued to screens. We keep buying new stuff that we don't even need. There's fish full of plastic and those sea cow things get hit with boat propellers and die all the time because there's too many boats and hardly any sea cows left. *And I can't have a baby!*' I finished with a yell.

She came over to the bed and put her arms around me.

'You smell awful,' she said, 'and you left a right mess in the bathroom.'

'Are you trying to make me feel worse?' I said, putting my head on her shoulder.

I missed physical contact – not the contact I'd got in the toilet last night, nor the previous nights, but meaningful contact, where the person expressing it cared how you were feeling.

All those worries. The endless worries. At the end of the day, *none* of them mattered apart from one. The desire to be a mum would never leave me. And no amount of writing it down or reading it out would dilute that feeling. I told June I'd come down soon and I just let the tears come. I was crying for the baby that wouldn't come. And for Mum. And the fact that I missed her. Then I cried for Carl and wondered whether he was really that awful or whether I'd just made that up to feel better about splitting up with him. I cried about never being a mum. About the terrible sex I'd endured, the risks I'd opened myself up to and the ways I'd humiliated myself. I cried for the small girl who'd always watched other people having fun and been too sensible to join in herself. The one who worried about getting wet hair instead of jumping in the pool. The same one who wore leggings on the beach because her legs were too fat. The one who watched people dance and wondered how they were able to let their inhibitions go. And the one who didn't really enjoy sex and wondered what all the fuss was about.

Then I cried about the stupid worry diary that didn't really work for me because there were always new worries – and even if they *were* hypothetical, they were impossible to forget. I cried for Sarah because she'd tried so hard to make me better and it hadn't worked. Then I cried for the old women who were buying the serum that Meg had created at work and which would never work because we were designed to get old and it was the natural order of things and perhaps that was why I had wanted to do the plan in the first place, because I was too scared of IVF and too scared to go through that on my own. But in fact it was ludicrous, because the course of action I'd embarked upon was far more stressful – or felt that way at this moment in time.

I hadn't ever cried with that kind of intensity and it felt like I was finally letting things go...

Downstairs, I smoothed honey onto a thick wedge of fresh white bread. There was orange juice, eggs, and nectarines and it was all delicious; people said food always tasted better on holiday. June was chatting about the new book she'd started reading, obviously trying to make the best of things after my drunken night.

'I had no idea you had so much on your mind, Kate,' she said, 'and it's not healthy. You need to *talk* more. This writing it down is fine, but none of the people around you, none of the people who care about you, have a clue what's going on in your head.'

'That's true for most people though, isn't it?'

'Well, yes, but these are important things. And yes, your counsellor is right. The majority are things you can't do anything about. They might happen or they might not. Even the pregnancy thing … *especially* that. You can't make it happen. The plan is flawed, Kate. I didn't want to tell you that initially because I knew you had to find it out for yourself, but the emotional fallout is too harsh.'

'Maybe if I enjoyed sex more it wouldn't be so hard.'

'Or maybe if you were having sex with people you loved?' she said, smiling kindly.

We ate the rest of our breakfast in silence. I was still hungover but oddly uplifted. The crying had helped to acknowledge that yes, things were essentially shit and that no amount of planning and strategy could make the impossible happen. And there was also the beginning of a feeling inside that perhaps motherhood wasn't the answer – or not the only answer, anyway. I wanted a baby but I didn't have to kill myself in the process. I didn't have to be so obsessive, did I? I drank as much water as I could and slowly my hangover lifted. I kept looking around to see if I could see the man from the toilet. Maybe I'd invented him? But no, I knew it had happened and I had a bruise on my cheek where my face had bumped up against the sink. I tried to shove the memories away. June had gone into the sea and was paddling up to her knees. She looked up and waved. I fell asleep and woke up with the sun lounger imprinted on one side of my face.

I drank more water. I was slowly putting myself back together.

That night we got the coach to a distant taverna. I didn't want to talk about anything meaningful and June seemed to sense that.

'I can't decide whether I like feta or haloumi the most,' June said, her cheeks flushed from the red wine. 'Like, imagine it was your last meal? Which would you pick?'

'Feta, I guess,' I replied.

'I want you to swim with me tonight in the pool,' June said.

We were quiet for a while, just watching the singer on stage.

'Is that a wig or their hair?' I said.

'It looks like a wig. Nobody has hair that straight. Why do men do that? It just draws attention to the fact they're bald.'

'What was your husband like, June? You never talk about him.'

'He was perfect. He was like Elvis. His hair was thick. And it was jet black – right up to the day he died. He knew how to treat a woman. Born before his time. He was feminist from the day he was born. Six sisters, maybe that helped. I loved him, Kate. I really, really did.'

'I wish I'd met someone like that,' I said mournfully.

Even when things with Carl had been good I'd had a sneaking suspicion that he wasn't *the one*. It was hard. We had lots in common but he often irritated me to distraction. I found that the further along we got, the more his habits (one of them was picking his feet) drove me bonkers. I couldn't see the good bits any more. And he definitely wasn't a feminist. He tried to dress himself up as such but underneath he was just like Sid the Sexist from the classic *Viz* magazine.

'I've spent enough time thinking about myself anyway,' I said. 'The whole reason I want to have a baby is to switch that off: the noodling and imagining and worrying.'

'Yes, it just unleashes even more worries! In many ways it makes you even more self-absorbed, love,' June said. 'Just try not to think about it. It has either worked or it hasn't.'

Try not to think about it. That was what Sarah the counsellor always said. Or schedule in a specific time to worry about it. People seemed to believe that emotions were something you could control, switching them on and off whenever you fancied. Was I the only one who found this impossible?

That night June woke me up.

'I'll join you tomorrow,' I said.

'It's always tomorrow,' she whispered, 'never today.'

She sighed and walked off with her towel wrapped around her. I hesitated for a moment, thinking about maybe following behind. Then lay my head back on the pillow.

In my dream, a baby rose out of the swimming pool and into my arms. I looked around to see if anyone had seen it happen and then hid it under a towel. It was wet and I dried it then sat on a lounger, the towel wrapped around it to keep it out of the morning sun.

'That was easier than I thought it would be,' I said.

'This is a dream, you imbecile,' the baby replied.

Chapter Twelve

The coach was relatively empty. We were on our way to Paleokastritsa for the day and the coach was slowing down as it mounted a steep curve. The views were dizzying. I was thinking about a technique that Sarah had taught me, how to remain in the moment by focusing on the details. So here was the furry coach seat with the tartan pattern. And the smell of June's hairspray. And the sea was just over there and it was shimmering and there was a sheer mountainous drop on the other side. And there weren't any pregnant women or babies to get distracted by. And maybe it had worked and maybe it hadn't. And there were the trees and some had broken off at the roots and rolled down until their progress was halted by thick bramble bushes. There was the Greek music. There were the trees. I felt fingertips on my wrist.

'Thank you for coming on holiday,' June said. 'I know it's not been easy, but it's done me a world of good.'

'I'm sorry if I've been a bit preoccupied,' I said, 'but I have enjoyed it too.'

It was true. Sort of true. There had been a few moments here and there that had made me forget myself and my never-ending list of woes... No, it hadn't been great. It had definitely been mixed.

'Have you really?' June said, looking hopeful.

'No. I mean, I enjoyed it up to the part where I had sex in a toilet and woke up with the worst hangover of my life.'

'Well, that's not my fault, is it?' June laughed. 'How are we going to get you back on your feet?' she said then. 'What can we do?'

She looked around as if an answer would present itself and then shook her head.

'A holiday. Nice food. Swimming. I mean, it's the perfect recipe for happiness in my book. What else would make you feel better?'

'I'm afraid I don't know,' I said.

The truth was I was feeling more robust than I had in a long time. I felt like I could cope with whatever outcome the Goddess of Impending Motherhood was going to throw my way.

We arrived at the Theotokos monastery which sat atop a rocky bluff above the beach and sea. It was surrounded by a complex of courtyards, archways and storerooms. Aside from one or two black-clad Orthodox priests with long beards and robes, it was deserted. The heavy scent of incense filled the air and there were intricate mosaics of biblical scenes. We stopped next to a painting of the Madonna. The baby Jesus had a strangely adult expression. I dropped three euros in the collection box. One for Mum. One for each of the babies I'd tried to have that hadn't arrived…

———————————

That night I got into the pool with June. It was deliciously cool and I closed my eyes and for a few seconds I thought about nothing but the sensation of the water on my body and how refreshing and cooling it felt – and how I didn't want it to stop because, once it did, the mind chatter and the worry would all creep back again.

'I'm going to act out something and you have to guess what I am,' June announced, making a strange shape in the shadows.

'I just want to relax,' I said, but looked up.

June had stuck her bottom out of the pool and craned her neck up so she was the shape of an S.

'A boat?' I said, hopping from one foot to the other.

I had played these kinds of games with George as a child.

'No,' she said, spitting out a mouthful of salty water.

'An alligator?'

'The Loch Ness Monster.'

I lay on my back, bringing my legs up to my chest. I jutted my jaw out.

'You're Tommy Cooper,' June said.

I shook my head.

'A crab,' she said.

'I'm a jellyfish,' I replied.

'Ah, good one,' June said.

We lay on our backs and looked up. The number of stars up there was dizzying. Were these stars always out but we just didn't see them? I knew that in London there was so much artificial light that we didn't notice them at all – but I couldn't remember looking up. I never looked up, in fact. I spent all my time looking at women and their tummies and whether they were pregnant or not or staring into their buggies and feeling that incessant tug inside. It became clear that, since Mum died, I'd enjoyed very little. There was a line of Shakespeare that came to mind, but I couldn't quite remember it. Something about everything beautiful feeling like a pile of dust.

But the veil of dust that had covered my eyes was

slowly disappearing. We talked. I tried to stay positive and not let my thoughts drag me under.

Chapter Thirteen

'D o you have any books about mindfulness?' a woman asked.

I'd been back for a week. Everyone said I looked better. George said he'd never seen me look so relaxed and Lesley immediately asked whether I'd had Botox as the frown line between my eyes had flattened out. The truth was that the holiday had changed my mindset. June had recognised exactly what I needed. I felt overwhelmingly grateful. There was, of course, a chance that I was pregnant and I was trying not to obsess about it, but I could feel my hope was building.

The fact that I had had somewhat of an epiphany on holiday – i.e. the joy of living in the moment, appreciating nature, swimming at night, feeling the cool water on my body, enjoying food, enjoying being outside, and even beginning a book and getting beyond the first few pages – didn't change the stirring inside, the voice that muttered: it might have worked, it might have, you know; maybe this time you're actually pregnant!

There was something about the fact that I felt more resilient, as though I could possibly survive the disappointment if it hadn't worked, that made me think it had.

The customer kept looking from her phone screen, into my face, back at her phone screen and into my face. Stress was an epidemic. I'd noticed it more since coming back from Greece. Everyone was on their phone. It was unhealthy; everyone knew it was but was powerless to stop themselves.

'I think you'll find our mindfulness section over here,' George said, appearing from downstairs and pointing to the back of the store. 'We have two new books all about morning meditations which you might find useful.'

While I'd been away, George had been doing brilliantly at Franklin's. Lesley was over the moon and I was envious of his enthusiasm. Had there ever been a time when I'd felt this way about anything? I'd opted for a job that was safe and stable. I loved books but there was no route to progression – I'd never make a store manager because I lacked the drive. It would have happened five years ago if it was going to. George was manager material because he had new ideas and was genuinely dedicated to selling and improving the store environment. Today he'd arranged for a famous mumblogger, Hannah Heart, to come into the store. The event was sold out.

It was difficult not to compare our two lives.

Hannah Heart

- Three beautiful kids (with exactly two years between each one).
- A husband who looked a bit like Robert Downey Jnr.
- A massive house in the countryside.
- A designer whippet.
- 500k followers.
- Two books published – her second, *Perfectly Imperfect*, was all about how her life was a shambles, how she was making it up as she went along and didn't think being perfect was any big shakes. (Why was it always perfect people who said it wasn't good to strive to be perfect?)

Me

- No kids.
- No husband.

- A shared house with my brother. (OK, I was lucky as most didn't have any house at all.)
- No pets.
- 150 followers.
- No books published, nothing of note, a mediocre career.

The cover of Hannah's book featured her standing in a minimalist kitchen, a baby on her hip, sporting a bashful smile. Her mantra was *be authentic* but what if the *real* you was a complete ponce? The publishers had sent us a life-size cardboard cutout of her that we'd placed behind the till.

'Can you shout when she's here?' Lesley asked, running downstairs to the stockroom, 'I need to ring home to check if Billy got off to Scout camp OK. Can I also just say that I'm tired but that's overlaid with another bit of tiredness? I need to lie down for ten minutes at least.'

I rubbed my tummy. I was wearing dungarees and there would be plenty of room for the baby to grow. I was hanging on to the idea that it had worked this time.

Do you hear me embryo? I am trying not to think about you but I'm also thinking about you a lot.

I turned to Hannah Heart's cutout and gently shaded in the front two teeth with a green biro. I'd watched some of her Instagram stories and they irritated me. Each day she documented her first coffee, her walk to work, her office, her employees (who all looked slightly scared of her) and then her walk home again. She kept saying how ordinary she was, how anyone could achieve what she'd achieved, that she was just making things up, that she was happy to be true to herself, and yet the lifestyle she sold seemed fairly unobtainable to most. How did you afford such a lavish house? And how come the kids were never screaming in the background that they wanted a Kinder Egg? And she never filmed herself scooping up a giant dog turd and putting it into a bag. She never filmed herself vomiting into a sink after drinking too much after having sex in a toilet to get pregnant.

In essence, it was still the unattainable dream we'd been peddled for years and years – if you just tried hard enough and stayed true to yourself, you'd win in the end. There was a gloss that was the opposite of authentic. There were no nervous breakdowns and it was all very pleasant. The shop got busy with lots of attractive, young mums – well, in their early thirties – with buggies, shunting one another out the way. Hushed and not-so-hushed chats about weaning – when was the right time? What if your baby had teeth? What if they were so advanced that they needed food as soon as they were born? Was ramen safe to eat at two months? What about organic breadsticks dipped in hummus? What if you made soup from breast milk?

When did you stop breastfeeding? Why not continue forever? Weren't there women out there that breastfed their five-year-olds? Was this OK? Wasn't that painful? Wouldn't it be better to stop breastfeeding? Actually, would it be OK to stop now? Because it was actually the worst thing in the world – but of course it wasn't, because you loved your baby and wanted to do the absolute best for it.

I wasn't sure how I would fit into this world of motherhood. I was tired thinking about all the different stages and how you had to guide the baby through each one. The first year sounded very intense but, then again, you could end up with a good baby, one that was easy and slept all the time. The thing was not to be too neurotic. A lot of these women were crazy. They worried about every aspect. They had no perspective, nothing else to focus on. Then I started seeing the different babies and realised that many of them weren't that appealing. Was that how nature was designed? Your own baby was gorgeous and irritable but other babies definitely weren't, so you could focus on your own offspring and its survival and not get distracted by all the other babies out there?

'Great turn out,' George said, sidling up to me as I stared at this group. 'I wasn't sure if they'd all come, but Hannah is obviously a big draw. I noticed what you did with her teeth, by the way.'

'I don't know, but there's something about her that makes my skin crawl.'

'Is it because you're not "authentic" enough?'

'Probably,' I said. 'I mean yes, you're right. I'm proud that you've pulled this together, mate.'

George gave my arm a squeeze. 'Thanks. I feel, like, super-inspired for the first time in ages. Are you OK? You seem quiet even by your standards.'

'Just post-holiday blues,' I said. 'Do you remember those holidays we used to have in the caravan in Cromer?'

'God, yes. We argued. We got sunburn. Mum used to go to bed at seven because she said she couldn't deal with us anymore.'

'Did she really?'

'Yes, she went to bed super-early and you and I used to sit up and watch that small TV that had no reception so we only got one channel.'

'I guess she was probably depressed. I mean, it must have been lonely sometimes.'

George nodded. This wasn't how I'd remembered these holidays at all. I'd thought we'd always had a marvellous time. It was funny how rose-tinted my vision of our childhood was, how I idealised Mum and refused to see anything negative about her. She had been perfect in my mind. It was useful to be reminded that no mother could ever be brilliant all the time.

'Do you like the tote bag?' George said, pointing to the bags he'd had printed up with a few baby-friendly goodies inside.

They said MEGA MUM on the side. Each mum who bought the book got a bag with a baby puree pouch inside (he'd contacted a baby food brand and they'd supplied the pouches for free). I was amazed how he'd got all of these things together. When Lesley had talked about events I'd struggled to see beyond an author sitting on a chair, reading from their book. George was getting a whole new demographic in and also creating excitement and buzz. The mums were taking selfies, holding up the book, and eagerly awaiting Hannah's arrival. Five minutes later a car drew up and she stepped out. She was wearing a luridly printed skirt, a pastel high-necked knit with the slogan *Happy as Hell* on the front and was scowling.

'Wi-Fi password?' she snapped.

'It's F5A6N7K.'

She was scrolling frantically through her phone.

'Shit, can't someone please just create an easy and memorable password?' she complained, barging past. 'I've got four stories to upload. For fuck's sake! The nanny has just texted to say Tobias has been sick. Shit!'

I followed behind as she walked towards the table where she'd be talking to her fans and signing books. I felt very subservient in her presence, as if I needed to curtsey or bow. She had expensive hair and her skin was gleaming (perhaps Botox, but *good* Botox that made you look healthy versus weird). George ushered her into her seat at the front of the audience.

'Latte,' she barked at him, 'and put the password into my phone please.'

He did it, handed it back, and ran off to the coffee shop. She rearranged her features into a lovely smile, and faced her audience who were all sitting down, bouncing babies and small children on their laps. The babies were making me sad. I was trying not to think about being pregnant but it was impossible. I was getting tired of it being the primary thought in my brain. Why did Hannah have everything? She was beautiful, successful, and had three kids! It was greedy. She had lots of money. She wasn't very nice but that didn't matter, I guess. I hoped she had halitosis and dodgy knees. There had to be some justice in the world.

'Hello, fabulous mamas!' she said grabbing the microphone. *'We're just doing our best!'*

A weary cheer went up.

'Anyone finding motherhood *tough*?'

Another louder cheer went up. I wanted to know how she'd managed to be so successful. How was it that I mooched about life like a woman in the knicker department with time to kill and everything she touched was an instant success?

'How did you launch your business?' I heard myself shouting.

I was genuinely curious. I wanted to know how you went from being someone who inspected the stuff that came out of the belly button to a big-business, award-winning career woman.

'Who are you?' Hannah said, looking over with irritation.

'I'm Kate,' I said.

'And you're a mum?' she queried in an accusatory tone.

My heart thumped. I hadn't had an anxiety attack for a while now but I felt like I needed the toilet/wanted to die/couldn't breathe. Everyone was looking at me. George had returned with the latte and put it down on the table in front of her.

'I'm not a mum,' I said, 'but I want to be a mum.'

'The target for my book is *mums*?' she said, voice and eyebrows rising on the last word. 'So really I want a question from *a mum*, if at all possible.'

The women in the audience all turned to study me more intently.

Hannah nodded in a patronising way.

'Well, you need to read my first book *Making Baby Magic*,' she said. 'It's about my struggle to conceive my first. It took three months for Tobias to happen. Three months of absolute panic and dread.'

Some of the women in the audience looked a bit aghast at this – three months was obviously very little time to try for a baby but it didn't seem to take the sheen off Hannah.

'Good luck and good vibes is what I say,' Hannah said and waved her hand dismissively. 'I mean, I had to go through hell in that three months but it made me stronger. That's my lesson for today. Trials only make you more resilient.'

One of the women raised her hand and I passed her the mic.

'But three months seems quite soon,' she said. 'I mean, it took us six *years* to have our baby.'

'It's not a competition. That's another piece of advice. Life is not a competition. Next question!'

I was feeling sick. The comment about not being a mum had hit me harder than I'd expected. It was the whole scenario: being surrounded by babies, seeing this successful mega-mum, feeling totally barren and useless on every level (no career, no baby, nothing) was kicking off some terrible chain reaction. The butterflies in my stomach, the sick feeling, the whir of dread, were taking over. I didn't have my notebook to hand so I just noted my worries one by one.

1. I will never be successful like this woman.
2. I will never be a mum like this woman.

3. I will never have my own book.
4. I will never have a whippet.
5. I will never have someone to get me a latte.
6. I will never intimidate anyone.
7. I will never have lots of followers and people who adore me.
8. I will be eaten by my own cats and be found wearing an old kaftan lying face down in my kitchen with a half-eaten cream cracker stuck to my chest.

I was in the midst of a panic attack and if I wasn't careful I'd create a scene by lying on the floor and panting. This had happened once at university during a lecture when I'd been unable to breathe and the nurse had had to be called. I had felt OK for the last couple of days. The holiday had done me the world of good; but now, amongst all these mums, I realised, yet again, that I was childless. I also realised that I only had a few days until I could do a pregnancy test and there was a high probability that it hadn't worked and I wasn't sure if I could deal with it, even though I'd felt, for a few moments, like I could. I tried to remember how I'd felt in the swimming pool that night. How perfect the sky had looked. How I'd managed to actually stay in a moment rather than constantly *fret, fret, fret*. It was so hard to grasp and hold onto.

'I'd love some tips on how you manage your social media following?' a mum asked, bringing me back into the present.

A baby burped loudly and everyone laughed.

'Does someone need a poo poo?' Hannah said and everyone laughed some more.

'I do three things,' she said. 'I engage with people, I block those who don't play fair, and I follow people who inspire. Engage, Block, Inspire. EBI. It's a good strategy and *always* be yourself.'

'So would you share a picture of yourself on the loo?' I called out, panting slightly, but hoping nobody would notice.

'Don't be silly. No one wants to see me on the loo.'

'What about when you have a bad cold and dry skin round your nose?' I persisted.

I had a bee in my bonnet about this whole *authentic* vibe. Nobody showed themselves as they truly were. Not the spots and the itchy fanny from too-tight trousers or the boring conversations where nothing happened.

'And what about trolls?' another woman asked, ignoring me.

Lesley was looking over from the top of the stairs. I was aware that I was behaving oddly but there was something liberating about just letting my mouth say what it wanted instead of being a goody two-shoes. More than anything, though, I wanted to introduce all these mums to my baby. I'd go downstairs and fetch her/him and bring them up and the whole room would be quiet as I held this perfect child aloft and I'd get my perfect breast out and it would feed, with zero hassle, and then it would fall into a peaceful sleep and I would look at it with the same adoring/frightened face with which these women looked at their babies and I would be part of the club, the exclusive club, and no longer judged as a no mark/flop/weirdo because I was in my late thirties and had no kids.

But was that why I was doing this? To fit in? Why did I want to be a sheep? And did any of these women look *truly* happy? For a moment I scanned the crowd, not listening to Hannah, and each woman looked more tired, more drawn, more stressed than the next. One mum had a small bald patch on one side of her head where it looked like she (or her baby) had torn her hair out in despair. Another had dark, purple, circles under both eyes. A third had a creamy substance all over one shoulder and was trying to brush it off with the back of her hand. And some of the smaller babies were still but these mums seemed to be very worried about them and kept lifting them up to their ear to check they were breathing, or lifting their bottoms to their nose so they could check their nappies weren't soiled. And the bigger babies didn't stop moving and grabbing and scratching. One baby reached up and tried to pull its mother's nose off with a small fist. The mum chuckled but I could see there were tears in her eyes and the self-same fear that Lesley sometimes exhibited – am I doing this right? Why is this thing behaving in this way? When will I sleep again? Why can't I visit the toilet on my own? Why do I hate my husband so much? When will it end?

Perhaps motherhood *wasn't* the best thing in the world. Nonetheless, I wanted to find it out for myself. Yes, there were women who didn't want children and wanted to carry on doing spectacular thing with their lives, but no, I wasn't one of those. I had to find out if it was the making of me.

Deep breathing. Deep breathing. The mums were all murmuring excitedly and taking photos now. I had to hold on to the counter with both hands or risk keeling over. It was the panic attack, the anxiety attack, the whatever you wanted to call it and it was jabbing me in my brain again and trying to finish me off.

'What's that?' Hannah shrieked suddenly.

I looked up and realised she'd seen the cardboard cutout that was sticking out from behind my head.

A few people gasped.

'Who coloured in my teeth?' she said, aghast.

Lesley walked up and got a closer look.

'What on *earth* is that?' she said, pointing.

I felt my face grow red but I also got a childish thrill inside. It was growing red because I was having trouble breathing and that had nothing to do with Hannah or the fact I'd defaced her visage. I would have coloured the whole thing if I'd had the chance and drawn a small dog poo on her forehead.

'Did you colour in my teeth?' Hannah said, looking over at me.

George looked over and gave me a sad, disappointed look but he was finding it hard not to smile.

'Well, like I said about trolls earlier,' Hannah said, 'I just keep on keeping on. If someone is insecure about their position then they're likely to hit out at people they're envious of.'

She gave me a pointed look. The audience clapped. My breathing was returning to normal.

Was I jealous of her? Yes, of course I was! But I also loathed her, despite wanting to have all the trappings of her success – perhaps minus the whippet as I wasn't keen on dogs who looked like bones with skin painted on.

After the questions, Hannah posed for selfies. She signed books. She shouted, '*Latte!* And this is my new friend Grant and he's getting me a coffee, aren't you?' she said, filming herself for her stories again.

George waved in the background and Hannah beamed, her expensively maintained skin glinting in the light, no signs of lost sleep or the types of worry each of these other women carried on their backs like a giant rucksack of troubles.

'What's your Insta-handle?' Hannah demanded as each woman approached. 'I can tag you if you like.'

Each woman looked a little insecure. With each name she checked her phone and then looked sad and disappointed when she saw how few followers each woman had.

'Never mind,' she said, 'you can grow your audience if you read my book. It's really easy. Remember what I said earlier – *engage, block, inspire.*'

'That's great,' one woman said. 'I've actually got an idea to launch beanie hats for newborns. Do you think that sounds good?'

'I offer an online course if you want to get my real opinion,' Hannah said. 'It's twenty-five pounds per five-minute session and I give you everything you need to propel your business idea forward.'

'For five minutes?'

'Yes, well, it's super-intensive. Also, I'm doing some life coaching next month – *How to Clear Your Head and be an Insta Social Media Star.*'

'That sounds interesting,' the woman said.

'It's forty quid a session but will be supercool.'

I went downstairs and took her cardboard cutout down to the stockroom and got out our largest pair of scissors. I chopped her hands off first, then her feet, then I chopped her hair off and made her head into a roughly constructed dartboard which I sellotaped to my locker and practiced throwing bits of Blu-tack at. It didn't offer me any satisfaction. Instead, it made me feel like I was losing my marbles and was going to be one of those old women who had a giant shopping trolley with a smelly Yorkshire Terrier inside, the kind who wore a Cliff Richard Fan Club T-shirt twinned with a kilt and wellies and drank so much tea that her lips had turned brown and she was constantly peeing into an incontinence pad.

Worries:

1. Should I try and be famous on Instagram?
2. How do you manage to charge £25 for five minutes of your time?
3. How will I react if I'm not pregnant?
4. How do you channel envy and jealousy and not end up going mad?

It was easy in theory not to worry about stuff. Yes, you could see on a pragmatic level that these worries were nothing I could actually do anything about, but they still haunted me. I had only a few days until I tested to see if I was pregnant. Three days if I did it early. I looked at the mums around me. The buggies cost £4-500 each. In the past, mums had worn frumpy clothes. Today, motherhood (like ageing, like everything else) had been rebranded so it was possible to be trendy, forward-thrusting and modern. The most successful mums on social media made it look easy with their diatribe of humblebrags and artfully messy hair. I knew the reality of parenting was different. It was more pressured. It wasn't acceptable to just walk about in a long, droopy cardigan with a Farley's Rusk in your pocket. You needed to make banana muffins and do this thing called 'baby-led weaning' (which Lesley had talked about incessantly) and meant you gave your baby giant pieces of food and expected them to eat it, despite the fact they had no teeth. Hannah finished signing and the women started to move away. George hovered.

'Make sure you hashtag Franklin's in all your posts,' he said to each person as they left. 'And we do a kids' story session on a Tuesday morning and we're hoping to do a Gruffalo event in October. Look out for that.'

Lesley winked at me.

'He really is a find, Kate.'

Please let me be pregnant. Please let something in my life go well.

June came in, pushing against the tide of buggies, pulling a new shopping trolley decorated with neon Yorkshire terriers. She still had her holiday tan.

'I almost got bowled over by a tornado of trendy mums,' she said.

'We've had an Instagram Influencer in this morning,' I said.

'What does that mean?'

Hannah was holding her phone high in the air, shouting about how the event had gone well, how mums were amazing, how we all needed to celebrate our femininity, our womanhood, how she was now on her way to her agent's and would post about the event later.

June and I walked to M&S for lunch. She was gabbling on about Lee Child's new book and the fact that she'd bought some tomatoes but they didn't taste as good as the ones we'd eaten on holiday. I wasn't really listening.

I would call the baby Greta. Or Mabel. Or Beth. If it was a boy, Max. I chanted these names under my breath like a magical incantation. It helped me breathe.

It helped me believe that life could be like the night in the swimming pool.

Simple, pure, abundant.

Chapter Fourteen

In the café I studied June more closely. We'd eaten our sandwiches and already discussed why M&S was very good for knickers, dressing gowns and jogging bottoms but never quite got it right with fashion. She looked tired, which surprised me as we'd not been back very long.

'So what day do you test?' June said.

'Well, I can do one in three days,' I said.

Already I thought I could feel symptoms. Swollen boobs, a strange cramping that happened at night. I had a surge of optimism whenever I thought about it. The whole thing had been kismet. It hadn't worked or it had worked. It *had* worked. Yes, it had!

'I'll wait till I hear from you. I'm hoping, darling. I know how much you want this to happen.'

I thought back to the toilet. I wondered whether he'd even thought about contraception or whether I was on the pill. It wasn't unusual on holiday, I guess, as you were so unlikely to ever see the person again.

'Some days I feel wobbly and other days I feel fine,' June said, 'but since we got back I've been wobblier. Maybe it's the fact that I don't actually like city life. I feel happiest floating in a swimming pool, staring up at the sky.'

I thought back to our holiday, how the tension had dissolved, and how it was only then that all my real feelings came to the surface. It had felt cathartic but now I was worried that the worries were starting to bed in again.

'That new thriller you recommended is brilliant, Kate. I hate the idea of being out in the middle of nowhere. Why do people live in a place where a killer can come and visit your house and nobody can hear you screaming?'

'Well, if my plan doesn't work, maybe we could move to Greece together,' I said, half-joking and half not.

I could predict that Meg and Tim were going to move in together and get their own place. I imagined George would probably meet someone soon (he was getting more confident, more attractive with each day). In an ideal world, I'd live with my child, but if that didn't happen then was I really going to live alone for the rest of my life?

'Wow, I'm tired. I get that heavy feeling sometimes if I eat too much cake. You're a bad influence on me. You make me stuff myself with cake.'

I was looking forward to finishing work and heading home. An early night, and before that some salad with some protein, something good for pregnant women. I saw June into a taxi as she said she needed a nap. She waved as it drove away.

I kept feeling waves of optimism followed by waves of sadness. It wasn't very pleasant.

That weekend passed treacle slow. Meg and Tim had gone on their first proper break together, to some sort of fitness camp which involved meditation, eating granola and running. George had gone off to a Franklin's sales conference in Manchester. I was glad he'd gone as usually it would have been my job and they were usually tedious affairs, with lots of 'blue-sky brainstorming'. The house felt empty and the more I studied all of Mum's old things, the more melancholy I became.

Here was the embroidered pillow that I'd cuddled up to when I had chronic earache and had to stay off school for a week. Mum had fed me jelly and ice cream every day and we'd watched TV and she'd bought me some Brambly Hedge stationery so I could write a letter to my pen pal, Janet, who lived in Montreal. Here was the teapot that she always drank her tea from, even though the spout had broken off and the inside had gone a deep brown colour. And here was the scarf she wore whenever the sun came out; it had pelicans on it and smelt of Shalimar. Why was it still hanging on the back of the chair? Three years it had been now. It didn't take a genius to see that June was a replacement for Mum in many ways. I picked up the phone and called her number but she didn't answer (I figured she was at the shops). I watched Netflix. I tried June again, but nothing. I worried that perhaps something had happened but it was also nine o'clock so it was possible she was asleep.

George sent a text.

Conference is insane. I have ideas coming out of my eyeballs.

Well done, I typed back. *You'll have to tell me when you get back.*

You OK?

So so, I typed.

I could have tested tonight but it was potentially too early and the pregnancy hormone wouldn't show up yet.

I needed to wait till the morning and use an early detection one. At night, the only sound was the kids shouting and the occasional police siren. I lay in bed and tried to stay positive. *The cells were dividing and growing. The DNA was doing whatever it was DNA did.* I came off the forums and tried not to google too much about symptoms. I heard a scrabbling under the kitchen sink in the middle of the night and I had to get up and grab a rolling pin, but when I opened the door there was nothing there.

Once Meg and I had watched a rat run out from under the bins, up a drainpipe and straight onto our neighbour's balcony. Would I cope if Meg moved out? And George? What if I never had children? Would I be OK living alone? Sometimes I imagined a future like this. I'd buy myself one of those foot spas with bubbling water and sit on the sofa in a kaftan. I'd eat white bread. I'd quit my job. I'd watch TV. I'd maybe start doing those Arrowword puzzles that old ladies did. Years would pass. My ovaries would shrivel and I'd die on my own in bed with an old crust of bread stuck to the side of my face and a rat readying itself to nibble my fingers off.

Mum had been blessed in that she'd never had to cope with old age. She'd been sixty-four. No morphine milkshakes for her, no bedpans or stairlifts or the indignity of being lowered into a bath and sponged in the privates by a stranger who was being paid less than the minimum wage. Outside, mopeds circled around like angry bumblebees. The spectre of the creepy donor DJ sprang to the fore. There were thousands of women who got pregnant that way. It was infinitely better than pushing men into toilets, wasn't it?

———

The next morning, I got the pregnancy test and peed on it. I went to make myself a cup of tea but my hands were shaking and I almost burnt myself trying to get the hot water in the cup. I went back into the bathroom. It was negative.

I walked out onto the balcony. It was early still and there were a couple of pigeons waddling about and the grass below looked like it was finally recovering from the 'scorched summer' weather conditions we'd had for two months straight.

'*I'm not pregnant,*' I shouted … but there was no one to answer.

I believed, in that moment, that you could kid yourself that things were getting better but they never were. I tried to ring June but it was only six-thirty and she'd probably still be asleep; she got up early but not that early. The initial shock of it being negative was wearing off, or I'd just gone numb, and all I could feel was this lump of disappointment in my throat like a piece of gristle you can't swallow. I got into bed and cried for a bit. It didn't give me the relief it usually did. It wasn't worthwhile to bother finishing this cup of tea or to get out of bed all day or watch TV or speak to anyone or go to work the next day. It was all just a farce when the thing I wanted *so* badly had failed to happen yet again.

Perhaps I had seduced a man who blew air out of the end of his penis.

Certainly he had seemed like a man who didn't make sense. No name. No real personality. No history. Perhaps I'd just made the whole thing up? I googled 'air blows out of penis, not sperm' and discovered there was actually such a thing as a 'dry orgasm'. This apparently happened after repeated orgasms and your penis would simply 'run out of seminal fluid'. The average amount of ejaculate, according to the World Health Organisation, was roughly 2.5ml. That didn't sound like much. I spent the entire day in bed. I tried to sleep. I didn't eat or drink. Instead, I browsed the forums and read post after post about women who'd also got negative pregnancy tests. Most of these were after IVF treatment. The messages were accompanied by sad emojis, crying emojis, screaming emojis.

I didn't think there was an accurate enough emoji expression to represent how I felt right now.

I tried to call June again because she was the only person who'd be able to understand why I felt so bad.

She didn't answer. I thought she'd mentioned she was going to the cinema with an old friend so that was probably it. I stayed in bed. I tried to masturbate as this sometimes helped me feel a tiny bit better but I couldn't focus. I kept seeing babies (which weren't sexy) or Mum (not sexy either) or June on holiday (*definitely* not sexy).

Worries:

1. Will I get pregnant?
2. Will I go mad?

I heard Tim and Meg come in at about seven. They were laughing and didn't bother checking to see if I was around. I felt sad that Meg and I were no longer close but it had been happening for some time now. George arrived later. He knocked on the door.

'Hey, you awake?' he said.

I sat up and turned my bedside light on. My tummy was rumbling but I was enjoying the sensation. It distracted me from the weight inside and the overwhelming gloominess.

'I'm having an early night,' I said. 'I've got a terrible headache.'

'Sorry. I'll let you sleep,' he said.

His face was flushed and full of excitement.

'I was thinking, there's no reason that we couldn't

serve samples in store, you know, if we did a cooking event with a local cook?'

I sat up and tried to smile but George felt very far away. He lived on a planet where people achieved stuff and made plans.

'Sounds great,' I said.

'Do you want some painkillers?'

I shook my head.

'Sleep will help.'

He closed the door. I knew I'd be unable to sleep. Apart from anything, I'd spent too long on my phone and this made me jumpy and sick. I waited until there was no noise downstairs and I went into the kitchen and made myself a cream cracker with cream cheese. And another. I ate the whole packet and returned to bed feeling even worse.

I did another pregnancy test at work around lunchtime the next day, just in case. Nothing.

'Did you see there's a new Cheryl Strayed book out?' George said, pointing at the display near the counter.

'I'll check it out. Thanks,' I said.

I loved Cheryl Strayed. One of my favourite books ever was *Wild* and I sometimes wondered if this was what I needed, to get lost in the wilderness on my own so I could find the 'real me' but also knew I was hopeless at surviving with no hot water or nice comfy duvets. Thank goodness there would always be books – one day I would read again. One day. If I was nibbled alive by rats while I lay stuck to the lino on the kitchen floor in my kaftan. Books...

———————

I'd never babysat before but Lesley was desperate to go to the cinema to see an arty French film and Toby was travelling with work so I agreed; I figured it would be good practice for having kids, of course, although the timing wasn't great as I wanted to get home and wallow but there was also part of me that said it was good to be distracted and not hiding. When I came into the hall there were piles of shoes, cardigans, and coats that you had to step over to get into the house and the hallway was covered in jammy fingerprints and scrawls of Biro. I'd been to Lesley's before for lunch, but hadn't noticed these things. Perhaps I was only looking at them now because I was interested in mothering myself.

'I've got a donut in my butthole,' one kid said, coming up to me. I think it was Billy, the eldest.

'You don't have a donut in your butt,' another kid said. Was it Coco?

Lesley just walked past, unfazed, looking for her

jacket. I sat on a kitchen chair watching as she excitedly got ready and dabbed fragrance behind her ears, just like Mum had if she was going out, and then she applied some really awful blue eyeshadow out of a tube onto each eyelid. She poured a glass of wine for herself and one for me and finished the first glass before I'd even raised mine to my lips.

'I love Gérard Depardieu,' she said. 'I mean, he's getting on a bit now, but don't you think he's perfect?'

I'd never really considered him attractive and was much more enamoured with lead singers in rock bands.

'He's OK if you like that kind of thing,' I said without enthusiasm.

'Right, you've got my number so call if any issues. Billy goes to bed last and the others should all be down by seven. Are you sure you're OK? I've left some nice bread on the counter and you can help yourself to wine. There's a few episodes of *Big Little Lies* on the planner if you want to catch up.'

It sounded rather nice, sitting on Lesley's sofa, no Tim or Meg snogging, then a glass of wine and some distracting TV.

'I farted on my hand and then ate it,' Billy said, clapping in front of my face.

'Stop that, darling,' Lesley said, swooping down and kissing him on his nose. 'Now, be good for Kate and do what she says.'

'I'm eight so I don't have to do *anything* anyone says,' he replied.

'That's clearly nonsense,' Lesley replied. 'You're a lifesaver, love,' she said, looking at me. 'I so need a trip out. Toby is never home and when he is he's locked in his office – probably looking at porn and pretending to work.'

'What's porn?' Coco said.

'Oh, sorry, I shouldn't have said that. Mummy's excited because she's going out *without children*!'

Lesley swung out of the kitchen, grabbed her bag, and I heard the door slam. She was behaving as if she was off to Vegas for a week, not going to the local cinema with a couple of mums. I was already wondering how to get these children into bed. Did they need a bath first? Where were their pyjamas? Did they drink cocoa and have biscuits? Have hot water bottles? Under the table two kids were fighting over a plastic toy, a stretchy action figure whose arms looked close to snapping right off.

'Did you eat?' I asked, looking up at the clock.

It was six-thirty so only half an hour and they'd be in bed and I could watch TV and chill out.

'No, we're starving,' they both said.

'And where's the other one – is it Polly?' I said.

I remembered there was a very young one but Lesley hadn't mentioned her and I hadn't seen her when I got in.

'She's in bed already. She's a baby,' Coco said.

I figured the other girl with Coco must have been Sammy, then. That was all four accounted for.

'We're starving,' Sammy said. She looked about four but it was hard to tell as her hair was in her face and just her mouth was poking through.

'I'll make you a snack,' I said.

'How about some toast?'

Half an hour later and the three kids had eaten an entire loaf of bread. The Beastie Boys were blaring out of the kitchen radio and Billy was flinging himself from the sofa onto the carpet and shrieking, 'Monster Magic!' over and over.

'Now we watch TV,' he said.

'I think it's bedtime, right?' I said hopefully.

I looked at the clock and it was seven, so yes, it was definitely time.

'Mum lets us watch TV,' he said.

'What, before bed?'

'Yes, we always watch TV and then bed.'

I turned the TV on in the front room but CBeebies had finished its programming for the day.

'You're having me on,' I said. 'Come on, upstairs and get your pyjamas on.'

I heard a shrill, high-pitched noise from upstairs.

'It's the baby,' Billy said.

I'd forgotten the baby. Lesley had said something

about a bottle at seven, that she might wake up and need it as she'd fallen asleep too early and hadn't finished her last one. It was coming back to me now. I looked around the kitchen for bottles and found the steriliser. I presumed these were clean and poured hot water in and then studied the side of the formula box. It was very complicated and had precise instructions based on how much the baby weighed and therefore how many scoops of powder versus water needed to go into the bottle.

'How old is the baby?' I asked.

The noise was getting louder. The other two children had disappeared upstairs so I hoped they were getting ready for bed.

'She's seven months,' Billy said helpfully. 'I can do the bottle. Mummy usually lets me.'

'Really?' I said, feeling reassured.

If Billy could do the bottle then that meant I could relax downstairs and have a glass of wine and cheer myself up with some TV before Lesley returned. We went upstairs, armed with the bottle, correctly measured out, based on the instructions on the pack. We went into the nursery and Polly was screaming her head off. Tears were running down her red face. I felt a sense of panic. I'd never really dealt with a crying baby before. I'd only really seen the ones on TV which tended to be smiling or giggling happily as they weed into their highly absorbent nappies. I picked her up. She felt very hot as I held her against my shoulder and tried to rock her up and down.

'Are you sure you do the bottle?' I said to Billy, realising that this was a stupid idea. Billy didn't seem like a reliable person.

'Look, you go to bed and I'll come in and see you in a bit,' I said. 'Can you check the other two are in bed already?'

'They're downstairs,' he said.

'What do you mean? I thought they were up here!"

'They're in the garden.'

'What?'

I looked out the hallway window at the top of the stairs and they were indeed in the garden and standing over what looked like a rock which was walking across the grass. Polly was still screaming in my ear and I realised she still needed the bottle.

'Go and tell them to come in immediately,' I said, realising I was sweating and my anxiety was picking up.

Was this really what it was like to be a mother? I knew it was sometimes challenging, but how were you supposed to do several things at the same time? How did you tend to one child while chasing another? It was good that I was only planning to have one! I'd be fine with one. Lesley was mad to have had more.

I sat on a chair in the nursery and gave the baby her bottle. She kept staring up at me with brown eyes and I felt nervous that she'd start crying again but the minute the bottle was finished she fell asleep in my arms. I sighed. This was going to be fine. I sniffed her head – and felt my stomach turn over. It wasn't the idyllic smell they described in books. It was the smell of poo. It took me at least five minutes to get the Grobag contraption she was encased in undone. The poo had gone all the way up her back and was all over her Baby-gro so I had to get her completely undressed, locate a pack of wet wipes, use half of them to clean the shit up, and then seek out a clean set of clothes. She was fully awake, not crying but definitely not sleepy either. I put her in her cot and went into the other room where two kids were still fully dressed and staring at the rock they'd bought in from the garden.

'Gordon has died,' one of them said.

I looked again and realised the rock was, in fact, a tortoise. I went over and picked it up. It did seem to be very still but then it craned its neck out and I dropped it on the floor with a shriek. I wasn't a big fan of these creatures. Luckily Gordon seemed to be fine and I managed to convince the children to put their pyjamas on and get into bed. I had no idea whether they were going to sleep and realised it was now eight o'clock and my evening was rapidly evaporating in front of my eyes. At least the baby was quiet so I flopped onto the sofa with my glass of wine. I was beat.

The sofa had originally been grey but was now covered in grubby marks and the windows had sticky finger prints all over it. I'd somehow forgotten that babies got bigger and turned into mess machines. Would I be well-equipped to cope with this kind of mess and disorder? I enjoyed a sense of routine and order – perhaps this was why I'd stayed at Franklin's so long. It made me feel safe, knowing that each day would pretty much be the same as the last. I felt a whoosh in my stomach – another anxiety attack on the way. What was I thinking? I would be a *useless* mother. I could already hear the baby crying upstairs but she'd had her bottle so I had no idea what she wanted. Did they cry just for the sake of it? I went to the toilet and changed my sanitary pad. I'd read somewhere that your periods got heavier before they stopped. The baby crying seemed to be making me bleed. Was it my body telling me, yet again, that I needed to get a move on?

My brain was leaping from one worrying thought to the next. *Heebie-jeebies!* But worse, much worse. I needed John Denver, my mum's hand stroking my head, calm, a friend, a cuddle, something to help me feel normal again.

Could this be menopause on its way?

How on earth was I going to get pregnant before that happened?

How would I cope with IVF?

How would I manage a child when they were so unpredictable?

'Ow! Billy hit me in my face,' Coco said, rubbing her eyes.

She'd opened the toilet door and was standing in front of me.

'Can I have some privacy, please?' I said.

Was it not even possible to have a pee in peace?

Billy had followed her downstairs and was about to whack her around the head with the stretchy man but I grabbed it from him, pulled up my pants (luckily they didn't spot my pad) and frogmarched them up the stairs.

'Mummy said *fuck* today,' Billy said.

'Yesterday she said *bugger*,' Coco added.

'*Fuck bugger*!' they shouted.

'That's not very nice,' I said, sounding very prudish.

Was it normal for kids to swear this much?

'Shall we put the TV on?' Billy asked.

'No, this is *my* time now,' I said. 'Grown-up time.'

'Mummy lets us watch TV.'

'At eight thirty?' I said.

The baby was crying, but slightly less. I wondered whether to go in and check and decided that yes, I needed to do that. With the kids back in their rooms I went into the nursery to find the baby on its front and struggling to turn itself around again. Was it suffocating? I quickly turned her over and patted her tummy which made her start roaring again.

'What's up?' I asked. 'You OK?'

I bent down and sniffed its nappy. It smelt fine. Almost nine and the baby wasn't asleep. Was Lesley strict enough? Why wasn't it sleeping properly? Was this something that happened often?

'You were drinking Mummy's special drink,' Billy said, coming into the nursery, 'Only Mummy is allowed.'

'Can you go back to bed, please?'

I could feel myself getting angry. No wonder Lesley was so exhausted. How did you deal with this level of disruption every single night? How did you sit down and watch your favourite TV show?

'You're not a mummy, are you?' Billy said poking my tummy, which, to be fair, looked like it had a small baby inside already. 'Have you got a boyfriend?'

The baby had stopped crying and seemed to be settling as I patted it on the tummy.

'No, I haven't,' I hissed. 'I'm happily single.'

'So you can't be a mummy,' he said. 'The daddy has to make the baby with the mummy.'

'Yes, but they don't have to be your boyfriend,' I said.

'Oh,' Billy said. 'So you can have a baby with a stranger? Mummy says we can't talk to strangers.'

'Goodnight,' I said.

I wasn't about to explain my plan to this inquisitive child. Then I remembered I'd left the tortoise somewhere. Patting the baby one last time – luckily she'd gone to sleep – I got the tortoise, went downstairs, put it in the garden and collapsed on the sofa. I was beat.

It made no sense.

It was *lunacy* this parenting lark.

My life was *easy*. At the moment, I had massive amounts of sleep. I could watch films all night. I could go to a museum or an art gallery on the weekend (not that I ever did). With children it was clear that all your needs and concerns came second – *you* were no longer a priority. And so many questions! And they didn't do anything you told them to. Did all babies not go to sleep till nine? How did you manage to have an evening to yourself then?

Then again, there was a side of me that was sick of doing what *I* wanted – especially as my plans were always so dull. I had lots of freedom but didn't take full advantage of it. I didn't backpack around Asia or go scuba diving at the Great Barrier Reef. Arguably, I already lived the life of a parent, just with more sleep and more TV, perhaps. I sipped my wine but the nervous tension was still brewing inside and I realised I was listening out for the baby. Perhaps some people were natural parents and had instincts, and then there were people like me who'd struggle.

I watched TV for a while but couldn't switch off the 'intrusive thoughts', as Sarah called them.

1. You will be a rubbish parent.
2. You have no parenting instincts.
3. You can't even take care of yourself.
4. How are you going to do this alone?
5. You're too old.
6. You're *way* too old.
7. You have no patience.
8. You'll be in a wheelchair at your kid's graduation (this wasn't strictly true).

Lesley came home at eleven and I was already in the hall with my coat on. She was beaming as she took off her scarf and earrings.

'Going already? Don't you want a quick drink?'

'No, I'm knackered. I'll head off now.'

'That film was brilliant. I must do this more often. I feel human again! Was everything all right?'

I hoped she wasn't relying on me to babysit again. I hadn't charged her anything as she was my boss and besides, she deserved a break, didn't she?

'It was fine,' I said, realising I hadn't checked upstairs but the silence had reassured me that all was OK.

'Can you stay for a sec, Kate?' Lesley looked shifty. 'I need to have a quick chat with you.'

We went into the front room. Sitting down on the sofa, she motioned for me to join her and then patted my knee.

'You know that I love working with you…' she said.

I felt a wave of apprehension.

'But I need to be completely honest and tell you I'm going to have to make some cutbacks. Don't panic – all I'm saying is that everyone will come under more scrutiny.'

'What do you mean?' I asked.

Had she purposefully got me to babysit and *then* decided to sack me?

'I mean, jobs are no longer for life… No, hang on … that's too flippant… No, I shouldn't be saying this to you now. It's the wrong time and I'm tired and I've had a couple of gin and tonics.'

She patted me on the knee again.

'Forget we spoke. Everything's fine,' she said, 'all fine. Will you get an Uber?'

I nodded. It was clearly *not* fine. I knew Franklin's wasn't doing brilliantly – I knew each month we had higher and higher sales targets – and I also knew that George was doing brilliantly. Me? Well, I was treading water and had been for many a year. Had George's arrival made my apathy more obvious?

My entire existence revolved around getting pregnant and I'd put Franklin's on the backburner.

'Anyway,' Lesley said before she waved me out the door, 'it's not something that's looming. Or ... it is *kind* of looming. Yes, well, it *is* looming but let's talk another day.'

I went outside and the Uber was waiting. I had mixed emotions. The nervousness in my tummy persisted – the aftermath of dealing with all the kids possibly – but also now with the fear that my job wasn't a dead cert any more. The thing was, I didn't love working at Franklin's but I had absolutely zero idea of what I'd do instead. Yes, I'd once, years ago, wanted to make documentary films, but it was too late now. I was thirty-eight! Who made documentary films at that age? Or, more accurately, who started a new career when they were middle-aged? If I wanted to have a baby then it definitely wasn't a good time to embark on a new job. I needed something stable and straightforward that I could do with my eyes shut. I would probably go part-time once I had my maternity leave and I'd continue treading water, but motherhood would be my main priority anyway, so it wouldn't matter anymore.

I looked out at all the cosy homes, children in bed – or playing up, perhaps – parents sitting on sofas with their glasses of wine, Netflix playing... I wanted that. OK, maybe not the partner part, but the family life. OK, the babysitting had been stressful but I could easily cope with *one*. It was good that I'd been exposed to the coalface of parenting, the reality that they didn't show you in the adverts: the clean cars with kids sitting happily in the back playing or the tidy mealtimes where everyone ate food off their plate and said thank you and nobody swore. Yes, Lesley's house was a mess and it was chaotic – but it was also fun and full of noise and life. Increasingly, it felt like Mum's house was full of people who were moving on with their lives while I just stagnated.

I wasn't progressing.

I was too old to change course.

I was too old to do something new.

I went straight to my room and heard George talking to Meg in the hallway. I was sure they were gossiping about me.

I looked down at my phone. I'd somehow managed to miss a call and I didn't recognise the number. Usually I didn't call back if this was the case, but I was curious so I dialled.

'Hello,' a female voice said, 'is that Kate?'

'Ye-es,' I replied.

'I'm Julia, June's daughter,' the voice said with a hint of an Australian accent. 'June's in hospital,' she said. 'She always talks about you and I found your number in her phone so thought you should know.'

'Has she had a fall or something?' I asked.

I knew that sometimes June could tire herself out and try and do too much. Then she tended to get unsteady on her feet. Perhaps this was what had happened.

'It was a stroke. She's been unconscious. I'm afraid it doesn't look good.'

She sounded surprisingly calm and collected but I also knew grief didn't always happen in the same way. I'd been very removed from it all when Mum had been in hospital and had wondered what was wrong with me because I wasn't crying all the time.

'Can I come and see her?' I asked.

'Of course. Come tomorrow if you can. She would like it if you came. She's not awake, though. Just so you know.'

I felt my stomach flip. I wasn't sure I could deal with seeing June now. Everything was taking a nosedive and I wasn't sure I had the emotional resilience to deal with it. In fact, I was pretty sure I didn't.

Chapter Fifteen

The hospital ward was busy and it was visiting hours so lots of families sat huddled around each bed. I kept squirting the sanitising gel on my hands as I'd read a lot about how hospitals were dangerous places in terms of spreading germs. It left a sticky residue which I found reassuring – it was offering me protection. Next to June's bed sat a middle-aged woman with bright pink hair, the trendy kind of pink that lots of people had and I knew would never suit me. She stood up and I noticed she was dressed in a more modern version of June's clothing – everything co-ordinated, so her trainers and her sweatshirt were both grey and she had off-white, hoop earrings

'You must be Kate,' she said.

I went to the other side of the bed. June was

unconscious and her face looked weird, more sunken in than usual.

'How do you know Mum?' Julia said.

'I guess we're both really into books and she comes into the bookshop all the time.'

'Yes, Mum said you liked the same kind of books,' Julia said.

She looked a bit suspicious of me. Was it because I was younger? Was it odd that we were friends? I'd never really felt that way as we tended to just enjoy each other's company. June's hand felt cold so I rubbed it between my palms. She was hooked up to a monitor and was being fed through a tube. Julia was probably thinking I'd adopted June as a mother figure. The truth was, June was very different to my mother. June was always well put together and she liked new stuff more than old; she didn't wear old cardigans with holes in the elbows or steal junk out of skips. She also had more joie de vivre than Mum had ever had. Mum had rarely worn make-up and it wasn't uncommon for her to forget to brush her hair. The truth was June had been trying to bring me out of myself; she'd recognised that I was flatlining, that my life was stationary and she'd invested her energy in me, trying to make me feel more alive, more spontaneous, more capable of fun. And a couple of times she'd (sort of) succeeded.

'She wakes up now and then,' Julia said, sitting down

on the other side of the bed, 'She asked for you once. She said something about a baby. Does that make sense to you?'

'Not really,' I replied. 'I guess she may have been a bit delirious.'

'She said she hoped you'd had the baby.'

'That's weird,' I said.

'Do you have kids?'

'No, not yet.'

'I'm lucky in that we just squeezed two in before I hit forty. I mean, that's if you want them.'

Why was it that people who had kids assumed that the idea of having them yourself had never occurred to you? That you were just sitting about and had somehow forgotten? Oh yes, thanks for reminding me! Kids! I knew there was something I needed to do. So grateful that you brought it to my attention! I hadn't spoken to June after the negative pregnancy test so perhaps she thought it had worked.

'Has anyone ever told you that you look a bit like Goldie Hawn?' Julia said, perhaps realising that the kids thing was too personal and she needed to back off a bit.

'Yes, but I'm a less chirpy version, perhaps,' I replied,

She laughed. 'Mum said you were funny. I can see why she likes you now. I guess you think I'm a bad daughter because I never kept in touch very much. The thing is, Mum had very high expectations. She wanted me to be a successful career woman and when I decided to stay at home with the kids, she was disappointed.'

'She never said anything negative. I know she wanted to see you more often.'

'Well, that's kind of impossible when you live where we do.'

I'd always vowed to stay near Mum – I couldn't have imagined moving so far away.

'I'll get you a coffee,' Julia said. 'The coffee here is awful but I've got jet lag so need to drink buckets of the stuff and I also need to ring the kids. Will you stay for a while?"

I nodded again. I wasn't sure how I felt about Julia. There was a weird part of me that was envious of her, even in this situation with June looking desperately ill. She still had a mum. Then, on top of that, she had kids and, presumably, a husband. Again, I got the sense that my life was not as it should be, and wasn't different in a positive way, either.

I held June's hand again. Her nails were long and painted mint green which had chipped off at the ends.

'I bought you a new Jack Reacher book,' I said, patting her arm. 'I haven't read it yet, but it was part of the Richard and Judy book club this month so I think it'll be good. Would you like me to read you some?'

I opened the book and started.

'Mum wasn't easy to live with,' Julia was saying as we walked to the lift an hour later. 'Like I said, she wasn't always the nice old lady.'

'Maybe she just wanted the best for you,' I said.

'I've *got* the best.'

'I suppose she didn't see it like that. She's very modern. She was of that generation who started to do things differently.'

'Well, it's none of her business how I live my life, is it?' Julia said.

I didn't want to get sucked in to all this. I could see Julia's perspective. Mum had always badgered me to plan my life more, to strive and not just settle. I knew she'd have been disappointed to see me still at Franklin's, still sharing the house with George and Meg, no further forward than when she'd died. I thought back to a day that I'd gone to the Natural History Museum with Mum and George and seen a whole hall with animals preserved in jars. They were each perfect and suspended in time, captured exactly as they'd been in the moment they'd died. I'd remained stuck since Mum's death. I thought about something Carl had said before he'd left.

'I'll never be able to compete with your mum,' he'd said, 'it's not normal to be so close to your parents.'

He didn't understand the bond we'd had. I knew I'd put her on a pedestal, that I'd perhaps remained stunted because I'd not done what most people did and created distance between us, but I'd been proud of how close we were. I'd never anticipated that she'd not be around. I couldn't relate to Julia because I couldn't imagine having a mum that was still alive and choosing not to see her. It seemed strange.

'I'll let you know if there are any changes,' she said as I went down in the lift.

I went to work as usual the next day.

'I heard about June,' George said, 'I'm sorry…'

The next couple of days passed slowly and I waited for news. By the next visit she'd improved and was sitting up in bed, but her speech was slurred. I thought about our night in the swimming pool, how alive I'd felt, how simple life had been – the sensation of the cool water on my body, my focus solely on the physical sensations and not eternally overthinking everything. I wondered whether June thought of that night too.

'Hey, how's it going?' Meg asked the following morning.

Things felt strained between us. Her job was going

really well and she'd been promoted. 'Were you up late last night? I heard the TV.'

I'd been watching a documentary about women in punk in the seventies. It had a band called The Slits in it and in my normal mindset I'd have found it inspiring (they were massive feminists, faced lots of prejudice from men and seemed to have been born before their time), but instead I looked at each woman who was interviewed and wondered if they'd had children or not. I wondered how many. My focus had become very narrow. I was also unable to plan ahead. I didn't want to even think about another candidate, another shag, another disappointment.

'You don't seem yourself,' Meg said, patting my back. 'I'm sorry, Kate, I've not been around lately but shall we plan something nice to do together?'

The words *too little, too late* sprang to mind. Tim came in and squeezed her around the waist, then kissed her on the neck. She laughed, distracted again by this stupid, fitness-loving, idiot. They were both wearing running gear. Meg had embraced fitness now. They stared into their digital fitness monitors, they wrote down their times, they discussed what kind of high-protein mulch they'd have when they returned.

On the way to work I scrolled through Instagram but all of it seemed even more meaningless than usual. People uploading photos of their coffee, their toast, their baby eating toast, their crowded commute, and then labouring to write a comment that glued it all together and made it engaging. I'd stopped posting a long time ago. For a while I'd tried to share my opinion on books but that had stopped when the reading had stopped. I planned to share my pregnancy when it arrived. Not the scan, but just a nice comment about 'good news' and maybe a photo of something sweet like a teddy bear. I called Julia and she said June was asleep and hadn't eaten so they were changing her feeding tube and giving her more sedation as she seemed uncomfortable.

'Tell her that I'm still going to try,' I said.

'Try what?' she replied.

'Tell her that I still have the plan and I think it's going to work,'

'OK, but it doesn't make sense to me,' she said.

'She'll know,' I said, 'tell her I'm working on the heebie-jeebies.'

I felt tears rolling down my cheeks as I sat on the bus.

I tried to make more of an effort at work but I had no energy. I was already accepting the fact that I was going to lose my job. George was fresh. He was green. He cared. It was impossible to fake that kind of thing. And I *didn't* care that I'd put all the books in the wrong section and not priced them correctly.

In my lunch break I scrolled through Facebook. One of my old school friends, a frizzy-haired girl who'd once stolen my bus pass so I'd had to walk three miles home, had put a status update – a visual of her twenty-week scan. She already had two children and was on her third. It was greedy, so damned greedy. She'd hit me over the head with her folder and given me concussion. She'd always had the latest clothes and the best trainers and the newest pencil case. She'd even gone out with the fittest boy from the local boys' school. I'd had rows of pimples around my eyes because I'd shaved my eyebrows off in an ill-advised, early morning DIY beauty treatment.

I tried to look at Carl's profile but realised it was blocked. Then I found a photo of a mutual friend. They were at a baby's christening. The father looked like a guy Carl worked with. Carl was in the background of one photo. He was smiling and had his arm around a woman who was pretty and looked about twenty-four. I tried to figure out who she was. She had dark brown hair, olive skin, and almond-shaped eyes. She had very thin legs. I realised I didn't care. I was starting to believe that when one thing went wrong, this set off a whole chain of wrong stuff and I was just waiting for the wrong stuff to stop.

When I got to the hospital, Julia was walking up the corridor.

'You've missed her,' she said.

'Oh, has she gone out? Is she feeling better? Walking around?'

'No,' she said shaking her head like I was crazy. 'I'm sorry, Kate. I was about to call. She died. She didn't suffer but she had another stroke this morning.'

'Why didn't you wait for me?' I said, feeling sick.

There was no part of me that had been prepared for June not making it.

'What do you mean?' Julia said, her eyebrows raised in exasperation. 'Did you want me to ask her to *hang on a bit*?'

'Did you tell her that I might have a baby?'

'Why would I do that?' she said, looking at me now as if I'd lost my marbles.

I had to steady myself by hanging onto a nearby wheelchair that had been abandoned in the corridor. Images flitted through my brain – negative pregnancy tests, Carl and his new Eva Longoria lookalike girlfriend, Meg and Tim getting married, George being promoted to store manager, me living all alone in a giant kaftan and shuffling off to the Londis every morning to buy cat biscuits and Arrowwords.

Julia seemed calm. That was how I'd been just after Mum died. I'd been putting on a front. Inside, the darkness had swept everything away, leaving the sensation of being pulled underwater and everything else feeling far, far away, as if I was looking up at the surface but couldn't get there.

'Did you tell her?' I asked, grabbing her arm.

'Tell her what?'

'That I might be a mum?'

'I don't know what you're talking about! She wasn't awake, Kate. She was asleep the whole time – you know that!'

She was getting annoyed now.

'Listen, I need to ring our relatives and start sorting stuff out. I don't know whether you're having some sort of mental breakdown, but kindly take it elsewhere. I have enough on my plate right now, thanks.'

'You said she'd been conscious a bit.'

'A few hours maybe, yesterday.'

'Did she ask for me?'

'No. She was just staring and then she pointed to the book by the bed.'

'She wanted you to read to her.'

'Read to her? Her brain was fried, Kate! You're starting to get on my nerves now,' she said with growing agitation. 'She's *my* mother. I think I know what *my* mother needs more than you do.'

'You didn't like talking to her on the phone,' I said.

'I did. I always talked to her on the flipping phone.'

'She said you made her book in a FaceTime ahead of time.'

'Jeez, what is this?'

Julia started to walk away.

'I'm not being called out on my relationship with Mum. You aren't even family! Why don't you just go home? Who hangs out with an old woman? Who chooses to go on holiday with an old woman?'

I felt a lump in my throat. June had been right. Julia wasn't a very nice person. She had none of the kind, warm qualities of her mother. She was cold. Even in the heat of this moment I could understand what June had been trying to tell me. Your kids might grow up to hate you and there was nothing you could do about it. Julia went out to make phone calls and I walked into June's room. Her head was cocked to one side as if she was considering something. Both arms were folded stiff over the blanket. The novel I'd left was by the table. We'd only got to page 23. I sat on a chair by the bed and squeezed her hand. I turned to the last page and read aloud. She didn't respond at all.

I got a taxi home. I didn't feel the same heaviness that I'd felt after Mum had gone but it was the self-same category of misery. I thought of the evening ahead and couldn't imagine how I'd get through it, or the next day, or the next month.

Meg and Tim were watching *Fatal Attraction* when I

got in. Meg had her feet resting in his lap and he was massaging her calves. There would have been a time when me walking in, then going straight up to my room, would have seemed weird but I didn't want to talk about June or what had happened. I felt like the two of them were steadily taking over Mum's house. I didn't care too much, but there was also part of me that wanted them to move out so I didn't have to be confronted with how content they were.

This had been Carl and me. We'd sat on the sofa watching old 80s films. We'd argued about John Hughes and whether he was a good director or not. Carl said none of his films stood the test of time and were all super-cringy now. I was a Big Fan. Before Carl, Mum, George and I had sat on the sofa and watched TV together. If we fast forwarded again it would just be me, on my own, with no family, no friends, nothing. I knew I was being self-pitying but the wallowing was actually distracting me from the fact that June had gone. It was easier to just focus on my failed life than think about how I'd never got a chance to say goodbye properly.

George was out and had texted me earlier to say he was on a date with someone he'd met at the Franklin's conference – she apparently managed another London branch. It was exactly as I'd predicted. Everyone was getting their lives together.

Despite the wallowing, thoughts of June in her funny

matching shoes and bags popped into my head. In her weird, flowery swimming hat squinting into the sun. On her back looking up at the stars in the swimming pool.

I went back down and made myself some toast and took it back up. I ate half a piece but it tasted like nothing so I ran a bath. Meg had left a magazine next to the loo. Apparently, if I dedicated myself to ten minutes of body brushing each morning and evening, I'd no longer have cellulite.

I felt like this world, where such things mattered, was a long, long way away.

NEWS FLASH: Girls, cellulite is not as bad as death. It's not as bad as losing your mum. Or your best friend. When you are low you won't give a shit about the fact that you have dimples on your knees.

I crawled into bed. I looked in the book where I'd written down my plan. It was the rantings of an imbecile. What kind of person really thought they would get pregnant from a one-night stand? Why had June not pointed this out? Had she seriously thought it would work? Or had she hoped I'd just come to my senses eventually? I was on day seven of my cycle right now which meant I was almost fertile but not quite. Was I going to try again this month? I didn't have the heart. It wasn't respectful to June, either. I would take a break for a month and decide what to do next. I couldn't focus on babies for a while ... I must have fallen asleep but woke up again and looked at my phone. It was eleven.

Tim and Meg were fooling around in her bedroom. I tried to put the pillow over my head but five minutes later their headboard kept banging against the wall. Then five minutes after that the hall light went on. I heard someone pee in the bathroom and I half dozed again but I needed the toilet so I got up. In the bathroom I blew my nose and tossed my tissue in the bin under the sink. I saw the condom nestling amongst a bunch of screwed-up tissues.

I picked it up. A condom full of semen.

Part of me wanted to vomit but then there was also a little voice inside that said, *'Think you've lost all self-respect, mate? Not yet! You can sink even lower! Come on, a holiday shag in a toilet is nothing! How about trying to fertilise yourself with your mate's boyfriend's sperm?'*

'But this is your friend's boyfriend,' another voice argued.

'But she isn't really my friend, not anymore. June was my best friend.'

'But it's not right, is it?'

'Isn't it right? Is June dying right? What about Mum? What about Carl? What about every person I ever actually loved? Because right now I feel like the universe is crapping on

me from a great height and I am entitled to anything I want to make my dream happen. Anything. So back off.'

The other voice was silenced.

The spectre of the creepy DJ flashed before my eyes. Sperm donors who looked like DJ's from the 70s. Sex in toilets with men who didn't like me. Sex with hairy men who talked about *Game of Thrones* too much. Fitness fanatics who slept with fat girls because they were bored of skinny girls. Where would it end?

I got the nail scissors out of the wicker basket on the shelf and sliced a very tiny hole in the condom. I lay on the bathroom mat and hitched my legs up, squeezing the tip of the condom so the contents went inside. Some of it dribbled down my leg but I kept my hips raised so some would go inside. I tried to relax as much as I could. I was simply taking something Tim didn't want. It was ethical. It didn't need to upset anyone. Soon Meg'd go off and have a new life and I'd have my new flatmate.

It would be a tiny flatmate with no hair, teeth and chubby legs.

I lay on the bathmat with my pelvis pushed up for another five minutes. My back was aching, but this was the important part.

I flushed the remains of the crinkled condom down the loo. The baby, when I visualised it in my mind, still half-believing, *wanting* to believe that manifesting might work out if you persevered with it, had soft and delicate skin. It had brown curly hair. It had good physical stamina. The rest of the personality traits it would inherit from me.

I went back to bed. I slept well. I whispered into my pillow, *'I think I've finally done it June. I think I really have.'*

———————————

The next morning Tim was up early and standing in the kitchen stuffing green leaves into the NutriBullet.

'Hey, Kate, how's it going?' he said. 'Want a spinach smoothie?'

Already I was full of regret. Then Meg appeared from nowhere and Tim slunk off. I couldn't even look at her, I felt that guilty. What on earth was I thinking? OK, Meg and I had grown apart recently but Tim was out of bounds.

'Look, this probably isn't the right time to say this,' Meg said, 'but I'm getting a flat with Tim. I wanted to tell you a few weeks ago. I sometimes feel like you're my child and I've been tasked to look after you.'

Her face was flushed. She'd obviously been brewing up these thoughts – in fact, they didn't sound like her thoughts; they sounded like Tim's. I knew he thought I was too dependent on her, that I rarely remembered to cook proper food for myself, that I didn't plan things on the weekend and had just fallen into line with whatever

Meg was up to before she was occupied with him all the time.

'You're actually moving out?' I asked.

She nodded and reached into the fridge to get the almond milk which she poured into a glass. I couldn't think of anything to say. This was probably for the best. If I was pregnant (the chances were slim), then I never wanted to see Meg again. It would be a constant reminder of my betrayal. If I wasn't pregnant then I still didn't want to be reminded of how low I'd stooped. It was also obvious that our friendship wasn't the same anymore. I missed the times when we sat watching *RuPaul's Drag Race* together, or reading magazines and eating white-bread toast. When I'd first embarked on the plan I'd imagined Meg and I living together. The baby would slot right in with the lazy weekend mornings reading the supplements and putting rings around the things we wanted to buy, the Sundays spent moaning about work and then going to the supermarket to choose something comforting to eat.

'We have to move on with our lives, right? And it's not normal for you and George to live with all your mum's stuff everywhere.'

This definitely wasn't Meg talking anymore. Meg had loved Mum. She'd also understood that three years wasn't that long ago, that it was still too early to get rid of her stuff, that it was comforting for me to have her things around because it made it feel as if she was still alive. Meg grabbed her phone and scrolled through her work emails and angrily fired off responses. I wondered what George and I would do next. We needed a flatmate to get the additional income – the house was too big for two people. Meg had been perfect because we knew her so well. Then Tim had come along and the whole vibe had changed. It wasn't possible to come downstairs in your pants in case he was lurking about. There was always a sense he was judging what you were eating or the fact that you weren't getting up extra early to do a HIIT workout. The problem was I couldn't think about any of this now.

I just saw myself on the bathroom floor, basting myself with Tim's old condom.

And there was simply no way of justifying my behaviour.

Chapter Sixteen

'So how is the worry diary going this week?' Sarah asked.

I'd missed a couple of weeks and was feeling disengaged with the whole thing now. Yes, writing the worries down helped but still I was feeling no better. The anxiety when it came was just as strong.

'I've kind of stopped doing it,' I said.

'That's not great, Kate,' Sarah said, looking concerned.

'I just feel like it's going nowhere.'

'What kind of thought is that?' she said.

'Pessimistic?'

'That's right – and when we get those thoughts we have to remember that we're trapped in a cycle of negative thinking and move on.'

'I am trying, but there are an awful lot of things going wrong.'

'But *are* they going wrong? Or are you just thinking they are?'

'No, they really are. I mean, literally, they are.'

I left Sarah's office feeling no better than when I'd gone in. There was a small sliver of optimism inside that told me the tools she gave me would work if I only persevered a little longer. There was another part that couldn't face it anymore. I was born to feel down and that was it.

June's funeral was on a Thursday. It was usually the day we'd go for lunch together. The crematorium was a strange, anonymous box with watercolour painting of seascapes. Julia had chosen all the music and readings. The hall was quite empty – Lesley, George, her neighbours who were an elderly Italian couple, and Julia.

'How are you doing?' I asked when I saw her outside.

She was vaping some sort of strawberry and mint concoction which was very sickly. My heart sank into my feet somewhere. 'Song to the Siren,' came into my head and I thought about how we'd played it at Mum's funeral at the end and I'd finally felt myself unravel. It had been the lines, *Let me enfold you. Here I am waiting to hold you.* With Mum, it had been the physical absence I'd noticed first, because we'd always been affectionate – the feeling of her hand, which was always cool, on my forehead, the squeeze when I got in from work, the bear hug when things were getting too much. Again, I was struck by how the feeling someone left behind could be so strong that it was impossible to accept they weren't here anymore. June's voice had always been so distinctive, and the way she dressed, her movements, far more co-ordinated and graceful than many people her age ... all that was gone. I'd never believed in God apart from desperate moments when I'd tried to pray (when Mum had been ill) and I knew that if he or she did exist they'd not listen to anything I said because I was clearly only a believer when it suited me.

The coffin arrived and the pallbearers carried it in. One was a woman and for a split second I was distracted from the heavy-heartedness of the moment and started thinking about whether a funeral director would be a good career or not. It was regular work. It never went out of fashion. It was unlikely to be replaced by an online service unless we started having virtual funerals on social media and our remains were diced up and injected into a smartphone.

'I'll fly back tomorrow,' Julia said, cutting through my thoughts. 'I'll have to sell the house and get everything cleared out.'

'Can I have her books?' I asked.

I had a feeling that I was going to start reading again. That I'd *have* to start reading again in order to survive the next few months.

'All of them?' she asked. 'There's an awful lot.'

'Maybe not all of them, just the thrillers. Those were her favourites.'

'Do you want me to go through all her books and pick out the thrillers?' Julia said grumpily.

'No, sorry, I mean just give me the ones by her bedside. She always had a few on the go at any time so I'll be happy with those and any ones you come across when you're packing up. We used to talk a lot about them, you see.'

'Sure. I mean, I'll put the rest in the charity box. Who bothers with books? I've got a Kindle but barely have time to read anymore unless it's a little comment on my social media.'

Mum's house was already crowded with stuff. It made me sad that Julia didn't seem to have any sentimentality around June's belongings but it was her mum and her choice. I already had plenty of memories of June and didn't need to start collecting up all her bits and bobs too. I wanted the copies June had read, the pages turned over, the bits where her eyebrows had shot up at the unexpected plot twist, the tears in the paper where she'd been too fast in turning over because she was so absorbed in the narrative. I would hopefully remember the parts she'd mentioned to me – the times when I'd pretended I'd read the book already but was faking it.

It struck me that June had been the only person I'd been almost totally honest with. It made me feel lonely to think that that was all gone now. Was this purely selfish, though?

I hoped that at least having June's books would get me interested in reading again; maybe on a broader level make me more involved in life and, most importantly, involved in things that pushed beyond getting pregnant.

What had I been interested in before I'd embarked on this plan? I found it hard to recall. I realised that whether it worked or not was irrelevant as I was still the same person, a person who didn't know how to create happiness, who arguably might struggle to create happiness for her child, who was like a zombie, shut off from the world, who rarely laughed unless it was something cynical, who never found joy in much, who didn't enjoy sex, hated most men, had a long list of things she didn't like but struggled to come up with anything she did.

The heavy feeling continued for the rest of the service. I kept thinking about June inside the coffin. I imagined her in her swimsuit with her flowery hat and a towel wrapped around her midriff. This would have been the most apt final outfit, I felt. We stood and listened to 'Ava

Maria' while June's coffin disappeared behind a pair of cream curtains. I kept thinking back to Mum's funeral and how we hadn't had many people there. We'd lived a fairly insular life, George, Mum, and I, and she'd had a couple of friends that she went to the odd film or theatre night with, but that was it.

I fast forwarded to my own funeral. Who would come to that? George? Meg? Two cats, perhaps? Why was it that once you got on a negative spiral, your thoughts so naturally followed behind? I tried to remember what Sarah had advised me about these moments. What were you supposed to do when you felt yourself sinking lower and lower? It was hard to believe that you just disappeared and all the thoughts, feelings, anxieties, and hopes went too. Where would I feel June's presence now? It would be difficult to wean myself off the ritual of picking out books I thought she'd like. With Mum, I'd spent months afterwards thinking about things I would usually tell her – the fact I'd noticed a young guy not giving up a seat for a pregnant woman or that there'd been a woman who'd come into the shop who'd spent over £200 on diet books or that I'd read in *Metro* that one Death Row prisoner had requested an olive as his last meal before he was killed the following morning. I'd always feel a little surge of excitement at the thought of telling her, and what her expression might be, what she'd say, how horrified she'd be, and then that would

314

dissipate because there was nowhere for the story to go. With your mum you don't worry so much about how interesting the story is. You just tell the story. Everyone else gets a more curated, cleverer version, one that you make more effort constructing and maybe exaggerating the details to make it more sensational.

The only thing I had to hold onto was the fact that I might be pregnant – but then there was also the fact that it would be Tim's baby and I'd betrayed my best friend. It was funny, but I had no guilt about Tim – I didn't care that I'd taken his sperm without permission. This illustrated how little respect I had for men generally. I loved George, yes, but he was my brother. The rest of them could go to hell. Dad, Carl – they were all useless.

'Work will be a good distraction, mate,' George said squeezing my arm. 'I know how much June meant to you. I'm sorry.'

'It's not just that, George. It's my life. The whole bloody thing's a disaster.'

'Don't be stupid,' he said as we got outside.

It was raining and I realised June would have been happy about this. It was supposed to rain at your funeral.

'You're getting your life together,' I said. 'Lesley adores you. You've pieced everything together while I'm no further along than three years ago. I'm *worse*. I can't seem to move forward.'

I realised it felt good to say this stuff.

'I hate seeing you like this. You've got loads going for you.'

'Bollocks.'

'You're funny – I mean you're mean at times but you make me laugh. You're pretty, which is obviously a weird thing for me to say but it's true. And you're good at your work. You might not be so enthusiastic but you were probably just the way I was a few years ago.'

'I was never like you. I never wanted to work in a bookshop. I just ended up there.'

A taxi drew up and we got in the back.

'You keep it in,' George said as we drove away. 'You think I can't see how sad you are. But I'm your flesh and blood. I know grief is hard, Kate, but life goes on.'

'I have been trying to get pregnant for ages and it isn't happening,' I said. 'Why's that?'

George looked at me. 'What do you mean?'

'I've been sleeping with men without any protection.'

'Which men?'

'Just men, generally.'

'Why?'

'Duh! Because I want to be pregnant, *I want to have a baby*.' I was crying now and shouting and there was snot coming out of my nose. 'I want a baby because it's the only thing worth having. My life is total *shit*! *I have no life*. Not even a shit one.'

George put his arm around me and pulled me tight.

'You are actually alive, right?'

'But what's the point? I haven't done any of the things you're supposed to do. I haven't got a partner, I haven't got an amazing job. I don't have any desire to travel or climb mountains or do yoga camps. I have no family of my own. I have no passion. No lust for life. No meaning.'

'What about me, then? I'm family, aren't I?' he said, getting a tissue out of his pocket and handing it to me. 'And I don't understand what you mean when you say you've been sleeping with people to get pregnant,' George said, studying my face. 'I mean, why wouldn't you have IVF? Isn't that the normal course of action?'

'This felt more natural in some way.'

I could tell George wanted to say something but he bit his tongue.

'I hate seeing you like this,' George said, shaking his head. 'You're only thirty-eight. Jesus, didn't Janet Jackson have a kid and she's fifty! And Nicole Kidman!'

'She used a surrogate. And it's too expensive.'

'But you have some money, right? Look, I was thinking. We need to think about selling Mum's place sometime. Meg told me they're moving out and I can't imagine finding someone we like as much as her to live with. And besides, don't you think it's time?'

George was right. It *was* probably time. He was also right about the surrogacy and IVF. These were possibilities I'd simply bypassed. I'd carried out my own hairbrained scheme which had left me feeling broken. There was something inside me that wanted to be punished.

'Do you think you feel so bad about yourself because of Dad?' George said. 'Because sometimes I get that feeling too. Like I'm not good enough. I wonder whether that's what happened. He was a complete jerk though, you know? I mean, anyone who leaves their kids and never bothers to stay in touch must be.'

'I wonder if he's even alive any more,' I said.

'I don't think about him at all,' George said, but I knew he was lying.

Had my relationship with men broken down because of my dad? Certainly, there was unfinished business, a sense that I would always be disappointed, so there was no point bothering. I'd understood that for some time but hadn't taken any of it on board. Perhaps, if I stopped anticipating the worst from men, I could finally start having a proper relationship…

The day at work was like many. Long and tedious. Sometimes customers only had very vague notions of what they were looking for. 'It's the one about lemons' or 'the one set in Greece with Keeley Hawes?' Or 'Suranne

Jones – she's on ITV and it's a book now.' Or 'It's the one where she's Japanese and goes travelling, and she's a Geisha, no hang on, I've read that one already – something like that.'

I kept looking up and half expecting June to walk in with her bright pink lipstick and turquoise handbag. There was a new crime writer who'd just written a book about the Italian mafia in Sicily in the 50s. I knew June would have loved it as she was especially keen on crime set in the past.

'So I thought we could approach people,' George was saying to Lesley at the till, 'people who are browsing and get them to do a short quiz to refine what kind of books they like. Then we could give them some recommendations, like they do on Amazon. You know, if you like this then you'll love this too?'

'Mmm, I'm not sure that'd work,' Lesley said. 'We could try it, I guess. What do you think, Kate?' she called over to where I was tidying up the kids' area which had a mashed-up banana that had been left inside a Peppa Pig book.

'It sounds like a good idea to me,' I said without much enthusiasm. 'We do get a lot of customers who don't buy anything.'

Later, downstairs in the makeshift office, Lesley pulled up one of the battered office chairs and sat down opposite me.

ANNIKI SOMMERVILLE

'I'm sorry about June,' Lesley said, 'but when George joined the team I was worried about whether it would work out and I'm now under pressure to make some cutbacks. I mean, our sales are up but it's not enough.'

I could see where this was headed.

'I'd hoped that having him around would inspire you, make you step up a gear, but it's done quite the opposite. You're just flatlining these days. You've even told a few people that they'd be better off going to the library. And there was the guy who wanted to buy the *Top Gear* book and you said Jeremy Clarkson was an idiot.'

'Well, he is, right?'

'But you can't make those decisions, Kate – we lost a sale because of that comment. We need to stay objective. The whole queue heard you. You've also been pricing books down by accident.'

'I don't remember that.'

'You took Zadie Smith and made it £3.99.'

'The covers looked the same so I got muddled up.'

'Do you actually want to be here selling books?' she said.

It was obvious that Lesley had been weighing all this up for some time now.

'I love reading. I love my job.'

Her phone rang in her pocket.

'Hold up a minute.' She grabbed it. 'No, I can't talk

320

but I need Billy's violin to be picked up. Can you do that? He's going to miss his second lesson in a month otherwise.' She pocketed her phone and turned to me again. 'Where was I?'

'You want to offer George my job?'

'I'm sorry, but I'm going to have to let you go. I hate doing this – you have no idea how much – but it's not working out. I need a different kind of person now. Someone who wholeheartedly embraces books and can come up with new initiatives to get a different audience into the store.'

I didn't say anything. I could see Hannah Heart's decapitated head staring down at me from my locker. Even with no hair and no body and coloured-in teeth she looked more of a winner than me.

I went back upstairs. It was a kick in the teeth but I deserved it. I'd not put in any effort for a long time. I'd been distracted. I no longer read so rarely had an opinion. I was bored with the customers. I'd only liked June and she was gone. I was going to have to watch as my brother became the CEO of Franklin's.

I decided to hit the nearest pub. The fact that I might be pregnant didn't bother me anymore. Truth was, it probably hadn't worked. How much sperm did you get in an old condom? And didn't sperm die the moment they came out of the body? I was grasping at straws. I needed a drink – I needed to do the thing that people did in films where they went up to the bar after losing their job/wife/home and then said, 'Give me something strong, and keep them coming, barman.' The barman wasn't really a barman, though; he wasn't fit and good-looking like he might have been in a film. He was a bald, overweight pub landlord eyeing me with some suspicion as I was the only woman in here. It was one of the few pubs that hadn't started offering smashed avocado on sourdough and craft beer.

'Can I join you?'

I looked up and there was a guy standing next to me. In a film he would also have been good-looking and it would have been the part of the narrative where I finally met the man of my dreams and he showed me that life was worth living or somesuch and brought me out of myself. But instead this man was in his early fifties and looked like a more haggard version of Gary Barlow, if he hadn't been in Take That and had spent a lot of his life in pubs smoking and drinking and eating carbs. Still, it was company. And somewhere in my deranged brain I was thinking that sleeping with this old Barlow dude might double my chances of getting pregnant, even though it wasn't the right time of the month.

'Mine's a double vodka,' I said.

'I've had this mega client meeting today. This client basically confirmed a £650k piece of business, so I'm celebrating.'

'What line of business are you in?' I said, really not caring much at all, just wondering whether he sprayed air out of his penis or real live semen.

'I'm in property development. So I'm doing up an old place and selling it on. You know, rip out all the original features and get nice modern stuff in. Concrete over the garden and put some plastic bushes in the front. Perfect.'

The conversation didn't get more exciting than that.

We went back to his flat – a new build and the whiff of paint was strong. The place looked like a show home. There was a photo of the Eiffel Tower that looked like the kind of thing you bought in IKEA when you had no personality. He put Kings of Leon on. Was I going through with this? I felt like I was somewhere on the ceiling looking down at my body.

The man talked.

You look like you're up for it. You must be what – late thirties? You have lovely hair. Did anyone ever say you look like Goldie Hawn? Do you like my flat? What do you think? It's very modern, yes. All mod cons. Have you ever been to Paris? You have, but I bet you've never seen the Eiffel Tower up close? Oh well, I mean I like the photo, that's all. And I can tell you're not married. I used to be but I prefer the single life. I never wanted kids. I won't ask about you because it's personal and I know it's a bit dicey once you get to your age, right? And I love Ibiza! No, you don't look like the kind that enjoys that kind of thing. You had some bad luck or something? It doesn't cost much to smile, love. It can't be that bad. I always say that the best thing you can do each morning is to decide to be in a good mood. We're not here that long, really. What, you fancy another drink you say? You're keen! Not got a problem, though, have you, love? It's not nice when a lady drinks too much.

I miss June.

The man, who was called Keith (which was one of those names that you rarely heard anymore), was just pointing out how erotic the song 'Sex on Fire' was. I knew he was trying to make a move as he'd switched the dimmer on in a very unsubtle way.

'Why are you doing this, love?'

It was June's voice. Or was it Mum's?

Or mine?

I wasn't going through with it. The self-destruction button had been disabled. The toilet sex had been bad. I couldn't go through it again. I hated this man and his jaunty, silly life philosophies. He probably shouted out of his car window *cheer up, love, it might never happen*! He had no idea. He thought a fucking photo of the Eiffel Tower was good taste. He also – and I could tell this just by looking at him – had comedy boxer shorts on which he'd been given as a Christmas present by his niece or his sister-in-law.

'Sorry, I've just got a text from my brother,' I said,

standing up and grabbing my handbag from behind the sofa, 'he's not well. I have to head home.'

'But you just got here, love. I thought we could watch a film together. You know, *Netflix and chill.*'

Just the very suggestion made me shudder, and yet this felt good as it meant my self-esteem was improving and I thought I was worth more than a quick bunk-up with the first man that approached me in a grubby, men-only, watering hole. He looked disappointed. Nonetheless, I think he could tell that I wasn't quite right, that I might be a bit flimsy mental health-wise and not worth the trouble. These things have a habit of shooting you in the foot, he'd say to his friends. She was odd and didn't laugh at any of my jokes. And she drank vodka. That's always someone with an alcohol problem, right? Funny how women go on the turn when they get to that age, don't you think? It seemed like 'Sex on Fire' was on repeat and he walked over to the Alexa and said, 'Stop playing Kings of Leon, Alexa.'

I somehow found myself on the tube. I had no real idea where I was. As I went up the escalator I kept thinking about what a relief it would be if I just let myself fall backwards. It wouldn't take long to fall all the way down and then surely the chitter-chatter would stop. The incessant thoughts about being pregnant. The anxiety each morning. The jealousy. The comparisons. All gone as I lay at the bottom of that escalator and people stepped over me, playing on their phones and complaining that my body was slowing them down and they were going to be late.

For a second I took my hand away from the railing and fell a centimetre backwards. It didn't feel good. It made me want to be sick. It didn't matter how miserable I was, I didn't have the balls to end it all.

Whatever happens, you have to keep going.

When I got in, Meg had left a tray of blueberry muffins out on the counter. She knew instinctively when I needed comfort food. We'd always made muffins when were hungover or hurt in some way. Everyone was in bed and I opened the fridge and stood there for a while, breathing in the cool air.

The next morning I found it hard to get out of bed. The vodka had left me with the feeling that someone had sucked my brain out of my nose, washed it in toxins and then injected what was left of it into my eyeballs. I'd tossed all night like a character in a romcom who's having an epiphany. All night I'd had visions of penises of various sizes. They came up to my face and slapped against my cheeks. Big penises, small penises, ones snuggled up in a halo of hair, others completely bald, some half-mast and other fully erect. It was like one long porn film, but there was nothing erotic about it.

I realised that the plan had been torture because I hated sex. I wasn't sure why this was, but it had something to do with the fact that I hated myself and so felt I didn't deserve any pleasure. Carl had only gone down on me once and even then he'd complained that it made him tired because it had taken me so long to come. It had been about ten minutes because I'd found it really hard to relax and not think about him down there. Was I actually having an epiphany or was I just careering from good mood to bad over and over? I was done.

'Do you think Lesley is 100% sure?' George had said when I told him that morning that I was getting the boot.

'She told me. Listen, you're doing brilliantly. You're great. Unfortunately, I've lost my mojo so it makes sense. She would rather have you and your ideas than me and my non-enthusiasm.'

'I think maybe the Hannah Heart dartboard might have sealed the deal, mate. I feel bad. I never meant to take over. You found me the job in the first place.'

I felt surprisingly calm about the whole thing. The thing was, if I'd been passionate about work and felt like it was my calling, then I would have been devastated. Instead, there was something inside that told me it might finally give me the impetus I needed to get off my ass and do something else. What this might be I had no idea at all, but it was a start to know that I couldn't shuffle around Franklin's forever. George would soon be promoted to Deputy Manager. He deserved the success. I'd taken my job at Franklin's for granted and thought it would always be there.

Chapter Seventeen

'**K**ate, have you finished your worry diary this time?' Sarah asked.

'Um ... sort of.'

'So no. But have you actually written all your worries down and classified them?'

'No.'

'I feel like we won't progress unless you take this work seriously,' she said, looking angry and then recovering her expression so she was looking chirpy again.

'I'm sorry,' I said.

'Don't be sorry but do the work. It's important. I don't just make this stuff up to make your life more difficult.'

I knew that some of it worked but the problem was

when things got *really* bad I didn't believe it and it was almost time to test again. The time had passed more quickly than I'd imagined. I'd actively avoided Meg because I couldn't stand seeing her and thinking about what I'd done.

Saturday morning and I set off to Sainsbury's to buy some ingredients to whizz together in the NutriBullet as I was trying to be healthy again. I was in the queue paying when I recognised the back of someone's head. He had two straps over his shoulders and his hair was longer and messier, but I could tell instantly it was Carl. He turned around as if sensing me looking at me.

'Kate!' he exclaimed.

I looked at his face and then immediately noticed that he had a sling ... and inside, with its head just poking over the top, was a baby. A baby with unruly hair.

'I know!' he said, laughing and pointing at the baby. 'It's funny, isn't it? It's been a bit of a whirlwind. I mean, I had no idea that Katya wanted kids and we'd only been on two dates but then she found out she was pregnant and the timing felt right!'

I looked at my basket and tried to focus on how nice and green everything looked and how good all these ingredients were and how happy I'd feel and that my body would be nourished and the fact that Carl had a baby didn't make any difference to whether I was happy or not. He had a baby and that was fine. We weren't going out anymore. We'd been separated for three and a half years now. I knew he'd met someone else, but I'd had no idea she was pregnant. But just because he'd had a baby didn't mean *I* couldn't have one. There were lots of babies everywhere. This thing had no impact on me and my happiness at all.

'So, are you on a bit of a health kick?' he said following my gaze and looking at my basket of virtuousness. 'You always used to say you hated that healthy shit. Mind you, it helps, doesn't it, as we get older? I can't cane it like I used to. Anyway, you don't really want to when you're a dad. The night-times are the worst. Man, I mean, I never thought I'd feel this tired. But how are you, Kate? I'm sorry I blocked you, but Katya didn't feel comfortable that we were still friends. It's odd, really. Even your names are similar – but Katya is ten years younger. It's like we were in the beginning… No, that doesn't sound right. I mean, you know, before everything happened … you were fun. No, that's not right either.'

Carl put the divider down so I could load my shopping onto the belt. Already I felt like running away, straight out of the shop and into the canal, perhaps managing to entangle my feet in an old bicycle wheel and drowning quickly and painlessly without anyone noticing I'd gone. Katya. More fun. Younger. Carl a dad. A baby on his front. I couldn't absorb it all and despite the fact that I rarely thought about him, this news, this update – far more hurtful than any status update or coy post on Instagram – shook me to my core.

'Well, good luck, mate,' I said as we parted ways.

He looked very tired. He'd definitely aged. I would google Katya later. She must have been the one from the christening that I'd seen. The one who looked like Eva Longoria.

This doesn't impact me. I will be OK.

Carl won't be happy.

Even if he is happy, it doesn't change anything. There he is in a loving relationship and here you are, not in any relationship, and using your best friend's boyfriend's sperm to impregnate yourself like a depraved animal.

———————

When I got home I lay in bed, leaving all the green stuff on the counter, not even bothering to unpack it all, and fantasised about being in a coma. There was no such thing as 'reaching your lowest point'. There was always a downwards trajectory mapped out for you. I got up. I ate toast. The green stuff had been put in the fridge but I hadn't heard anyone come in.

Where was everyone?

They all had lives and were out living them.

I wanted to hold my own baby. If I was entirely

honest with myself *this* and *only this* was what I wanted. But there were no encouraging pregnancy symptoms…

That night I watched a bit of *RuPaul's Drag Race,* but it didn't feel right without Meg sitting next to me. I went to the loo and there it was. No drumroll. No grand announcement. A spot of blood on my pants. *My fucking period had arrived.* The bathroom walls were closing in. Why was I lying on the bathroom floor now? I had a sense that everything was tumbling. Was this how June had felt just before she passed out?

I heard the sound of Meg and Tim coming in. They were doing the happy, loved-up couple chuckle. I bent forward and placed both hands on the cold, tiled floor. There were times in life when you could leap up, make the best of things, put the kettle on, have some toast, talk to a friend, reassemble yourself. Then there were other times, when all you could do was lie prostrate in a semi-child's pose with the cold eating its way up your legs as you stared at a cobweb under the sink and counted how many earbuds were left on Meg's shelf – forty-seven but it looked like she'd half used one and put it back in again; that was possibly Tim as Meg was very hygiene obsessed.

Forty-seven ear buds. Two lipsticks – one looked like Rimmel but the other was more premium. Nail varnish remover. A bag of cotton balls. An electric toothbrush. A cream that promised to 'maximise glow'. A deodorant that was tropical-fruit scented. Dry shampoo. Hair conditioner that promised to 'Tame Those Tangles.' I couldn't even raise my head to look at it. Each day we got up and used this stuff, under the illusion that it made our life better, our bodies more heavenly scented, our hair perfect. In the end, did any of it really matter? Wouldn't it just be more honest to walk around in our own disgusting stink? There was something so exhausting about the charade of being civilised. Better to lie and wallow and be done...

Eventually I sat up; there was some blood on the tiles. I grabbed a sanitary towel out of the cupboard and stuck it into my pants. This would be the first step in putting myself back together.

Towel in pants. Pull pants up. Pull trousers up. Wipe blood off floor. Flush toilet. Go downstairs. Put kettle on. Make tea.

This would be the new plan. Putting myself back together.

Chapter Eighteen

T here was something liberating in letting it all go. So nice to drop the pretence and just settle into hopelessness. I went straight to bed with an enormous sanitary towel wedged into my pants.

Dear Womb,

You're a fucking idiot!

I've tried to create a baby and you've repaid me with a large, vacant hole. I know it's not strictly your fault (eggs – I hope you're listening, you FUCKING WANKERS!) but how come all the other wombs of women my age have babies inside? How come you can't be arsed?

Thanks for nothing.

Kate

I had another few days at work and then I'd need to look for a new job. We had another event that George had organised – 'Healthy Living Vibes'. There were canapes (little sushi rolls stuffed with sprouts and the like) and the celebrity yoga instructor – Susie Moon – was appearing to sign books. Her latest was *Be Honest with Yourself and the World Will Open for You*. A man walked into Franklin's with two Boots carrier bags on his feet instead of shoes. He had a jumper with worn leather patches on the sleeves and was clutching a range of old newspapers under his arm. He had a slick of what looked like cream cheese on one cheek and one strand of greasy hair that was wrapped from one ear to the other like a soggy mouse's tail.

'Are you here for our event?' George asked. 'It's not starting yet, I'm afraid.'

The man shrugged and went to the back of the store to browse. For a split second I wondered if this poor man was still producing sperm and, if so, just how viable it would be. The thing was, without children to shift the tempo of your life, you were staring into a long, straight line of monotony. The sun came up, you went to work, the sun went down, you went to bed. The hair grew. The hair was cut. The dresses came into fashion and went out again. New books came in, trends, then these books went into the promotional pile. Authors were celebrated and then forgotten. The celebrities stuffed fillers into their cheeks until they resembled plump toddlers and people were surprised when these celebrities died but then realised they were actually in their nineties and so it made sense. You menstruated. You stuck a towel between your legs. The eggs disappeared. You stopped menstruating. You sweated and felt crazy. You died. A smattering of people came to see your coffin disappear and someone read out an extract from a book you didn't like and would never have chosen yourself.

Did Susie Moon not feel this way too?

Susie Moon was lovely and had that kind of aura where you could tell that she'd never had a bad day or a bad week or sworn or wanted to cut the head off a cardboard cutout of someone she hated. I wondered what it took (more than yoga, surely?) to be this calm and happy. Had she never got up in the morning and groaned at the prospect of the day ahead. Had she never had a worry tree that went on for fifteen pages?

She was perfect in her Lululemon leggings and bronzed glowing skin *and* she genuinely seemed nice. She brought her own coffee, put down her phone and listened to people, even feigned enthusiasm (or perhaps it was real) when George talked to her. She'd brought along some nettle brownies which she'd baked at home. I was in awe of women who could cast all the bad things aside and choose positivity. They seemed to come from another planet. She was wearing a T-shirt that said, *Powerfully Feminine*. I fought the urge to say something mean because I wanted to be more like this woman – bright, open to opportunities, happy, forward facing. Instead, my instinct was to crawl under the table and eat a bag of cheesy Wotsits.

It also struck me that I was too old to be part of this new wave of optimism and healthiness. My generation had lived in the land of beer, chips, and fags. I didn't really like the taste of healthy food. It felt like deprivation and sacrifice. I liked macaroni cheese too much.

'It's all about staying optimistic and believing in yourself. Dreams really do come true,' Susie said to the crowd.

The audience was different to the mums in that they were wearing expensive sportswear and were drinking strange concoctions that they'd mixed together at home from giant bottles.

'How do you stay so positive?' said one of them slightly nervously.

'I'm bowled over by how amazing women really are,' Susie answered. 'This is what motivates me each day. I'm inspired every day.'

I could hear the same words over and over. Inspiring,

powerful, miracles, self-belief, amazing, amazing, amazing. None were in my vocabulary. When was the last time I'd felt amazing? Or inspired? Why was I so at odds with the zeitgeist? Plenty of people went through tragedy in their lives. They lost their parents or were diagnosed with terrible illnesses but they weren't consumed by self-loathing and pity. Aside from the generational thing, it just wasn't in my DNA to behave like her. Meanwhile, the other women were rapidly filling their notebooks (each from Susie's exclusive stationery line 'We Got This Shit', only available via Instagram).

Still, I had to believe that luck played a massive part in success. If Mum had lived I would have been different. If Carl hadn't left. If I'd grown up with a dad around the house. What if you did all the vision boards, the meditations, the affirmations, the gratitude lists and you got knocked over by a bus? Did that still mean the universe had your back?

'Kate, are you feeling all right?' Lesley whispered, leaning towards my chair. 'You're talking to yourself.'

'No, not really. No, actually, not all right at all.'

'The one key thing I've learnt,' Susie continued, 'is that you should *never* give up. Something will change so it's about patience and hope.' A few women smiled and nodded. 'I remember the day it all changed. I'd lost my job and was three stone overweight. I was eating a

McDonalds. Yet something drew me to this community hall and the "mindfulness class" they were advertising outside and everything fell into place.'

'I want to have a baby,' I said quietly.

'What was that?' Susie asked brightly.

'Sorry, I wasn't sure if I actually said that out loud, but all I want is a baby. Is that too much to ask?'

She smiled kindly. She was no Hannah Heart. She genuinely believed that you could choose the course of your life purely through having a positive mindset.

'Well, you need to start thinking positively. And instead of saying "I want a baby", why not say "*I have a baby*?" Act as if it's already happened.'

The women in the audience nodded madly. They all believed this was possible. You could wish something and it happened. That simple.

I thought about the tarot reader and the acupuncturist who I'd stopped seeing because she was far too expensive. They believed getting pregnant was just a matter of trying hard and being positive. At lunchtime I left the store and walked around the shopping precinct. I saw the man with plastic bags on his feet. He was eating an apple core and then tried to trample a pigeon underfoot. I didn't like him but I knew he was right. Sometimes you just had bad luck and there was nothing you could do about it.

Chapter Nineteen

I missed the routine of getting up and going somewhere. Routine had always been important to me. I was an old lady inside. I liked to know what I was doing each day, so that when I wrapped up at work things felt very disorientating to begin with. I had enough money not to worry for a couple of months but not much to keep me busy. I opened the box of June's books and started reading again in earnest.

'I can't remember the last time I saw you with a book,' George said as I sat on the sofa, barely looking up.

It felt amazing, like when I'd first learned to read properly and would sit on my bunk bed, my cat Kipper on my lap, and slowly it would grow darker and Mum would come in and switch my Snoopy desk lamp on and I'd get aches because I hadn't moved in so long. I read six thrillers in three days. I read through the night. I let the stories wash over me. Some of the plots were ludicrous, some intricate and awe-inspiring. I saw the small corners of each page where June had turned them over and it made me feel as if I still had some kind of connection because we'd read the same thing.

In the evenings, the bathroom was now free because Tim wasn't in there for hours oiling himself up with Deep Heat bath oil or whatever it was he did in there. He and Meg had found a small flat in Dalston. So I sat in the bath and read some more, a glass of wine balanced in my other hand. There was usually a girl who did something stupid, like decide to take a shortcut through a deserted subway tunnel late at night. Then there was a lonely, persecuted guy who lived in a caravan or a truck and he'd abduct the girl and keep her hostage and then she'd be found in a swamp and the detective would find some very minute pieces of DNA under her fingernails. And the whole thing was so far removed from babies and pregnancy – if anything, it was the opposite of these things, as these books were dark and full of death instead.

My phone rang unexpectedly one evening. It was on the washing basket so I leant over and grabbed it, careful not to drop it in the water. It was Meg.

'Your instincts about Tim were right,' she said. 'He never had any intention of settling down. I just don't know why he waited till we moved in together to chicken out.'

'What do you mean?' I said.

'He's moving back to Australia,'

'But you've only lived together for three weeks!' I said.

It felt strange to be talking to a person rather than absorbing words through my eyes. My voice felt a bit sluggish, as if it needed more exercise.

'He said London was bad for his energy, that it was full of negative people. In reality, I think he's going back to be with his ex-girlfriend! I found a couple of messages on his phone. I never even knew she existed.'

I'd genuinely thought the two of them would be very happy. I'd never liked Tim but it had always seemed like he loved Meg.

'I'm texting you a photo of his ex. I found her on his Facebook.'

'Oh. Well, she looks quite empty and not very interesting.'

'She's studying to be a doctor.'

'Well, her hair's thin – she looks like she might go bald.'

We paused. I turned the tap on with my foot so I could get more warm water into the bath.

'You're a good friend,' she said. 'I ignored you for a long time, basically.'

'It's normal. I did the same when I was with Carl, and yes, of course you can move back here,' I said.

We were our little family unit once more. Meg and I spent our weekends drifting around the flat, toasting bread, slathering it in butter and staring gormlessly at the TV. I carried on reading and found my brain was no longer eaten up with thoughts of being a mum. Yes, it was still there, and there were times when I saw a baby in a buggy and felt a dull ache and a twinge of anxiety, but nowhere near as bad as it had been a couple of months previously. The jobs I applied for were in retail as I didn't have experience in anything else. I went for two interviews and was demoralised to discover that the interviewers were ten years younger than me and talked in a sales-speak that I wasn't familiar with. It was all about digital strategy and 'creating a linear customer journey'. Lesley had never mentioned this stuff. I felt out of my depth, like I'd been living in a cave for years.

'Why don't you do a refresher on media?' George said on one of the rare evenings he was home.

'I wouldn't have a clue what that even means,' I said.

It had been years since I'd studied anything, but there was also part of my brain that felt as if it was waking up.

'You always said you wanted to make films. A few

lessons on how to get good footage and the whole thing is far more accessible,' George said.

Meg looked up from her phone for a moment. She was obsessively following Tim and it wasn't healthy but it was also part of a process – you almost needed to immerse yourself in the pain before you could move on. I started to think that George was incredibly clever. I wasn't sure what I'd make a film about but I had a hunch it would be something around my longing to be a mother, maybe not documenting the plan (that would be too shocking) but more around how obsessed we'd become by motherhood, how women would stop at nothing, how I'd almost lost my sanity.

The constant, raw desire.

Apparently, Buddhist teaching said that fifty percent of life was suffering. That left twenty for boredom, twenty for watching TV and ten for eating, sleeping, washing, etc. So far, the percentage of my life dedicated to suffering had been too high and I knew this had to change.

In a few days I would be thirty-nine.

Worries:

1. Will I ever find something else to do with my life?
2. Are my eggs still there?

3. Would I consider fertility treatment?

'So how has your anxiety been this week?' Sarah asked.

'Probably a five,' I said.

The morning attacks where I had to rush to the loo had stopped but there were still days when my tummy ached all the time. It was a tightness, a sense that my abdomen was a hard ball and no amount of breathing or positive self-talk helped.

'So that's an improvement,' she said cheerily.

'I feel like I'll always have it, though,' I said.

'Well, you will. We all get anxiety. You can't just eliminate it from your life. We feel anxious for a reason. It's just about trying to accept those feelings, cope with them, and get on with your life.'

Was I ready to get on with my life?

There were still so many holes everywhere. The Mum-shaped hole. The June-shaped one. The baby one was the biggest. The fact I had no clear path mapped out and was nearing forty. The lack of routine. The lack of romance. All these holes. What did it actually leave me with? Two arms, two legs, a head, and a body. A friend. A brother. Enough money not to work for a few months. A roof over my head (that was a big one). It was a start. It was more than a lot of people had.

'This is going to hurt, OK?'

I'd returned to the fertility clinic that I'd visited a few months before. I wanted to check again to see if there was anything wrong and to take the first step towards having a baby in a more conventional manner. The female doctor slathered a plastic dildo with lube (it wasn't a dildo but was exactly that shape) and slipped a condom over the top. I tried not to look her in the eye because it felt so awkwardly intimate. I winced as she moved the probe inside and pushed down on my abdomen.

'Your womb looks healthy,' she said, pointing at the screen. 'See the outline? You've got a follicle growing on this side which is about right for this time in your cycle.'

'How does it look?' I asked. 'Does it look like there are still eggs in there?'

I squinted at the screen. It was hard to make anything out but I could see a big sphere and then a smaller one right next to it.

'The eggs obviously deteriorate as you get nearer forty but you can still get pregnant. My advice would be to make it a priority.'

I nodded. I'd heard this before of course. There was nothing she was telling me here that was a surprise. My womb was small and curled up like a cat that had fallen asleep. Time was of the essence.

'How often would I need to have sex to get pregnant?' I asked.

'Ideally, you'd have sex every other day – especially over the most fertile part of your cycle,' the doctor said, withdrawing the probe, removing the condom and taking off her gloves. 'There's some paper towels over there to wipe yourself. I'll also look at those blood tests we did earlier this year.'

She smiled. I sensed a bit of pity in that smile. She had kids. She had a career. She was thinking *thank God I'm not this poor sap.*

'If you want to start fertility treatment then we need to get you in again in the next couple of months.'

I nodded. I needed to think about it. The treatment would be invasive and expensive. But I would probably give it a go. The desire to have a baby was still there. When I thought about the future, I was unclear about what path I'd take. I wanted to learn new skills, to do something that wasn't just absorbing content and watching other people get on with their lives. It wasn't too late to start something new – I just needed to find out what that might be.

I remembered happiness. I knew what it felt like.

'Can you see the stars?' June had said, paddling on her back, her flowery swimming hat glinting in the moonlight. 'There's literally millions up there – the oldest anti-anxiety medicine that exists.'

'You're right,' I'd replied, gasping as I took a step into the swimming pool, the cold shooting up my legs and making me shiver, 'but I think there might be a dead mouse in here. Didn't that woman's husband say lots of mice drown in the swimming pool because they're thirsty and need a drink?'

'Look at those stars, Kate,' she'd said. 'Just for a few minutes focus on the good stuff.'

'Is that a song lyric?'

June had laughed.

'It's not a very catchy lyric if it is.'

She'd started singing: 'Don't focus on the bad stuff, darling, just look at the stars. And maybe there's a dead mouse about to bob up in the water any minute.'

She'd squeezed my arm. Looking up, the moon lighting up her profile, June had looked years younger, like a teenager. I'd loved her in that moment, so grateful that she'd brought me to this place. I'd floated onto my back and closed my eyes. The cold dissolved as my legs paddled up and down. I saw a baby with inky, dark eyes and sticky out ears, grabbing my hair and tugging, skin so soft I couldn't stop rubbing my cheek up and down its tiny arms.

Exhaustion. Anxiety. Was it going to happen? Then Mum stroking my hair out of my eyes as she'd always done, Carl and me belting out karaoke and forgetting some of the words to 'Tainted Love', Meg stuffing buttered crumpets into her mouth and licking her fingers, George scrawling his ideas down and feeling like he'd finally found the thing he was passionate about, Lesley surrounded by kids who kept shouting *bumhole!*, exasperated but happy, June turning the first page of her book, licking her lips in anticipation…

'You felt good for a bit, didn't you?' she'd said.

'Yes, I did…'

Acknowledgments

Thanks to Paul, Rae and Greta for supporting me as a writer and putting up with me flouncing off with my laptop. Thanks to all my friends who have provided inspiration. To all my extended family. Also to all the women out there who are just about hanging on in there but feel like they're really in need of a break quite soon - it's coming. And to my dad. I love and miss you x

ONE MORE CHAPTER

One More Chapter is an
award-winning global
division of HarperCollins.

Sign up to our newsletter to get our
latest eBook deals and stay up to date
with our weekly Book Club!
<u>Subscribe here.</u>

Meet the team at
<u>www.onemorechapter.com</u>

Follow us!
 @OneMoreChapter_
 @OneMoreChapter
 @onemorechapterhc

Do you write unputdownable fiction?
We love to hear from new voices.
Find out how to submit your novel at
<u>www.onemorechapter.com/submissions</u>